NEXUS

Starship Hope Book Four

T.S. VALMOND

The Starship Hope: Nexus

T.S. Valmond

PRINT ISBN: 9 7 8 1 7 7 7 5 4 4 7 3 7

EBOOK ISBN: 9 7 8 1 7 7 7 5 4 4 7 2 0

Cover Design by: Goerz Designs

for Grandma

THE MANIFEST

The Crew

Captain Dana Pinet

Commander Wade Chance - ex-boyfriend to Dana and ex-fiancé to Maggie

Lieutenant Commander Adrian Valente - Security Officer

Lieutenant Nancy Westlake - Pilot

Commander Eric Rogan - Chief Engineer

Commander Esme Rogan - Chief Engineer (pregnant)

Ensign Cliff Harden - Communications officer and language specialist

ARI Three - (Artificial Robotic Intelligence) the android also known as Ari

Dr. Randall Jabar - Medical doctor and surgeon (twin)

Rido Jabar - Healer and therapist (twin)

The Passengers

Eartha MacLaren Singh - (stowaway adopted by the Rogans with mysterious origins)

Maggie Brooker - Reporter and ex-fiancé to Commander Chance

Luke Geyer - former CAH member and genius friend to Eartha

Franklin Jennison - Oldest passenger and amateur historian

Peter Barnes - former SO and escaped prisoner

The Fashin Teku Aliens

Aswin Zeppel - Captain of the The Des Freighter (blond-haired)

Tovar Vaziri- Second in command (red-haired)

Oli Serei - Security Officer (black-haired)

Members of the Intergalactic Consortium (IC)

Major Croft Adams

Lead Agent Vandermann

Telepathic Agent Sorel

CHAPTER 1

Captain's log: 4327.10.21 via Relay Unit A.R.I. Model 95643.

The Nexus is like a bag of candy in the front window of the most expensive place around. We can look, but we can't touch. Everything we need is out of our price range. Of course, when you've got nothing, that means you get nothing.

The Hope is desperate for repairs, and because of a lack of credits, I've had to loan out my two best engineers to nail down some work on my ship in exchange. The Fashin Teku were taken into custody by the Intergalactic Consortium for—well, for being who they are, and have since added a child to their band. It's going to require four thousand credits just to get them out of confinement. Wade and Maggie seem to be stuck in some kind of virtual programming that has gained station-wide popularity. I can only assume it's for Maggie's benefit. However, an investigation of the circumstances seems to be warranted. At this time, I'm also following up on a contact who may have spotted more people from our home world of Zelenia. Successful or not, after our conversation with Major Adams of the IC, there's one thing I'm *certain of: we're no longer facing extinction. We know there are other humans in this galaxy. Though, at the making of this recording, I am facing imprisonment if the IC finds out I'm roaming around the space station with a human-looking android. End recording.*

"Thanks, Ari. Store that one under the same code as the previous and upload it to the ship's storage when we return," Dana said.

"Does this mean we are going to retrieve Commander Chance and Maggie Brooker?" Ari's blond head inclined to one side, as if considering her potential responses. He could do millions of calculations a minute while scanning her vitals for signs that she might be lying. She counted four of his programmed blinks as she considered his question.

"I want to know what they're doing in this virtual fantasy. If they're in trouble, I need to get them out."

Dana led Ari around the Ring away from the IC and followed the direction of the crowd until they reached the building displaying a large marquee of Wade and Maggie, surrounded by flashing lights. It kept replaying the same scene over and over; the Nexus crumbling around them as they ran for their lives. The sight was more horrifying knowing that Wade and Maggie thought it was real.

The virtual program had gained so much popularity that a small crowd had gathered outside the doors, requesting entrance. A small white booth with a duroplasty-protected guard was positioned outside the theater, dealing with a queue of those interested in viewing it live, there to purchase tickets to get inside. Dana joined them. Perhaps if she made it inside, she could find someone in charge and find out what was going on with her people.

The bored attendant didn't make eye contact with the patrons as he called out over the crowd, "The live showing is fully booked. Come back for the replay tomorrow. You can make a reservation, but there's still no guarantee unless you're here on time."

Several members of the crowd groaned. Some began filing out, not bothering to add their names to the wait-list. When it was Dana's turn, there were still people jostling in behind her. He repeated his instructions for the new individuals.

Up close, she saw the man behind the transparent duroplasty had gray skin and sharp teeth. His bright pink mohawk fell to one side of his face, and matched the pink tie he wore with his shiny graphite suit. He had two eyes, a nose, and a mouth, but his elongated neck bore a metallic, braid-like necklace. He questioned her without taking his eyes off the screen in front of him.

"Name?"

Dana heard a scream and leaned forward against the duroplasty. He was watching Wade and Maggie on a tablet in front of him. Maggie was hanging off the side of a cliff.

"Those are my people," she told him sharply. "Where are they being held?"

"Name?" he repeated.

"Captain Dana Pinet."

He gave her an exasperated sigh, as if he'd heard this line before. "The actors are inside, experiencing a virtual environment. They'll be paid once the show ends."

"Are they safe?"

"They're perfectly safe. They have also given their consent

to be a part of the program," he said with as much indifference as he could muster.

"When does it end?"

"It ends when it ends," he said, still not looking at her, watching the tablet screen.

Dana squared her shoulders and put on a commanding tone. "I want to speak to your boss, and I want my people back now!"

The attendant looked up for the first time, meeting her eyes. He glanced back down at the screen, then back up to her. "What did you say your name was?"

"Captain. Dana. Pinet," she gritted out, enunciating each word. She tapped the toe of her boot, holding one hand on her hip while ignoring the plaintive murmuring behind her.

He seemed to register her agitation, at last. "Sorry," he said, holding up his hands in surrender. "I wish there was something I could do, but Magnus is in the middle of monitoring your people. I wouldn't suggest distracting him, as the program is doing well. He'll compensate them well for their work."

Understanding dawned over Dana. Wade and Maggie must have figured out a means to get credits on the Nexus and had gone for it. That explained why they were in the same virtual reality, and from the look of it, they must have reconciled.

She shook off her concern. Perhaps they didn't fully comprehend what they were getting themselves into, but if they were getting paid, then at least Wade's portion would help the crew.

"How much will they be paid for this?" Dana asked.

The attendant shrugged his thin shoulders. "I don't know,

but we haven't had this much enthusiasm for a fantasy adventure for some time. I suspect this one is going to be all over the station for more than a month. If they came out with a million credits, I wouldn't be surprised." His eyes went back to the screen. "You can't write a script with this much character and heart."

"How long will it last?"

"Until one of them dies or kills the other. Half the fun is trying to figure out which it will be. These two are exceptional together. The sexual tension is tremendous, and yet they fight each other as hard as they fight their feelings. They could be in there for years. In our time, it's just a few hours, but for them it could be a lifetime." The man stared back down at the screen in dismissal. "My technicians will see that they have everything they need, but they're perfectly safe, I assure you."

"Pardon me if I don't accept your assurance," Dana said stiffly. "I want to see my people. Now."

An expression like boredom crossed the guard's features, and he tapped a button on the device at his ear, speaking into it using a language she didn't understand.

"Please stand aside," he told her. "Someone will be here to attend to you in a moment."

She waited nearly ten minutes before approaching the booth again. The attendant barely noted her presence, pointing instead to a door behind him. There, a female version of the alien she'd been dealing with had appeared, nervously looking from left to right as if she expected to be surprised. She sported the same long pink tendrils on her head, but dressed in a gray skirt and suit jacket with pink pinstripes.

"Sorry to keep you waiting," she said to Dana, "but Magnus is extremely busy. I am his assistant. Please follow me, and remain silent through the theater." She gave a wary look at Ari, then turned and disappeared into the black beyond the door.

Dana followed with Ari on her heels. It took a moment for her eyes to adjust to the pitch black of the theater. The beam of a small red pen light turned on in front of her, held in the assistant's palm. Dana focused on the light, following it until they reached another door. Once they were all inside, she pulled open a second door and escorted them into a brightly lit room decorated as an office. On the opposite wall from where they entered were two other doors, one on the left and one on the right. Dana watched as the assistant moved to the door on the right, peeking inside before waving them forward.

"Magnus will see you now."

She ushered them in, then closed the door behind them.

Inside, a large wooden desk surrounded by monitors dominated the room. Each screen showed a different vid. A monitor at eye level held the attention of whom Dana assumed was Magnus. He didn't acknowledge them as they entered and stopped in front of his large wooden desk. He popped something green and furry in his mouth and laughed at the screen. On the screen, she recognized Wade preparing to set his leg. It sat at an odd angle, the uniform ripped away from the calf, and the skin underneath was scratched and bruised.

"Those are my people you're holding," she said sharply, interrupting his mirth.

"Oh." Magnus tore his eyes away from the screen, looking

up at her from his chair. After taking in her form in a slow up and down, he grinned. Dana locked down the immediate shiver the look sent down her spine, steeling herself against his gaze.

"I see why he's in love with you. You're gorgeous and strong. Would you like to join them? I can have it arranged. It would only take a few moments to get you all set up and placed into the program." He leaped from his seat in excitement, coming around the table to get a better look at Ari. He poked a finger at Ari's face before frowning and shaking his head. "No androids."

"I'm not here to get into the game," Dana said. "I'm here to get them out."

"That's not possible," Magnus said, shaking the tendrils on his head for emphasis. His brightly colored suit was hurting her eyes. "We haven't had this much interest in this world for years. Have you seen their chemistry? You can't fake this."

Dana glanced at the screen, showing Wade and Maggie again, and rolled her shoulders. They were injured and fighting. She wasn't sure what this game was about, but she wasn't going to keep them in there at the cost of their lives.

"I want my people out now." She felt like a broken record.

"Captain Pinet, right? Come with me," he said, shuffling around her and over to the wall. He opened a small door and led them into a small room. Inside, two technicians were monitoring Wade and Maggie from one side of a glass booth. They also had monitors displaying their activity inside the game.

"What are they doing to them?"

"They are unharmed," Magnus explained. "These technicians are the best in the business. They adapt the world around the characters. The weather, the wildlife, the water—everything in the world around them, we create and change based on the needs of the characters."

Dana watched as one technician altered the level of the sun and the temperature so it felt like dusk on the screen. She could see Wade and Maggie lying on beds in the center of the other room, their heads partially covered by virtual headsets like the ones they used on the *Starship Hope* in the gymnasium. Though they both looked injured on the screen, she saw in real life they were untouched and unharmed, as promised.

"They went into the experience voluntarily," Magnus continued. "The only thing we changed was the environment. What they experience is real to them. Over the years we've found that forcing them out of the adventure too soon can cause unwanted, and permanent, brain damage. As long as they play the game out to its end, whatever that is, they'll wake up fine, and can go about their lives." He looked to Dana. "Did I mention you'd also be paid? We do not enslave our characters. They are honored guests, and often go on to find substantial work outside of the Nexus."

It was certainly something that would benefit Maggie, but what about Wade?

"What if something goes wrong?"

"My technicians can keep the simulation running for as long as needed. There hasn't been a technical difficulty in ages. We've even installed our own backup system. Should the Nexus lose power or be damaged, the adventure can continue to run without interference."

Dana bit her bottom lip. She didn't like the idea of leaving them. It seemed they'd both climbed into the chairs of their own accord, and brain damage was serious. *By the Majestic, what had they gotten themselves into?*

"Fine, but if something happens to them, I guarantee you'll have a much more serious problem to deal with than a technical difficulty."

"Are you sure you don't want to go inside?" Magnus' hands twitched at his sides as if he were experiencing withdrawal. "It could raise your rate substantially. You're already getting half a million credits for this adventure. It will play out for at least another week, maybe two, the android can't go in, but if you join—"

"No." Dana crossed her arms and lowered her voice. "Look after my people. I'll be back for them when they're done. If you harm either of them in any way, there won't be enough credits on this station to make it right. Do we understand each other?"

Magnus gave her an anxious nod. "Of course, Captain. There's nothing to worry about, I promise."

Dana stormed out of the room, Ari following close behind. Magnus' assistant met them and brought them back to the entrance of the theater. Wade and Maggie were safe for now, but she and Ari had more business to take care of, and the sooner they finished, the sooner Dana could get her ship repaired and get off this space station.

CHAPTER 2

Dana didn't like breaking the rules, but there was a time and a place for everything, and this was not the time to turn themselves in to the Intergalactic Consortium. She'd already had a bad first impression with the IC, a significant step up from the local authorities that regulated activities on the Nexus, the implication that she shouldn't ignore or disobey Major Adams' IC regs. However, Captain Dana Pinet wasn't accustomed to following someone else's orders, and she didn't intend to start doing so now.

In truth, she and Ari hadn't purposely done anything wrong. The only thing they had asked was that she return Ari to the ship, and she planned to do so as soon as it was convenient. Considering their current circumstances, it seemed prudent to make a log of her current circumstances for later retrieval, as she had no idea what was in store for them.

The all-hands call for the IC Agents to the docks sounded serious. The IC's local base of operations on the fifth ring of the Nexus put them near the communications hub. Dana was going to use that to her advantage. Ashwin Zeppel, the former Fashin Teku captain, had given her valuable intel leading to someone who had dealings with people from Zelenia. It was time to track down his contact and find the other survivors. After her attempts at getting credits from the financial district had been a dismal failure, perhaps she could get help from her own people. All she had to do was find them.

The communication hub sported several terminals along the Ring that individuals could use for local calls within the Nexus. There were two currently open, and Dana approached one, then glanced over to see how the being beside her was operating the device. It seemed to work using a touch screen interface, though, when she tapped on the screen, it remained black.

"I believe these machines require a certain number of credits to work," Ari offered.

Dana groaned. "Is there nothing on this space station offered as a public service?"

"There is an interface. Would you like me to determine if it is compatible with my system?"

"Yes."

Ari lifted the tip of one mechanical finger and plugged himself into the terminal. A couple of pink and blue creatures, alongside two with gray skin and long black hair, stared at them. Dana couldn't resist gawking in return. It was only as they passed that she noticed they didn't move on feet, but an undulating mass of tentacles, as if they belonged in the water.

Her translation module implant behind her right ear picked up their muttering as they passed.

"Aren't those things illegal?"

"The authorities will deal with them."

Dana hadn't thought anyone else would be bothered by Ari. He was an android, not the unauthorized weapon the IC had accused her of bringing along. If his mechanical hand matched his synthetic one, most species probably wouldn't have known he was robotic at all. The bleach-blond hair and bronze skin of a surfer could fool an alien, but to a human, his head tilts and precisely timed physical movements made his mechanical nature obvious.

It seemed together they were already drawing too much attention. A small crowd had gathered around the two blue beings who had grumbled past them, staring and pointing in their direction.

"We need to hurry," Dana said. "Let's start with the *Hope*. Can we get a call out to them?"

A full minute passed before Ari turned to her. "I cannot reach the ship from here. It seems they've temporarily suspended all communications to the port."

"What about locating Rohath? Is there any such name in the public directory?"

She waited another agonizingly long minute while the crowd pointed toward the IC. A few of them seemed intent on blowing the whistle on her illegal android.

"I found a contact code. It pinged back with a location on the third ring. I assume we are to meet Rohath at the location to speak in person. Would you prefer I try again?"

Dana glanced over and saw the crowd growing more animated. She tugged at Ari's sleeve and backed away from the communications hub.

"We don't have time for that. We need to get on the nearest lift and get out of here."

Ari cocked his head. "The nearest lift is through that crowd you seem to be avoiding."

"Then we'll need to find another one. Let's go. I don't want to be stuck in the IC waiting for someone to come get us."

"Considering the situation, it may be more prudent for us to be with the authorities than on our own."

"No, the Agents have their hands full, and we need to find our people before we're sent back to the ship. Let's go, that's an order."

Dana dashed around the Ring, following the walking path around until Ari called out from behind her.

"Captain, there is a lift on your right."

She saw nearly a dozen figures already queued up, waiting to enter the next car. With that crowd, they'd never make it on. Dana knew they'd have to get creative if they were going to get off the fifth ring and away from the IC.

"Ari, you're going to need to plow through the crowd and get us to the front so we can board the next car."

"Yes, Captain," he replied easily. "How much force do you suggest I impart to achieve our objective?"

The Nexus was working on a currency exchange system. She hadn't grown up with such a concept, but knew of it from Blue Earth's history. It usually began with trade and worked up from there. Thankfully, they'd never needed it before, but she imagined that most of these species wouldn't take too well to being injured. They might even charge for something like medical care here, the way they did everything else.

"Only the minimum amount needed to get us on. Let's try not to injure anyone. We owe enough credits as it is."

Ari took a position in front of her and easily cut through

the crowd, using his synthetic skin covered hand to nudge aside the creatures waiting for the lift. By the time the doors of the lift opened, she and Ari were at the front, pushing their way on. Ari did an about-face, and Dana followed in behind him so he could repeat the maneuver to get them out. She watched as the crowd that had followed them from the communications hub got left behind.

Dana took a breath and sighed in relief, though immediately regretted it when she realized the mix of odors in the lift were emanating from the other beings inside. She coughed roughly, and a couple of heads turned, bodies shuffling away from her. At the next stop, several beings shuffled out, and were quickly replaced by more bodies.

Dana leaned toward Ari's ear. "The next stop is us."

"You are incorrect. This lift is going up."

"How many more rings are there before we're going down again?"

"We started on the fifth. This lift will go up to twenty-five before it comes back down again."

"Twenty-five?" she echoed sharply. "Why didn't you tell me that before we got on?"

"It seemed imperative that we board the next lift. You did not ask me in which direction it was traveling."

Dana huffed out a breath. "Isn't Rohath on the third ring?"

"That is correct."

"So why didn't we get off at the last ring and find another lift going down?"

Ari's head tilted to one side. She could practically see the gears turning in his head.

"I did not consider time as a factor, as the terminal did not give us a specific time, only the location."

Dana sighed. "He's probably not going to wait forever. Let's get off and find another lift going the other way." She wedged herself between a creature on her right whose head was grazing the top of the lift and something soft and squishy on her left.

"As you like, Captain." Ari made it to the door and claimed enough space for the both of them to spill out with the next group before the doors closed again.

Dana glanced back, watching the doors shut firmly in front of the surging crowd. "Do people ever get caught in the doors of those things?" she asked.

"There are no reported incidents of anyone experiencing an injury," Ari answered immediately. "However, there was an incident in the early days of the space station where the lift doors refused to open. Its load of passengers were stuck inside the car for several hours."

"Was anyone injured?"

"No. However, there were two creatures eaten by a larger being before they managed to get the doors pried open."

"What? That's awful."

Ari thought for a moment. "I suppose you are correct. Although the doors themselves did not fatally injure anyone."

"You have a strange sense of humor."

"I have no humor at all. Eartha tells me that is something I should work on."

"No, stick to your programming." Dana looked up at him, the gray eyes and the programmed blinks. His abnormal movements and mannerisms couldn't pass for human, but he'd already proved he differed from the other ARI's with whom she'd had interactions. "How is your programming? Since you teamed up with Eartha, you seem... different."

"How do you mean?"

"I mean, did Dr. Walker ever learn why you kept her hidden from me?" she clarified.

"Eartha was in potential danger. As she explained it to me, it was obvious she needed my protection."

"What about obeying basic commands given to you by a member of the crew?"

Ari seemed confused. "Have I disobeyed an order?"

"Not exactly, but I'm wondering if you can disobey an order for the sake of your friendship with Eartha."

"It is my function to care for the crew and to obey all direct orders from you."

"But you're able to go outside of your function. Like with Eartha."

"Yes, but there is a certain stability in knowing one's duties. Going outside of that is less than ideal."

Dana nodded to herself. "Sounds about right."

They made their way to another lift, a crowd already forming outside its doors. Several beings were jostling for a position at the front, but Dana whispered to Ari, "You know what to do."

"Yes, Captain."

Ari made his way to the front of the crowd while Dana held on to him. Behind them, a transport vehicle stopped. A dozen more individuals disembarked and lined up for the lift, pushing and shoving from behind them. They could not shove Ari in either direction. Dana stepped in front of Ari-the-unmovable-wall and waited for the doors to open. She ignored the looks and whispers the mechanical nature of his exposed hand got, standing firm as if they had every right to be there.

They boarded the next lift going down. Strange enough, the odor was identical to the last one they'd been in. Though she had more shoulder room this time, Dana still had to press herself against Ari's back or risk being separated from him by those crowding in around them.

They reached the third ring's level and climbed out of the lift with most of the crowd. The smells of fried meat and baked pastry drifted through the air in her direction, and her stomach growled in complaint. They were on another food-service ring. The commotion of people coming and going and the steady thrumming of the Nexus generators mostly hid the sound of her stomach growling, but Ari turned toward her.

"When was the last time you ate, Captain?"

Dana felt heat climb to her face in embarrassment.

"Never mind that," she said with a dismissive wave. "Where are we meeting Rohath?"

Ari inclined his head to the right. "I believe we need to get to the other side of this ring before we will see it."

She groaned as she joined the flow of the crowd circling to the right. There seemed to be more shops serving fresh goods and an assortment of prepared dishes on this level. They passed a vendor with an interesting looking yellow fruit that bore angry spikes on its skin. Next to him was another vendor with a dark blue fruit twice the size of the previous one which required two hands to hold. Dana couldn't stop her mouth from watering and steeled herself against the onslaught, but when she smelled freshly baked bread and pastries, she thought she'd melt into a puddle. She imagined herself crawling into the shop and begging for just one slice...

Ari tugged on her sleeve. "Not that one, Captain." He pointed to a small cafe with a bowl of steaming soup and a slice of pie on the digital sign outside. "That's the one, up ahead."

"What does the sign say?"

"'Sweet and Savory Eats'. It claims to have the best Buk To on the Nexus."

Dana pressed a hand to her empty stomach. "Of course it does."

CHAPTER 3

EARTHA

Eartha reached the cargo bay, where people came and went from the ship in a steady flow. She knew the rules. If you wanted to get off the ship, you had to be going in pairs or in a group. Eartha scanned the crowd and found a couple with mahogany skin and vivacious manners. Gliding up to them, she stood just out of their sight, but within view of the security guard without making eye contact. Her time in the ventilation system had taught her how to hide and blend in when necessary.

Her time as a stowaway had been long forgotten with all the other things happening on the ship. No one really cared about the one kid who wasn't on the manifest, snuck on board by the designer who'd long since died on their home planet. In fact, most days, no one noticed her at all.

Hadn't that been the problem all along? Her foster parents,

Eric and Esme Rogan, were the ship's chief engineers, and were currently pregnant with their first baby. Eartha had been an only child for so long that she didn't know what it meant to make room for a sibling, and bit down on the resentment of it. If they had officially adopted her, that changed everything. It meant they really wanted her. Not just for now, but for always.

She was walking down toward the dock when a firm hand grabbed her shoulder, spinning her around to look up at a firm faced guard. "What are you doing down here alone?"

Eartha glanced after the animated couple she'd attached herself to, her hopes of reaching the Rogans going with them. "I–I'm—"

"She's with us," Luke said, joining her and the tall guard. He looked to Eartha. "What happened to you? One minute you were right beside me, then next you were gone."

"I don't know," Eartha answered honestly, trying to keep up the ruse.

The guard didn't seem to buy it. Luke's parents waved him over. It was one thing for two kids to be trying to go off on their own; it was another for them to leave with a family. Luke grabbed Eartha's hand for good measure. The warmth of his grip distracted her, and she stared down at his fingers around hers for a moment before looking back up at his face. Luke was watching the guard as if daring him to call him out.

The guard waved them off with a warning. "Stay with your party. No one goes out alone."

Eartha let out a breath as soon as they were out of earshot. Even though they were away from the guard, Luke was still holding her hand. When he slowed down, he leaned over, dropping his voice so no one would overhear them.

"Where are you going?"

"I was looking for the Rogans."

"They're not in the engine room?"

"No, I checked there. They're working on alien ships down here in order to get them to help us with our ship."

"Which one?" he asked.

"I don't know."

"Well, you can't wander around here on your own."

Luke looked her up and down. When they joined his family, his parents barely glanced in her direction. Luke was the oldest of four, including twins, with another on the way. His mother's belly protruded a bit more than Esme's, though they were only a month or so apart. His parents walked arm and arm with their children, running circles around their ankles and clinging to them as they stared open-mouthed at the novelty of the new aliens. James stood waiting for his brother. From the red flush over his cheeks, he was still embarrassed about what happened to them during the virus outbreak.

Eartha didn't blame him for what he'd done. He'd been under the influence of a powerful alien virus, and he'd only grabbed her to threaten his brother. Luke didn't have any feelings for her, and he'd confirmed it that day. Though, she couldn't help but notice how he was still holding her hand as they approached. There was a time she'd dreamed of James holding her hand, but that felt like a lifetime ago. Luke was the one she wanted, but to her disappointment, he didn't feel the same.

"You can't be alone out here," Luke said in her ear. "It's dangerous, and if they catch you, they might arrest you."

"Where's she going?" James asked his brother, refusing to meet Eartha's eye.

"Nowhere. Go on ahead, I'll catch up."

James glared down at their joined hands, and finally Luke released her. Something unspoken passed between them before James turned to go.

"Come with us," Luke offered, attention turning back to Eartha.

Eartha scanned the docks. There were so many species of aliens, but so far, no sign of the Rogans.

"When we come back, I'll help you find them," he told her. "I promise."

Eartha bit her bottom lip. Technically, she was still grounded. She'd be in even more trouble if they found out she'd not only left their cabin, but ventured off onto the Nexus, though the temptation was hard to resist. A day with Luke and his family on the space station was a chance that might never come again.

Eartha nodded. She continued to scan the crowd and ships as they ventured away from the docks. Luke had his hands in his pockets, as if he didn't know what to do with them. Eartha's own hand seemed empty without his.

James threw her a side-long glance, then grabbed one of his younger twin sisters a second after she ran into someone made of goo. His parents barely noticed any of them, or seemingly the fact that they'd picked up another child. The bright lights of the shops were within sight when a commotion behind them got their attention. It was comical the way his parents turned, followed by their children, one at a time. It was so funny that it distracted Eartha long enough that she was the last to turn around.

A thundering beneath them shook the dock, making her stumble forward. A klaxon and yellow pulsing lights on either side of the large doors separating the dock from the rings of the Nexus signaled they were closing. There was a mad rush for them, and Eartha was pushed aside by several larger beings running for the doors. Luke called her name from the far side of the crowd, but she couldn't reach him. Then something rushed by her, jostling her off balance and knocking her to the floor. Something with tentacles slid over her legs, pinning her down.

"Luke!" The panicked screaming from all around her drowned out her cries.

A blur of red and black swooped her up, lifting Eartha to her feet and dragging her along. Somewhere behind her, she heard someone calling her name.

"Wait," she complained, pulling against the stranger.

The swell of the crowd was too much. His tight grip took her through the large doors a second before they closed. Only once they were on the Ring did they stop. The person who'd grabbed her from the floor turned around and faced her. His body seemed to be red all over except for a large black pattern that circled one eye. He let go of her hand and she saw he had black fingernails.

He put his hands on his knees and leaned toward her. "Are you all right, miss?"

"What's going on?" she asked, careful not to openly gape at him.

"Cargo shipment run amuck."

"But my family. I need to get back to my ship. My parents don't know where I am."

"Sorry, young one. If your parents are inside those doors, I hope for your sake they've got a safe place to hide."

"I need to get back to the *Hope*, my ship."

"Sure, love, just as soon as they clear the port. There were Buks in that shipment. You don't want to mess with them."

Eartha couldn't make much sense of most of the words he was saying. "Bugs?"

"Buks. They're like a type of giant beetle. They're a horrible nuisance. You'll be safer out here than in there until they call in the exterminator."

Eartha stared at the blast doors as the high-pitched screeching of something much larger than a bug reached her. The Rogans were in there. What if they were in danger? What would happen to her if the beetles got them?

The screeching and clawing grew louder, and something *thumped* hard against the doors. Eartha felt the vibration of the impact through her shoes. Her heart thumped in her chest even as she backed away along with the gawking crowd.

Most of the travelers on the Ring continued about their business as if the sound of giant beetles on the other side of the docking bay doors was nothing to worry about. When someone brushed past her and shouted at her in a language she didn't understand, the red man spoke up and pushed back.

"Watch where you're going." He looked Eartha over, turning her face from side to side with thin, red fingers. He pointed to the back of his own ear. "Where's your translator mod?"

"I don't have one of those," Eartha said. "They only made them for some of the crew. Kids don't get them."

"You should have one. Walking around the Rings without

one is just asking for trouble." His head darted around as if he were looking for someone to agree with him or hand him one, she wasn't sure. "Look, I've got someplace to be. See that shop?"

Eartha nodded as he pushed her in the shop's direction.

"Head in there and wait for me. I'll be right back. I'll help you get back to your ship as soon as things settle."

In the shop window dozens of shiny, sparkly, glittery things unlike anything Eartha had ever seen before were displayed. She caught sight of a bolt of material draped over a shapeless figurine in three shades of red. There was another swath in black with a golden swirl design. She wondered if Esme would let her get the material to make it into a dress.

When her mom had hidden her away in a ventilation shaft to survive the annihilation of their planet, she hadn't packed Eartha anything for parties. Until now, there hadn't been much worth celebrating. But Mrs. Hill had said they would have a dance in the Commons dining lounge at the closing of the school year. Eartha imagined herself in a ball-gown in the three shades of red like she'd seen in the old flat screen vids. What if Luke asked her to dance?

She stared a moment longer at the material, then shook her head. He wouldn't. He'd told James she was just a kid. When Luke had been under the influence of the virus, he'd been giving goofy eyes at the captain.

She turned to ask the red man his name, but he'd disappeared. She scanned the crowd a moment longer but saw no one with his bald red head or distinct markings. With a shrug, she decided that even though he was a stranger, he had saved her life and pointed her in a direction of safety. She ought to listen to him.

Eartha entered the shop. Something scanned her as she did and let out a pleasant chime. The shopkeeper, a small man standing on a ladder with a flat, pig-like nose and a crown of graying hair, waved a hand, directing her to one corner. There were others inside beside her. Most of them looked young, like they might be her own age. A young man with a mohawk stood a few feet away from her. A girl with blue hair and pointy ears stood with another being in a species that she wasn't sure how to gender. The closest familiar thing it resembled was a combination of a fish and a cat.

As she drew closer, she noticed they were all silently bobbing along to something. Eartha glanced down and saw there were rows and rows of disks attached to a central wire. Each of them had picked up a disk and seemed to be listening to it.

Eartha picked up a disk, turning it forward and back, but nothing happened. The boy with the mohawk pointed to the back of his large ears. He had a black TMI. She sighed, putting the disk back. They wouldn't work without the translator implant, it seemed, and she didn't have one. Turning away from the disks, she admired the rest of the items in the shop. She moved to an area with magazines covered in a thin film of duro-plasty. Eartha lifted one, staring at the young species of alien on the cover. The writing was unfamiliar. She turned it over and saw more of the same. Then she picked up another.

The feeling of eyes on her back made Eartha whirl around. The girl with the blue hair was staring at her. She had the most interesting eyes, one blue like her hair and the other green like Luke's. Eartha glanced around to be sure, then stared back.

"Hi," the girl said.

Eartha felt something in her stomach ease as she spoke. Something familiar and comforting she couldn't name.

"Hi," Eartha said.

The girl seemed curious about her, and went to reach out to touch her curls, but Eartha pulled back.

"What are you doing?"

"Your hair is a texture I've never seen before. May I touch it?" The girl's green eyes sparkled, but the way she looked at Eartha was the way a person looked at a pet.

"No, I don't know you that well."

The girl nodded, as if Eartha had just given her the local time. Her own hair fell in an ombre of dark to light blue wisps around her face.

"We don't look that different," the girl said with a glance back to the boy with the mohawk. Her pointy ears twitched as she smiled, as if she were holding back a giggle. It made Eartha smile as well. "Where are you from?"

Eartha stared at her a moment, wondering if she was being sincere in her question. "My name is Eartha, and I'm from a place called Zelenia."

The girl shook her head. "That's such an interesting name. I'm Bumi, from Trellis."

"Nice to meet you, Bumi," Eartha said, giving her a formal hand wave greeting.

Bumi did giggle this time, and she held out the disk she'd just picked up toward her.

Eartha shook her head and glanced down at her toes. "I don't have a TMI."

Bumi flashed her naked ears at her. She didn't have a translator mod either.

"How are you able to listen to it?" Eartha asked, surprised.

"My people don't need them. I'm talking to you, aren't I?"

Eartha hadn't realized the girl was speaking to her in her own language until now. In fact, her lips were forming the words as if she were a native speaker.

"How are you doing that?" Eartha asked, still staring at Bumi's mouth.

"Come on, I'll show you." Bumi held up the disk between two fingers and nodded at Eartha to do the same.

Eartha lifted one disk between two fingers.

"Now, open your mind, and just listen."

At first, nothing happened. Eartha stared at Bumi, whose smile was growing. Then she heard it, the faintest sound of music. She had to close her eyes to focus on it, but she could hear the music, a song without words played by string instruments that reminded her of a guitar and a violin.

Her eyes flashed open, and she picked up another disk. This one had a loud, angry sound. The words were a jumble of language until something switched and she heard them singing the words in her own tongue.

"How did you do that?" Eartha asked.

Bumi shook her head. "I didn't. You're doing it."

Eartha stared at her. She looked down at her fingers, then back up at the girl, holding her own disk. Could she be holding a different song while at the same time be projecting the ones Eartha had chosen?

"I knew you were like me."

"I don't understand," Eartha said. A twinge in her belly

responded to the impulsive lie. She did know. There had been something familiar about Bumi from the start.

"There's no reason to be afraid," Bumi assured her. "Isn't it true you can do things that the people on your ship can't?"

Eartha considered her words. She was asking her to reveal a secret she'd only revealed to one other person, and he'd made it clear if anyone knew, they'd treat her differently. Esme had been kind to her, but after she'd heard Eartha talking about being watched, things hadn't been the same. When she'd asked Esme if she and the baby boy could both call her mother, she'd been weird. Bumi seemed nice, but Eartha didn't want to be seen as different.

Eartha shook her head. "What do you mean?"

Bumi's lips quirked into a knowing smile, but she let it drop.

Eartha glanced at the door. There was still no sign of the red man. Why hadn't she asked him his name? Something on a sign moving outside the window caught her attention. She moved closer to the window and looked up. Bumi followed her gaze.

"What is it? Did you want to visit a virtual fantasy?"

Eartha shook her head. "No, I know them. That's Maggie Brooker and the Commander."

"It looks like they're doing well. Their vid is popular. It will be playing everywhere by the end of the day."

"They look scared," Eartha said, watching the expressions on their faces turn from concern to horror as people ran in all directions around them.

"Yeah, it's supposed to be fun, but I've heard that they sometimes bring in species that have never experienced it before just to see what happens."

Eartha frowned up at the marquee.

"I'm hungry, do you want to get something to eat?" Bumi asked, pulling her attention away from the window.

Eartha touched a hand to her stomach. She was hungry, but the red man had told her to stay in the shop. He was going to bring her back to the *Hope*.

"I'm not supposed to leave. I'm waiting for someone."

"No problem. We'll leave a message with the shopkeeper, and when your someone arrives, they can tell them where we went."

It made perfect sense, though there was still another problem.

"I don't have any of the local currency," Eartha told her regretfully. "I can't purchase food on the Ring."

Bumi waved a hand. "Don't worry about that. I'll share." She grabbed Eartha's hand, pulling her along. "I know a place with the best Buk To you've ever tasted."

"I've never had Buk To."

Bumi's mismatched eyes twinkled. "You're going to love it."

CHAPTER 4

"The sea, the stars, the sun, forever have been, forever will be.
They are the path to truth, light, and life."
-From the Faith of the Constants

DANA

S weet and Savory Eats was a smallish cafe with a grand total of five tables. Three of them were occupied, and two creatures were waiting for food to carry out with them. As the proprietor was busy, Dana directed Ari to slip over to a free table at the front, near the window. He sat with his hands neatly folded in front of him, his mechanical hand interlaced with the synthetic one.

"Keep your mechanical hand below the table," Dana said quietly, sliding into the opposite seat. "We don't want to draw any undue attention to ourselves."

He slipped his hand below the table just before the young

pink creature that had been behind the counter came over. She had large black eyes that took in everything. Her head swooped back into four columns, dark pink tentacles on each peak like a sea anemone.

"What would you like to order?" Her high-pitched words came out through her thin lips with a faint smacking of her tongue around the consonants.

"Nothing," Dana told her. "We're waiting for someone."

She made a shushing sound that indicated she wasn't pleased. "The tables are not free. You'll have to order something if you two want to sit."

"As soon as our friend gets here." Dana flashed the girl a smile, and she backed off with a huff. "What was that all about?" she asked Ari once the being was out of earshot.

"I believe your display of teeth may have either scared or offended her."

Dana lifted a hand to touch her lips. "What's wrong with my teeth?"

"Her species seem to have smallish teeth further back in the mouth. They are less menacing than yours."

Dana covered her mouth with one hand. She'd never thought of her smile as menacing before. As she took in the other patrons at the cafe, though, she realized many of them did not have the anatomy that favored large teeth.

Two patrons at a table near them had received their bowls and were slurping over them loudly. Dana did her best to tune them out as she waited.

"You're sure there wasn't a designated time?"

"I am sure," Ari replied. "There was no time given, only a location."

Dana groaned in frustration. Rohath could be on the way,

or have already gone. There was no way to know. She was about to suggest that they call again when a man with red skin walked into the cafe. His beady, black eyes scanned the room before he sat down at their table.

"I believe you are the patrons who requested to meet with me." He had a cool, formal accent that matched his long black coat and smooth crimson head. The black markings over his left eye only added to the overall pirate-like look of him.

The chances were very high that this had to be Rohath, but that didn't mean Dana was going to play the obvious mark in this scenario.

"How did you know?" she asked.

"The others here are regulars. You look like you need," his eyes raked over her and Ari before he finished his thought, "assistance."

Dana saw he had a TMI device for communications behind his right ear, though his mouth seemed to more closely match the words she heard. "Who are you?" she asked.

"You already know who I am. The real question is, who are *you*?"

"I'm Captain Dana Pinet of the Starship *Hope*. I believe you're acquainted with someone we know, an Ashwin Zeppel."

"Ah yes, Zeppel. Poor chap. How are he and the Tekus getting on?"

"He is currently in the custody of the IC," Ari interjected. "However, the lack of vital response would suggest you already had that information. Is my summation correct?"

Rohath sneered at Ari, then nodded. "Bad luck, that. Well,

if the Tekus are what you're here about, I'm afraid I can't help you, as I'm the one who got them pinched."

"You?"

Dana's surprise shocked him, and he lifted both hands in half a shrug.

"See, the IC and I are not on the best of terms. I had to give them something, or they'd have held on to me. I can't afford that kind of attention. Which brings me to you, love. What's a pretty brown morsel like you want from me?"

Dana bit back a quick retort even as her hand lifted to pull at the curls at the nape of her neck. She caught herself in the unconscious gesture and dropped her hand back to her thigh, his eyes following her every movement. She needed information from him, and he would be less likely to give it if she told him where he could shove his 'love' after betraying Ashwin and the others. He didn't seem the type to care that there was a child in holding thanks to him, so she didn't bother mentioning it.

"I need the information you promised Ashwin about my people from Zelenia," she said with her eyes level to his.

Rohath sat back in his chair, stroking his chin. He gave her another languid look as he licked his lips. She hated the way it made her feel self-conscious, as if she were on display.

The persistent cafe server came by again. This time Dana had time to stare at her unusual features as she greeted Rohath. Her large opaque eyes continued to scan the room. Her thin mouth pinched with impatience under two tiny nostrils. The center of her pink face was speckled with black freckles that made her look young, but in actuality, Dana didn't know how her species aged. As the only one waiting on customers, she might be the sole proprietor of the cafe, maybe the only one of her species on the Nexus.

"Bowl of Buk, Ro?"

He glanced at Dana and Ari, and when they remained silent, he shook his head. She turned her attention back to Dana and Ari.

"Not yet," Dana told her.

"We won't be long, Lalema," Rohath said. "Give us a bit of privacy, eh?"

Lalema shrugged her narrow shoulders and shushed through her thin, tight lips as she turned to go. There were still other paying customers that needed attending.

"I do know your people," Rohath continued, as if Lalema hadn't interrupted them.

"How?" Dana asked.

"They were here not two weeks ago. Said an asteroid named Harvey something-or-other destroyed their world." Rohath waved his long delicate hand in the air as if grasping for the name.

Dana's breath caught as she realized he might have the information she needed. Finding her people could mean the repair of her ship, the stabilization of her crew, that she wouldn't have to search for a new world alone.

She spoke around the fluttering anticipation in her chest. "Sounds like my people. What do you know?"

"That depends, love."

"On what?"

Rohath's lips stretched into a coy smile. "On how many credits you've got."

Dana looked to Ari, then back at Rohath. He was licking his lips again, and she wanted to crawl out of her skin.

"How many credits will it take?"

Rohath chuckled under his breath before his black eyes met hers. "For five hundred, I can tell you in which direction they went. A thousand, and I can get you a map to their most likely destinations." He leaned in a little closer. "For two thousand, I'll take you to them and show you where you can rebuild your alien homes."

"You know of a planet where we can settle?" She hated the desperation in her voice, but it was too late to modulate. If he knew of a place they could settle, their people would be safe. She wanted to find the other launched ships from Zelenia, but it would be so much easier to do so from a planetoid home base rather than wandering the galaxy like nomads.

Rohath nodded and grinned at her, showing off his short, blunt teeth. "Of course I do, darling. Don't you know who I am? What it is I do? Surely Ashwin has told you something of me–of the Forlo."

Dana sat back in her chair. Rohath seemed to have a lot of answers. How he'd come by the information and goods, she wasn't sure. If he'd had dealings with the IC, it was no doubt by illegal methods. Besides that, he'd turned on Ashwin faster than a two-headed gunther.

"We didn't have time to go into the details. As I said, he's being held by the IC." Dana crossed her arms over her chest. "Why don't you enlighten me?"

There was a gleam in his eye as he spoke. "I'm Rohath Karzenali. My people are the Forlo. We're traders and master negotiators within this quadrant of the galaxy. It's not bragging to tell you I'm famous for finding anything and anyone."

It was Dana's turn to grin. "For the right amount of credits, of course."

"I think we understand each other. Now, how about you lose the mechanical-man and the two of us find someplace more suited to discuss my price?"

She glanced down and found that his hand was on her thigh. She didn't know how long it had been there.

Her foot snaked out, her boot landing between his spread legs. She caught the flinch before he could hide it with a smile. Perhaps it was as sensitive for him as it was for human males. Whatever else he was, Rohath had a flirtatious nature. It might just be a Forlo trait, but she'd made her point clear, and he lifted both hands in the air before sliding his chair back several inches.

Dana stifled a laugh as her foot dropped back to the floor. "I think we understand each other. Look, I don't have any credits to spare at the moment, but I'm working on it. Give me some time and I'll have enough to make it worth the information you've got."

Rohath didn't bristle, but he took another measured look at both her and Ari before slowly shaking his head. "No promises, love. I'm due to leave the Nexus in eighteen hours. If you get your hands on the credits in time, be sure to ring me." He made a tsking sound against his teeth. "Too bad. I could really use an android. For him, I would give you a solid lead and throw in some extra credits so you can get yourself a bowl of the Buk To. It's well worth it."

"He's not for sale," she said immediately.

"Are you sure?" His sharp black eyes shifted from side to side. "You won't last long on the Nexus without something to sell. I won't last if I give away what I know for free."

"I'll get you your credits."

Rohath stood. "Suit yourself. It's been a pleasure." He

leaned forward and lowered his voice. "Oh, and a word of advice? Don't sit too long without ordering. Lalema is Nerimisa. If she offers you a special plate of Silver-Leaf Lichen from her home world of Ostea, politely decline."

"Sure, thanks," Dana said, tossing an uncertain look at the bar where Lalema was tending to a customer.

Rohath winked with the eye covered with black markings before bowing out, slipping out of the cafe and onto the Ring with the rest of the crowd.

"That did not go at all how I expected," Ari said.

"No, it didn't. Any idea what the Silver-Leaf Lichen might be?"

"It is a term synonymous with poison."

Dana looked over and caught the cafe owner giving her what might be her version of a glare.

"We'd better go. If we don't find a way to bring in some credits, we're not going to be able to do much of anything."

Dana stood and Ari followed her out.

"I am grateful that you did not sell me to the alien," he told her. "I am not interested in a change of crew."

Dana snorted out a laugh, thinking of all the people who'd requested to leave the ship. It hadn't even crossed her mind. "Me either." She looked from left to right along the Ring, where people were hurrying along to their destinations. She needed to secure some credits, and soon. Perhaps she'd find someone willing to help them if she looked hard enough. "Any chance there's a place on the Ring willing to hire a human?"

"There is a help wanted sign posted on this cafe. Would you like to inquire with the owner?"

"When did you learn to read their language?" Dana asked, taken momentarily aback.

"While I was connected to the communication terminal, I downloaded the necessary information to learn what they call Primary. It is the common language used here on the space station," he explained. "It was not difficult to learn the grammar, syntax, and structure, as they are not so dissimilar from our language. I suspect in this locale, people who can't afford the translation modulator implants are encouraged to communicate using Primary for daily activities."

Dana raised a hand to stop the language lesson just as her stomach made another loud growl. Ari looked down at her with one eyebrow raised.

"Fine. Let's see if we can earn ourselves enough credits for a bowl of the very best Buk To on the Ring."

CHAPTER 5

WADE

"Help me!" Maggie called out desperately.

The salt air was strong here, the crashing waves below making it clear how the cliff had come to be in existence. Wade peered over the ledge and saw Maggie around ten kilometers down, lying face down on a tree root jutting out from the rock face.

By the Majestic!

It was a miracle she'd landed on the root. If the jagged rocks and trees hadn't done the job, the six-hundred-meter drop had she missed that root would have certainly killed her. Wade had pictured her hanging on by her arms, but the reality wasn't half as bad as he'd feared. It was a good thing, too. He was still dragging the eighty-pound chute behind him. It had taken longer than he'd planned to reach her, and the slog had considerably worn him out.

"I'm here. I'm going to help you," Wade called down.

Maggie looked up at him. Her makeup had smeared down her face with tears, and her over-styled hair was hanging in a disarray of auburn clumps, strands clinging to her red face. "How are you going to get me back up?"

"I've got our faulty parachute. The one that should have slowed our entry into the atmosphere." He glanced around to see what he had to work with. "I'll need to secure it to one of these trees. Hold on, I'll be right back."

"Don't leave me!" Maggie screamed.

"I'm not leaving you. My leg isn't going to hold out forever, and I can't pull you up on my own. Save your strength. You'll be climbing soon enough."

Instead of answering, Maggie put her head down against the root and whimpered.

Wade calculated the distance again and realized it was going to be a stretch if he secured the parachute to the nearest tree, which was three kilometers away from the edge of the cliff. He looked around, testing the sturdiness of the brush and bushes nearby. They snapped under his hands, too young and fragile to hold the parachute, let alone Maggie. Nothing nearby seemed strong enough to hold them both, but he didn't want to attempt cutting the material of the parachute to make the material he had longer. It was extremely thick, but if it ripped beyond the seams, he could lose her. The easiest approach was tying the ropes to a tree and giving her the parachute end.

"Wade, I'm scared," she called up, a tremor in her voice. "I think it's getting dark again."

That was strange. She was right. The sun had already passed its zenith and was racing for the opposite horizon.

They were dealing with fewer hours of daylight than he was used to. From his gauge of the distance, they had less than a couple of hours before darkness covered everything again, and he still hadn't found a shelter for them.

As he secured the parachute ropes around the tree, he realized he'd also have to untie the thing and bring it with them when they made camp. His biceps ached and sweat poured down his face and back from the overexertion. At almost two meters tall and physically fit, he wasn't accustomed to being so weak. He dragged the heavy end behind him until he was at the edge of the cliff again. Below, Maggie was quiet, but still there.

"Keep your head down. I'm throwing the parachute down," Wade yelled to her.

He pulled the rest of the chute toward him, ropes stretched taut, before he threw it over to Maggie. It landed just above her. She'd have to stand up on the gnarled roots and leap up to reach it.

"It's too far," Maggie said, glancing at the parachute above her head.

"You're going to have to reach for it." Wade sat down on the grass near the edge. It was warm and soft, and he fought not to lie down and close his eyes in his exhaustion. The shot of adrenaline he'd received after their pod had crashed had gotten him this far, but the pain in his crushed leg was making him dizzy again. "Come on, you can do it."

"No, no, no." She was muttering something else between whimpers that he couldn't make out.

Wade groaned. It was bad enough that he could barely keep himself coherent. How in the *sou* was he supposed to get Maggie up the side of a cliff if she didn't do most of the work?

She wasn't a stranger to mental work, but physical work was something else altogether. Maggie hardly expended the energy to keep her quarters clean back on the *Hope*. She claimed the mess fed her creativity. *Whatever that meant.*

"You have to, or you're going to be stuck out there all night," Wade called down. "We have to find shelter." He left out the bit about the beasts he'd heard howling in the woods. He wanted to motivate her, not scare her to death.

Maggie sobbed. Wade shifted so he could look over the side. She was still clinging to the tree root, her head down.

"Come on, Maggie, you're stronger than this. Get up here. You're not the only one who needs help."

He watched as she inched her legs up under her. The fitted yellow dress, caked with dirt and ripped in the back, whipped around her. Her heels were long gone. *Too bad,* he thought. *Those might have been useful to help her climb.*

She had made it into a crouched position, but she still had her arms wrapped around the root.

"You need to let go of the root," Wade said. "Use the rock face. Find something to hold on to."

"There's nothing to hold on to," she shot back.

The defeat in her voice worried him. They were running out of time. The sun was going down faster than expected, and Maggie couldn't hold on much longer. The sky had gone from yellow to a dark orange. Wade tried to remember how long he'd been awake before he'd passed out the first time. *Maybe an hour? Or was it two?*

He rolled onto his back and closed his eyes. The chittering in the trees had lessened as the sun dipped down nearer to the horizon. This planet had a lot of similarities to Zelenia. What would Dana think of it when she arrived?

If she arrived.

He couldn't think about her now. He had to focus on Maggie, who was hanging on for her life.

"Remember that time we went rock climbing near Mt. Agnus? This is just like rock climbing back on Zelenia."

"I never liked rock climbing, that was all you." Maggie muttered something else he didn't catch. "You always loved traipsing around in the dirt. You almost killed me the last time we went camping."

It was true. She'd done a lot of things with him back then. He'd known from the moment he'd met her she wasn't an outdoor girl. If the high-heels and high-end makeup she wore weren't a clue, her first time putting up a tent would have given her away. He chuckled at the memory. She'd only played along because she was interested in him.

So when had she fallen for the cameraman? he wondered.

He tried not to dwell on the bitter taste of her betrayal. Wade would never get over her having a relationship with him and another man at the same time. But as angry as he'd been over the discovery, he didn't want her dead. At least not since the truth virus.

"You haven't got all day, princess. Let's go," Wade yelled down at her.

"Don't rush me!" she snarled back.

She's annoyed. Good. He'd use whatever he could to get her up that cliff. He leaned back over the side and glanced down. Maggie was next to the cliff face, her legs on either side of the tree root. It had to cut into the exposed skin of her legs, but instead of standing, she stared up at the wall of rock, unmoving.

"How about I go find shelter and come back and get you tomorrow?"

She glared up at him. "I can't wait to get up there and slap you in the face."

"We'll see," Wade said with a little more taunting in his tone.

He rolled back onto his back. He couldn't watch her creep up to the parachute. His head was still spinning, and he needed to rest if he was going to be able to help her. His left leg throbbed and burned as the shot he'd given himself wore off. He heard the fall of gravel before she called out again.

"I can't do this," she said. She was fading.

"Don't give up. Keep your eyes on the ledge."

"It's too far. I can't reach it."

"Find a nook for your left foot to boost yourself up. Put your hands on the rocks that are jutting out, and haul yourself up to the chute."

He listened with his eyes on the sky while she tried to do as he'd said. It was better this way. If she slipped, he couldn't watch her fall. Despite his feelings, he would never forgive himself if she died. The air was rapidly cooling around him, and it helped clear his head.

"If Dana were here, she'd have climbed her way up by now," he said, trying to sound bored.

Maggie muttered a curse. "If Bill were here, he'd have climbed down and helped me instead of fussing like a child."

Wade clenched his teeth. Okay, so he'd hit below the belt, and she'd done the same.

Maggie let out a yelp, and he rolled to the edge and looked down.

There she was, swinging from the end of the parachute.

"That's it, princess! Put the chute between your legs so you can place your feet on the rocks. Climb."

She slipped, her feet and knees scraping against the rock as she tried to keep herself from swinging backward.

"Climb!" Wade yelled down.

Maggie put one hand in front of the other. With slow, unsteady movements, she got her feet to the bottom of the parachute. It slipped again.

"For the sake of the Majestic, keep the chute between your legs! It will help you when your arms get tired."

"My arms are already aching, you moron!" she yelled, but she did it anyway, and she slowly started moving up.

Maggie cried, screamed, and cussed her way up the cliff. She was less than two feet away from the edge when she slipped against the rocks again.

"Just leave me!"

"I'm not leaving you. Hold on, I'm going to help pull you up."

Wade wrapped his arms in the chute and tugged, bracing his good foot against the trunk of a small sapling for leverage. It bent, but didn't crack. Wade tugged with everything he had left, his arms and leg trembling from the strain. When he saw the top of her auburn head, he called out.

"Reach for the edge!"

Maggie grabbed at the grass and flung one leg up over the edge, shuffling forward until she was prone in the grass. She inched toward Wade, then when she was a short distance from the edge of the cliff, she rolled onto her back. Too exhausted to move much further, he collapsed twenty centimeters from her, the parachute still wrapped around his arms.

The sun dipped closer to the horizon, and at some point, Maggie crawled the rest of the way over to him and lay at his side. She smelled of sea salt and something sweet.

An eerie howl in the distance brought Wade back to the moment. Maggie was still panting and trembling, staring up into the sky. He sat up enough to note her bloody knuckles and knees. The parachute still hung off the edge, but it was too heavy for even the two of them to carry now. They might need it for cover, or a million other reasons later, but it wasn't going anywhere tonight.

"Come on, I need your help now," Wade said, poking her in the side to get her attention.

"Help you?"

"I can barely walk, and it will be dark before you know it. There's no time to make a shelter of our own. We need to find cover, build a fire, and hunker down for the night. Have you noticed the drop in temperature?"

Maggie nodded. "What do I do?"

"Help me to my feet. I'll deal with the parachute tomorrow. Let's get back to the crash site. On the way, look for any large boulders or even a small cave we could sleep in for the night. Tomorrow, we'll search for other survivors."

Maggie shook her head and huffed.

"What?" he asked.

"Would it kill you to add a 'please' at the end of your demands?"

Wade sighed. "Look, if we're going to survive out here, we don't have time to walk on the eggshells of courtesy. Let's move."

"The last place in the world I want to be stuck in is in the woods with you," Maggie muttered as she limped away from him. She picked up the walking stick he'd discarded and brought it back to him. "Try this."

Even with the stick, she needed both hands to haul him up and keep him standing. As the blood rushed to his feet in a wave of pins and needles, Wade knew he was correct in his assumption that he was in no condition to carry the parachute. He'd need Maggie to look for firewood. In fact, she'd be doing most of the heavy lifting until he could get more use out of his leg.

A howl broke through the quiet and he scanned the area for some place safe. He started moving, not waiting to see if Maggie caught up to him. The two of them trudged through the trees, looking for more escape pods or something they could use for shelter. When they reached their crashed pod, Maggie let out a sob.

"I can't believe we survived the crash." She paused, trying to catch her breath as she looked around.

Wade limped over to where he'd dropped the gray case with the three remaining injectors. He picked it up and handed it to Maggie.

"Carry this for me."

Maggie took it and looked inside. She stared at the injectors for a moment, then looked back up at him as he struggled between his one good leg and the walking stick. "You look like you need another."

Wade shook his head. "Not until we make camp for the night. It's going to put me to sleep, and I'd like to enjoy it this time."

He bent down to check the pod for anything else of use. The pod had cracked in half upon impact, lying in two pieces. It was hard to know where the aliens would have stashed emergency supplies in it even before it had been so damaged. Frustrated, he beat a hand against the remaining side of the pod and looked up.

"Maybe we should just stay here," Maggie said. "What if someone's looking for us? It would be smarter to be closer to the beacon."

"There's no beacon," Wade said, tilting his head to indicate they should keep going, looking along their path for any place with cover.

Maggie eventually caught up, though she still seemed reluctant to leave the area. "What do you mean there's no beacon?"

"All the power in the pod is off. There's nothing, not even a signal beacon."

"Well, what if someone comes looking for us?"

"No one is going to come looking for us in the middle of the night. But something else might."

She took in a sharp breath. "What does that mean?"

"I didn't want to scare you, but we're not alone out here. Don't you hear the howling?"

Wade paused for a moment, and when a howl echoed through the trees, he gave her his best I-told-you-so grin. Whatever beast was making the sound wasn't too close. But if they traveled in packs, by the time they drew near, it would be too late.

Maggie, looking much paler now, nodded and scanned the area, searching for a place to settle. "There!" she called out, pointing to Wade's left.

CHAPTER 6

Less than ten meters from the cracked halves of the pod, Maggie had spotted a small cave. A moss-covered boulder blocked part of the entrance and made it difficult to spot, an ideal cover against predators. The sun cast a purple glow on the horizon as it started to sink below it. It would be a race against time now to get the damp cave inhabitable for the night.

"This could work. We need to start a fire, over there, now," Wade said, pointing to a low spot in front of the cave. Without sufficient light, he couldn't exactly march into the unknown of the hopefully empty cave. They needed a fire first. "I'll gather up some of these dried twigs and leaves. Go collect some wood, thin and thick pieces, then bring them back here as fast as you can."

Wade saw his own worry and fear mirrored on Maggie's face as she stood still, staring at the black hole before them, unmoving. Make-up and dirt streaked across her face where she'd wiped at her tears earlier. Even in the fading light, he could see the scratches along her limbs. He reached over and grabbed her by the shoulders, giving her a light shake.

"Hurry," he urged her, then added a stunted, "Please."

Maggie turned and tip-toed into the nearby trees to gather wood. He winced, remembering she had nothing on her bare feet. He'd have to remember to give her his boots. They'd be too big on her, but maybe they'd spare her from a more serious injury.

He used the length of his walking stick to feel around for the back of the small cave and encourage anything inside to vacate the premises. His heart leaped into his throat when a couple of bat-like creatures zipped out, just missing his head. The air blowing off their wings mussed his dark brown hair as he ducked to avoid them.

After testing the ground inside the cave and seeing nothing else slithering or climbing out, he dropped to the dirt to work on lighting the kindling. He hadn't made a fire by hand since Basic, but he was confident he could do it if he could keep the sweat rolling off his nose from landing on his little pile of dried leaves and twigs. His hands were raw by the time he saw a bit of smoke. He angled his head to one side and moved in close to encourage the fire with his breath, and soon the little pile was crackling with a tiny flame. Now all he needed was the kindling and wood Maggie was supposed to be gathering.

Wade stared into the growing darkness before he called out Maggie's name. There was no answer. He'd gathered as many twigs as he could find around him, and he now eyed his walking stick. If he broke it into pieces, he could keep the flame going, but then he'd be stuck there until morning. Maggie had left the gray case behind with him, and though its contents would help him, he'd pass out before he'd be able to go in search of her. She was all he had left, and it was only a matter of time before he was sitting crippled and alone in the dark.

He gathered several fist-sized rocks from nearer the cave's entrance to surround and protect his fire. A too-close howl caught his attention. He slipped out of his coat and removed his undershirt. He tied the cloth around one end of his walking stick and dipped it into the fire, then used the boulder and his staff to wobble to his feet. He had to find Maggie before something happened to her.

"Maggie!"

Silence answered his call. He painfully walked away from the safety of the cave and continued toward the trees, calling her name. He was well beyond the tree line when he heard another howl. The menacing night was as dense as it had been when he'd first opened his eyes on this world, the air cool and crisp against the sweat on the back of his neck.

He called out again, and then heard something like a whimper in answer.

"Maggie!" Wade whirled around, bracing himself so he could lift his makeshift torch above his head. He saw her a short ways away, her back pressed against the base of a tree. He raced toward her as fast as he could limp.

Pieces of wood were scattered around her bare feet, and she was shaking uncontrollably, her eyes on the darkness of the trees out ahead of her.

"What is it?" he asked.

He lifted the torch in the air in front of her, and a dark shadow bolted away from them. All he caught were a pair of yellow eyes and dark fur.

"Are you okay? Did it attack you?"

Maggie didn't answer, trembling with shock until he forced her to look at him.

"What happened?"

Without a word, she threw her arms around his neck, almost toppling them both over. Sobs racked her body. As the adrenaline wore off, he grew more dizzy.

"Come on. Let's head back." Wade kept his arms down careful not to hold her.

After a few moments, she eased away from him. "I thought they were going to eat me alive," she said through chattering teeth.

"I know. Let's not wait around for them to get any bolder. Grab the wood you gathered. Now that we know they don't like fire, we can encourage them to leave us alone."

It took Maggie two tries to get all the wood back into her arms, her hands still shaking. She whimpered as Wade leaned on her for some support. The top of his walking stick-come-torch had burned too close to where he had to hold on to it.

"I'm sorry, Maggie, I didn't think," he said, limping along. "We shouldn't go anywhere alone. I'm just so tired, and my leg is burning up..."

Maggie remained silent as they took a snail's pace back to the cave. The small fire Wade had built had gone out, but he used his torch to re-light it before he collapsed on the ground. Maggie almost toppled with him, the firewood scattering.

"Can you tend to the fire?" Wade asked as he grabbed the gray case.

Maggie nodded and rearranged the ring of rocks he'd

gathered, and fed a few pieces of the gathered wood to the small flames. She built up the fire outside of their small cave hotter than necessary. No doubt she would have a hard time sleeping without it after what she'd seen. The creature wasn't man-height, but he hadn't gotten as close a look at it as Maggie had.

Wade fumbled with the injector and placed it against his leg. There were only two doses left. If he lasted the night, he'd have to tend to his leg or it would never properly heal.

He had done his best to clear out the cave earlier, but used his torch to check the interior again. There were the bones of a critter the size of a mouse scattered over the ground inside, but nothing bigger to worry about. His eyes were already getting heavy. He put out the staff.

By the fire, Maggie was picking something out of her feet. She couldn't run around barefoot forever. They'd need to cover a lot more ground tomorrow, and without shoes, she'd slow them down. His eyes closed before he could mention it though, and sleep overtook him.

THE NEXT MORNING, HE WOKE UP WITH MAGGIE CURLED UP beside him. Again, he'd been dreaming of Dana, and it had taken him a minute to remember where they were. They'd left the space station behind them in an explosion. He and Maggie had crammed themselves into one pod. They'd been hurled down to this planet. They were trying to survive.

The chittering and songs of morning birds and animals brought him fully awake. His stomach growled, and Maggie moaned in her sleep. He pulled away from her, but she rolled toward him, seeking the warmth of his body. The pain in his leg had returned, but it wasn't half as bad as it had been the day before. There was probably something in the injector that sped up healing.

He eyed the gray box, debating whether to take another dose and go hunting for food. The thought made his stomach growl again, and this time Maggie yawned herself awake. As soon as she realized she was curled up against him, she scooted away and sat up.

"Good morning," Wade said. He continued to lie there, as if he were in no rush to move.

Maggie ran a hand over her hair. It was a bird's nest in the daylight, so out of character for her he had to stifle a chuckle.

"I don't suppose they left us any rations in the pod," Maggie sighed.

Wade shook his head. "I couldn't find anything, but I was working with limited light and a bum leg."

"Maybe I should go and check. I'm starving."

Wade's stomach growled again in response. His thoughts and physical state were like an open book. It annoyed him.

"Can we not talk about food right now?" he said as he moved to stoke the dying fire. They couldn't afford to let it go out, even in the daytime. Whatever they found to eat might need to be skinned, plucked, and cooked.

"Fine," Maggie said. "Just trying to make civil conversation."

"Since when do you care about civil conversation?" Wade's hunger was making him testy. That and the fact that he couldn't put too much weight on his leg before a shot of pain lanced up his hip. "Sorry. I just mean you'd better hurry.

If our days are as short as our nights, we're going to have some trouble adjusting here."

"What do you mean?" She asked.

"I mean we have about six hours of daylight. If nights and days are equal here, we won't have any more than six hours of night. Our bodies need seven or eight hours of regular rest. We won't be getting that for a while."

Maggie pushed herself out of the cave and to her feet. She winced as she stood.

"What is it?" he asked.

"I scraped my hip. I didn't realize it until now."

"We don't have an emergency kit. Maybe we'll run into some other survivors, and they'll be able to share their supplies with us."

Maggie stood staring out over where their crashed pod lay in pieces. She still hadn't moved closer to see if it had anything more they could salvage from it. He at least wanted to rip out the chair so he had some place to sit that wasn't hard ground or rock.

"Do you think the *Hope* will come for us?" she asked.

Wade continued to tend the fire without looking at her. The more she talked, the more she annoyed him. He knew why that was. He'd been thinking about Dana, and she was intruding on his thoughts.

"Of course they will. Dana's probably searching for us right now. We just need to be patient and survive until then."

Maggie picked up his walking stick and wielded it like a weapon.

"I'll be right back." She stalked off toward their pod in her bare feet.

Wade kept his true feelings to himself. Had Dana even

made it off the station before it had blown? Was she back on the *Hope* waiting for him to make contact?

In his heart, he knew she was alive. There was no universe in which she'd be dead and he wouldn't know it. Wherever she was, she was alive, and the love he felt for her made the ache of separation in his chest spread. He fueled that ache with memories of her, feeding it the way he fed the fire, bit by bit. No matter where she was, he wanted her to know he was thinking of her.

He looked down and saw he had written her name in the dirt with the stick in his hand.

CHAPTER 7

Maggie's Diary
Day 10

According to the daylight hours here, we've been here over a week, which seems to be half of what we're used to having. I'm exhausted every other day and wide awake every other night.

Wade's leg is infected. He's been in and out of sleep for days. I'm doing my best out here, but it's difficult finding anything that resembles food. Most of my training is for in front of the camera, not behind the scenes. I have no idea if the fruits, berries, and nuts I've managed to find are going to poison us or sustain us.

There's little I can do other than wait for Wade's condition to improve. Thank goodness for all those medical stories I reported on early in my career, or I'd know nothing of how to care for infections. It's been days since he saved my life, but I could see the resentment on his face. He's angry at being stuck with me instead of her.

She's never far from his thoughts. He calls out her name in his *feverish dreams. I want to smack him awake and remind him it's me saving his worthless life.*

In his more peaceful moments, I imagine what our lives would have been like if I hadn't been with Bob. If he had gotten over her. If we were truly meant to be together. I want to believe things would have been different. I want to imagine that our lives would have been something of a fairytale. The universe continuing to keep us together rather than the cruel twist of fate that stuck us with each other on this uninhabited planet. I would have been his queen, and he'd never look at me the way he does now. That was one reason I couldn't wait to be off the ship, but being stuck here on this planet, forced to fight off the dark and the creatures just outside the edge of the fire's light, is a fate worse than death.

When our rescue comes, I'll be glad to be rid of him and, and her, and the whole ship. He's not the one for me, and I'm not the one for him.

CHAPTER 8

DANA

A s they approached, Dana was sure the Buck To cafe's server was glaring at her from the opposite side of the counter.

"What do you two want?" she asked with a smack of her lips.

Dana inclined her head, hoping it wasn't another social taboo. "Sorry, to be a bother. Lalema, is it?"

Lalema cleared dishes from the counter then placed them in a larger bucket out of sight, then wiped the counter with her large eyes focused on her work. She made the same displeased shushing, but didn't respond.

"Well," Dana went on, "my friend and I noticed you have a sign posted out front."

"Have you got a local tag?" She asked without looking at her.

"Local tag?" Dana shook her head as another bowl of Buk To wafted past, on its way to another customer.

Lalema turned her back as she pulled a small hose from the wall and filled the glass with something pale and gold. "I don't hire from off station. Too many folks around here need the work."

"I'm not looking for anything regular. Just enough to get a few credits for the day."

Lalema looked them over, her eyes resting on Ari for a few seconds longer. Then smacking her thin lips as she spoke. "Well, I've got some crates in the back that need to be moved, but they're too heavy for someone as small as me." She gave Dana a significant once-over. They were about the same size, she had to admit. Even in her uniform, Dana couldn't hide her petite stature.

"Ari would be glad to help you." Dana slapped a hand on his back for emphasis.

Lalema looked down at his mechanical hand, seeming to consider it for a moment. No doubt it was just as illegal to employ a skin covered android as it was to walk around the Ring with one.

"If you're worried about the IC, don't be. They know who we are, and that we're here on the Nexus." It surprised Dana how easily the story came tumbling out of her mouth. It wasn't exactly a lie, but it was hardly the truth.

Lalema shrugged. "Come. I will show you what I need moved."

Dana followed them until Lalema held up a hand. "Wait here. I will bring you a bowl of the Buk To you've been drooling over while you wait. I don't want anyone to know you are here doing work for me. It would be bad for my reputation."

Despite Lalema's small stature, she had a firm hand, and she was insistent. Dana nodded to Ari, who turned and followed Lalema out. They disappeared behind a door to the left of the bar. There was a sign above it, Dana couldn't read. She didn't like knowing he was on his own, but as an android, there were few things strong enough to take him down, and she doubted Lalema was one of them.

Even a handful of credits at this point would be better than nothing. At least then they would have a place to start. Dana wondered if any other shops on the ring needed muscle. Renting out Ari for hire might be enough to gain them a reputation of their own. Once the locals learned who they were and why they were on the Nexus, they might offer them higher-paying jobs.

As promised, Lalema returned with a hot bowl of Buk To and placed it in front of Dana. It smelled divine. She wanted to bury her face in the spice-filled vapors.

"What is Buk To?"she asked before Lalema walked away.

"It's a hot soup with meat, vegetables, and noodles."

"What makes yours the best?"

"This is my grandmother's secret recipe. If I told you, it wouldn't be a secret." Lalema's laugh was a tight, high-pitched giggle, making her seem even more child-like. Though now that she'd seen the woman work, she figured she had to be an adult of her species.

"I'm not familiar with your species. Where are you from?" Dana asked.

Lalema's enormous black eyes scanned the cafe, checking on the two tables of customers eating before she answered.

"My people came recently through the Arch. We came from the water before we learned to survive on land. I am the first of my kind to venture this far from my home world." She blinked rapidly, as if holding back emotion.

"I am also far from my home," Dana confided softly.

"You look like the IC Agents."

Dana shook her head. "We are the same species, but they are from another part of the galaxy, one my people have never seen. Our world was on the far side of the Arch. It was destroyed by an asteroid, and my ship carries all that is left of our world. At least that's what we thought." Dana's eyes went to Lalema's face. "There are rumors that others may have escaped. Have you met any of my people traveling this way?"

Lalema shook her head, the soft fur-like tendrils on the four tips of her pink head swaying back and forth. "No, but that explains why you were meeting with Ro. He's probably seen them."

"Yes, so he claims. But we don't have enough credits to purchase the information he has." Dana huffed in frustration. "I guess it's not enough to lose your planet to get any help around here."

"No, it isn't. Too many who come here have the same sad tale. You'll have to come up with a better story if you want folks around here to help you. Keep in mind, most won't do it for free." She took a slow and long sip of the golden liquid before she put her drink back down. "Ro is a good man. He may seem a bit shallow on the surface, but he's had loss just like the rest of us."

Dana sat back. She hadn't considered that he might need the credits for something other than lining his own pockets. "What do you know of him?"

"Only that he deals in trade. If you need something, and it's hard to find, he can usually get it for you. He's also a regular customer, so if you're looking for dirt, you won't get it from me." Lalema smacked her lips and nodded in dismissal. "I need to return to my counter."

Dana hadn't noticed the two patrons who'd entered. Despite it being a small location on the third ring, the place's business was steady, and after trying the Buck To, she knew why. She had to force herself to slow down and use the miniature ladle provided to eat it, the hearty soup warming her belly. She listened as the other patrons slurped theirs down and did the same, the other patrons attending their bowls with the same vigor. Though she didn't recognize the meat, it tasted a lot like chicken, and the vegetables came in muted colors, but nothing she recognized. The noodles had a familiar chewy consistency though, and she was pleased to see that slurping them down was socially acceptable here.

Lalema came by with a glass of water and a pastry filled with a sweet red jam. She was biting into it as Ari returned. She frowned at the glove he wore over his mechanical hand as he sat down.

"Lalema insisted that if I was to be working in her establishment, I would cover my hand and not tell anyone I am an android. I agreed to the terms. I trust that is acceptable."

"It's fine," Dana said, flicking out her fingers to rush him to the point. "How did it go? Did you run into any trouble?"

"No, the crates were filled with berries. She needed them shifted to the shelves where she could reach them without climbing onto a ladder. The work was not difficult, or any trouble. I am glad that I could assist you, Captain."

Dana was still glowing with pleasure as she started in on

the second half of the pastry when Lalema returned. She placed a thin red disk half the size of her palm on the table in front of them.

"I appreciate your assistance today."

"How much did we make?" Dana asked.

"Fifty credits. The soup, water, and dessert are a gift from me in exchange for your discretion. I trust you will tell no one that you provided any service to me."

Dana slipped the disk into her pocket with a nod. "Thank you."

It wasn't much, but it was more than nothing in exchange for moving some boxes. Lalema moved to the front window and removed the help wanted sign before returning to her counter.

"Eartha!" Ari called out.

Out on the Ring, Eartha was walking along the row of shops with another girl. Her ombre blue hair went from a dark berry to arctic ice at the ends over her pointed ears. Neither of them had heard Ari.

Dana choked on the last bite of pastry as Ari stood and walked out the door without another word. "Hey! Where are you going?"

He returned a moment later, the girls following behind him, and sat back down as if nothing had occurred. Dana stared at him, wondering if he'd gotten his wires crossed. He'd practically leaped out of his seat, and the girl seemed unharmed. In fact, Eartha was giggling with her new friend.

"Hi, Captain," she greeted.

"Hello, Eartha. Join us, and introduce me to your friend."

"This Bumi," Eartha said, sitting in the chair next to Ari. "Bumi, this is Dana Pinet, the captain of the *Hope*."

"A pleasure," Dana said, lifting a hand in greeting.

The girl did the same with a nod. She and Eartha were the same height, though this girl had more delicate features. She had one olive eye and one sapphire blue. Her tilted gaze regarded Dana in a way that made her uneasy. It was the same feeling she'd gotten when she'd been in the Major's office with the telepathic agent.

"Where are you from, Bumi?"

"She's from Trellis." Eartha looked to her, then back at her friend.

"Hi," Bumi said. The response was innocent, but again, there was something beneath her mismatched eyes, as if she were far older than she appeared. Dana had seen similar mannerisms in Lalema. She stood with her shoulders back and her feet at the ready, as if she could pivot to bolt or fight depending on the situation.

The question was, how had she attached herself to Eartha? The young girl was alone on the Ring, and since she knew where the Rogans were working, that meant she'd found a way through the security officers she'd posted to control the comings and goings of her people. She wanted to know how.

"How did you get off the ship all by yourself?"

Eartha's eyes dropped to the floor, and Dana watched her squirm as she stumbled over her words.

"Well, at first I went to look for the Rogans in the engine room. They weren't there, so I went to find them. I got off the ship with Luke and his family, the Geyer's."

Dana nodded. They had four children and one on the way. It was only a month ago that their oldest Luke, had been on trial as a former member of the Coalition Against the

Hierarchy that had tried to sabotage the entire *Hope* project. The Justice Committee had cleared him of any involvement with terrorism, and he had helped get Ari functioning again when they had all been contaminated by the alien truth virus. In the end, he was a good kid. Dana couldn't imagine him letting Eartha go off on her own.

"How did you end up with Bumi?"

"There was this huge commotion on the docks with some bugs, and Luke and I got separated," Eartha explained, (action). I fell, and a man with red skin saved me from being trampled by everyone running. We ended up on the opposite side of the docking bay doors. I met Bumi inside of a shop nearby." Eartha's eyes lifted to the ceiling, as if she were looking for answers there. "We got tired of waiting and wanted something to eat, so Bumi's treating me since I don't have any credits."

Dana noted the possessive way that Bumi stood with her, but she wouldn't be taking Eartha anyplace else.

"Good thing we found you," Dana told her. "Let's get you some of their famous Buk To."

"That's where we were going," Eartha said, pointing at the door.

"No, you have to try Lalema's grandma's recipe," Dana insisted, laying it on thick. "I'm sure your friend won't mind us taking care of you."

Bumi's bi-colored eyes met Dana's in challenge, and she waited for the girl to respond. Instead, she giggled, her pointy ears twitching as if they were talking about boys instead of soup.

"I don't mind eating with your friends," Bumi said,

moving to fetch a chair from a nearby table until Ari stood, offering his seat to her and keeping his back to the wall.

"Is Ari artificial?" Bumi asked, staring up at him as she sat.

"He's an android," Eartha said. "He's my friend."

"Strange. I thought they outlawed those on the station."

It didn't surprise Dana that the girl knew of the laws on the station. She probably wasn't as young as she played at all.

"Speaking of outlaws," Dana interjected, "how old are you, Bumi?"

Bumi giggled instead of answering. At that moment, Lalema returned to take their orders.

"I've promised them your infamous Buk To," Dana said, glancing up. "You did say it was the best."

"Coming right up," Lalema said, then clucked her tongue in annoyance.

"I wonder when the docks will be clear," Bumi mused, effectively diverting the subject away from her age.

Dana nodded, her suspicion confirmed. She decided right there that this Bumi character wouldn't be allowed to continue running around with one of her young, naïve passengers.

"I'm not sure. Ari?"

"I believe they will send out an alert on all channels once the cargo is contained," he replied smoothly.

Dana looked to Eartha. "You said they were bugs?"

She nodded. "The red man called them beetles."

"I wonder why they'd need to shut down the docks for some little bugs."

"Dangerous things can come in small packages," Bumi said, casting a sly look at Dana.

Was that a threat?

"They didn't sound small," Eartha said softly. "Not the way they were screeching and banging against the doors." A shadow passed over her face and Dana reached out for Eartha's hand at the same time Bumi did.

Bumi pulled away, letting Dana's hand rest on Eartha's. "They're going to be okay," Dana assured her. "I know where they were working today, and if anything went wrong, they'd follow protocol and head straight back to the *Hope*."

Eartha nodded even as tears welled in her eyes. This time Bumi reached over, putting an arm around Eartha's shoulders and humming softly under her breath. The song seemed to calm her, and Eartha looked up with a smile, eyes lighting up in surprise.

"I know that song."

Bumi smiled and let out a giggle as if she were embarrassed. There was something about the exchange that didn't sit right with Dana. She had already made up her mind that no matter what, Bumi wouldn't be taking Eartha anywhere else.

Their bowls of Buk To came, and they ate and giggled over their meals like two young girls should, Ari standing over them and Dana watching.

"Did you like it?" Dana asked when they put their spoons down in unison.

"I'm stuffed," Bumi said.

"It was really good," Eartha agreed.

"Would you like a desert?"

"Dessert?" Eartha echoed excitedly.

"I can't eat another bite," Bumi said, rubbing her stomach.

Eartha looked at her friend, then back to Dana. She shook her head. "I probably shouldn't. I'm stuffed."

Dana was beginning to see how much of a hold Bumi had on Eartha. She was about to speak when a klaxon alarm interrupted her, sounding throughout the station.

"Oh no, what's going on now?" Eartha asked, leaping up and running to the protection of Ari's arms.

"It is an emergency shutdown of the Nexus," he announced.

A small creature came to the cafe doors, scratching at them. It had fur on its entire body and was no bigger than a small dog. Though it had fangs that hung out of its mouth, it didn't seem intent on using them. Dana noted that no one seemed to be with the animal and stood up to open the door. She let the animal sniff at her hand. Its small pink tongue protruded from its mouth, licking her hand before nuzzling against her. It seemed it wasn't going to eat her, so she picked it up and brought it over to their table.

"Hey!" Lalema shouted over the alarm from the bar. "Can't you read the sign? No pets!"

Dana looked down at the little creature, its beady brown eyes staring back at her as if it were pleading. She didn't like the idea of throwing it out to fend for itself with a shutdown in progress. Whoever it belonged to might come looking for it. Though, it was Lalema's cafe, and she couldn't afford to break the rules now. Lalema was a local and she could make it hard for Dana if she wasn't careful. She needed to acquire enough credits to have her ship repaired and continue their search for a new home.

Resigned, she stood up to put the small animal out. It

made a soft, keening noise that Dana took for begging, and she wished she'd left the thing outside in the first place.

Three short bells signaled a station wide announcement.

"Citizens and guests of the Nexus, please be advised that we are on emergency lockdown until further notice. Enter the nearest secure location and remain there until the threat has been contained. You have one minute to comply."

Dana looked out the window in time to see people running for their lives. As soon as the message had ended, and just as someone reached the door of the cafe, an articulated metal door slid down from the ceiling, falling into place over the windows and entrance, sealing them inside the cafe and keeping anyone else out. The person on the outside beat against the metal door, screaming, "Help!"

CHAPTER 9

ERIC

"It's been two hours, Eric. We need to find her." Esme clutched at her belly in her anguish over Eartha.

As soon as the alarms on the docks had gone off, Eric had gathered up his wife and raced them back to the *Hope*. In the commotion, they and the other passengers onboard hadn't realized what was going on until the Nexus announcement had been made over their comms. Something they called beetles, but these were as big as a personal transport vehicle, had escaped confinement and were now running loose on the Nexus.

Eric paced the length of their cabin. He ran a hand through his sandy blond hair, wondering what to do next. The official count was in. Everyone onboard had been sent to their cabins for check-in, but Eartha hadn't joined them. It was another hour before they got the message from her young friend, Luke, that she'd been separated from him and his family on the docks.

She'd come looking for them. Rather than do so on her own, Luke had insisted she stay with his family just in case. Trouble seemed to follow that boy wherever he went. No surprise there. As a former Coalition member, it seemed he was a magnet for it. Eric bit down on the resentment he felt towards Luke's parents for not doing more to keep Eartha with them when the crowd trampled their way off the docks, sweeping Eartha up and forcing her out the docking bay doors.

He wanted to believe she was safe, but they were already getting updated messages of these beetle things getting onto the station proper. If anything happened to Eartha, he didn't quite know what he was going to do.

Esme was worse for wear. She and Eartha hadn't exactly been on speaking terms since her punishment, and her first thought had been that the girl had run away. Eric knew better. She was a lot of things, but Eartha wasn't a runner. She was smart, and she'd do the right thing in the end. The only time she seemed to get in trouble was when she was with Luke Geyer.

Eric stopped pacing long enough to gather his wife up in his arms again. He'd done it twice so far, and each time it had seemed to work for a while until she worked herself back up again. She was trembling this time, and it took longer to get her to sit down on the couch than before. That's where they were when a chime at the door signaled that Lieutenant Commander Adrian Valente, their chief of security, had come.

"I've got news," Valente said without preamble. It was one

of his best qualities. "Eartha's safe. She's actually with the Captain and the ARI."

"Oh, thank goodness," Esme breathed, going slack in Eric's arms in relief. "Was she hurt? Are they on their way back here?"

"No, and I don't think so," Valente explained. "The Captain was able to get a message to us, but we weren't able to reach her on the comm channel she was using. They're somewhere on the third level of the Nexus, hunkered down at a cafe. They're out of harm and waiting this thing out, just like us."

Eric clapped a hand on his arm, just short of a hug. "Thank you so much for delivering the message personally, Commander."

He nodded tightly. "That's not all. We're being asked to prepare for departure."

"What? We can't," Esme said, shaking her head. "We're not leaving without Eartha."

"And why would we leave without the captain?" Eric added.

Valente ran a hand over his face. "The dockmaster, Fazil, is warning us that if these beetles get hungry enough, they'll start tearing into the nearest hold carrying food."

"We've only got rations," Eric said. "I find it hard to believe we're the tastiest option on the dock."

"Not the rations. Us."

Eric and Esme shared a look, then turned back to Valente.

"You mean... we've got the most people onboard," Esme said softly.

Valente's nod was grim. "The other ships on the dock are large, but they're not carrying over three hundred people."

"But we can't leave under our own power. We didn't even come in without help."

"I know. That's why I need you both in the engine room." He sighed. "The situation is going to be precarious. Fazil says he'll arrange for a tow out away from the dock, but after that, we'll be spinning in space. If the Majestic wills it, we're going to need all the help we can get just to stabilize the ship."

"Wait, what about the Commander?" Eric asked. "Is he back?"

Valente shook his head. "No. He and Maggie Brooker are apparently in some kind of virtual experience, but are safe for the moment. In his absence, I'm in command, and if it's a choice between waiting for the rest of them to return or losing the entire ship, I think you know which way I'm going to go." He gave both of them a significant look. "The safety of our people is paramount here."

Eric nodded, but Esme stood up again. He saw her reasoning it all out in her head.

"We'll wait, though, as long as we need to," Valente assured them. He inclined his head, then straightened his shoulders. "How long will it take you to be ready in the engine room?"

"Not long, as there's not much we can do."

"We'll join you on the bridge," Esme said. "I want to be there if there's any more news, and it doesn't take two of us to cover engineering."

Eric nodded in agreement. "We picked up a few new tricks working on the dock. I might be able to pull a rabbit out of a hat, but I don't think I can do much more here."

Esme reached for her husband, pulling him in. Over her shoulder, Eric watched Valente turn and step back through the open door into the corridor, giving them a moment alone.

"We're not going anywhere without her," he whispered into her hair. The words were hollow, though. They both knew that if it came down to leaving her behind, they wouldn't have much of a choice.

Esme pulled back and nodded, her eyes not meeting his until he lifted her chin. Her brown eyes were swimming with emotion. Her previously short bob had already overgrown the awkward length and now reached for her neck, like his own. They had far too much to do, with Eartha and the ship to worry about a luxury like haircuts. As soon as they were all together again, and things calmed down, he'd schedule some time for them to take a break. He needed to treat his wife while the possibility was still close.

He saw the resignation in the set of Esme's shoulders. There was no way to ease her worry, since he was struggling with it himself, but he could give her something.

"No matter what happens, we're going after her." The whispered promise was on his lips as he pressed them to hers.

"Oh Eric... I'm so scared for her," she whispered back.

"Me too. But we're her parents now. We need to keep it together until we're reunited."

Esme nodded, and after a moment, turned to slip out the door, joining Valente, who'd been patiently waiting to go up to the bridge.

Eric turned in a slow circle, taking in the empty cabin, thinking of his girls. Ari and the Captain were with Eartha. She couldn't be in safer hands. It was the *Hope* he had to focus on now.

Was it too much for the beetles to just ignore them and go about their business?

The screech of metallic scratching at the hull answered his question.

CHAPTER 10

The Order of the Prophet Dasha: Followers of Dasha, a being with unknown origins, who seemed to prophesy the future, including his own death. Those in The Order meet at the Tree of Abundance on level eight of the station, where Dasha planted a tree that continues to grow to this day.

The Faith of the Constants: Those who worship the heavenly bodies and love with wild abandon. They study the stars and their movements with great care. They have no book of truths, as they live by only one law, and that is to love everyone and everything to the best of their abilities.

The Chosen Ones of Winmur: A mysterious sect from the planet Winmur. They've created a utopian society with strict social rules. Many seek them out for their unique healing abilities.

-The three dominant religions practiced in the vicinity of the Nexus

DANA

. . .

Aren't you going to let them in?" Dana asked, standing to check the metal shutters over the door for some kind of release mechanism.

Lalema shook her head, shushing through her thin lips. "It's too late for them. Once the emergency doors are activated, we cannot open them until the emergency has ended."

"For the love of the Constants." The two local patrons dropped to their knees and hummed between muttered words, rocking back and forth.

"What are those things?" Dana asked.

"They're members of the Order of the Constants. Don't worry, they don't mean any harm," Lalema said with a wave of one hand.

"No, I mean the things outside."

"Those are the bugs that were down on the docks," Eartha said, burying her face in Ari's shirt. "They followed me."

Dana didn't like the sound of that. She hated bugs, spiders, or anything creepy crawly. She listened to the person trying to get in, the beating against the door growing increasingly frantic before a loud screeching replaced it. Whoever had been trying to get in ran away screaming. Several thumps later, the screams ended with an abruptness that made Dana's skin crawl. She suspected that whatever the bugs looked like, they were big enough to eat a person, though she kept that thought to herself as the screeching returned. Dana wondered if the rest of her people were safe from whatever was roaming the station.

Bumi stood up and moved to Eartha's side. To her credit, she exhibited extreme calm considering the situation. "They didn't follow you. The beetles are not intelligent. They run on instinct."

Dana nodded, agreeing with her. "They must be all over the station. That's why they're locking us inside, so they can round them up."

The other two other patrons who'd dropped to their knees in prayer were now standing at the bar near Lalema, discussing the situation in whispers. They dressed like the rest of the locals, wearing clothes and accessories in bright colors. They looked nothing like Lalema, though. These beings had gray skin with small, raised bumps that flowed in a pattern over their heads and faces. Dana wasn't sure if they were male or female, but from their stance, they weren't any more comfortable with the situation than she was herself.

Dana turned to Ari. "Are you able to access any other information about what's going on, or how long this is going to take?"

Ari shook his head. "Not without access to a communications terminal."

The other two patrons were now coming their way, leaving Lalema at the bar. She pretended to look busy, though her large black eyes followed their movements.

When they reached the table, she saw they wore almost identical clothing, making it hard to tell them apart. They wore matching black boots on their feet, cargo pants in a dusty copper color, and green long-sleeved shirts. Other than the pattern of bumps over their skin, they looked the same to Dana.

"I am Mox, and this is my mate, Pak," the one on the right introduced themselves. "We are from Frakmana, and serve the Constants."

"Captain Dana Pinet, Zelenia," she said with a slight inclination of her head, not bothering to introduce the others or bring attention to her own lack of faith.

"We should not stay here," Mox said, casting a glance around the table. "It isn't as safe as it appears."

Pak remained silent, but looked around as if expecting someone to come up from behind them.

"What do you know about our current situation?" Dana asked.

"Only that the beetles have taken over the docks. If we don't get back to our ship, the beetles may destroy it. They inject a kind of enzyme into their prey that breaks down the fibers that hold it together so they can eat what is inside," Mox said. "We love all creatures, but that doesn't mean we'll let them destroy us or our home."

Dana frowned back at them. "Why would they destroy your ship?"

Pak and Mox looked back and forth between themselves as if silently determining if they should say anything more. Pak gave a slight head shake that Mox interpreted in the negative.

"You don't know?" Mox asked.

"Know what?"

"The metal doors will deter the beetles, but it won't keep them out. Our ship carries," Mox paused, as if searching for the right term, "food. Depending on which breed of beetle has gotten loose, they will use their poison to liquify the shell of our ship, or any other ship, to get what's inside."

Dana's stomach clenched in fear as she imagined them destroying the *Hope*. If the beetles got hungry enough, they'd probably go after the closest food source they could find. It didn't help matters that they were sitting in a cafe. However, the Nexus hundreds of shops and ships. Why would they go after one specific one over another?

"Lalema, another hot drink please," Dana called out as she settled back into her chair, turning her attention back on the Constants. "We're not going anywhere. There are lots of places the beetles will look for food. The chances of them coming all the way up here on the third level when they've got the entire dock level to hunt through is slim to none."

Dana felt all the eyes at her table on her. The girls were looking to her for cues on how to react. As soon as she seemed to relax, they did the same, as did the hairy creature she'd saved waiting under the table at her feet. It curled up under her chair, and before long, it was sleeping. Before long, the girls were huddled with their heads together, whispering and giggling. They didn't need to know how serious the situation was becoming. Mox and Pak didn't seem to take the hint, so Dana stood up and tapped Ari on the shoulder, signaling he should join her as she walked them all to the bar.

"Perhaps you do not believe us," Mox continued. "We should be more clear about the dangers."

"No, I do believe you, but not in front of the children," she said with a nod to her table.

Mox cocked their head. "They are your young?"

"One of them is," Dana said, feeling the need to clarify the situation. "In our culture, these things are not discussed in front of children. They are easily frightened and hard to calm in situations of distress. I don't want them scarred by any of this. She's had enough trauma in her life. You two do what you have to do, but we're staying."

"We mistook you for one in The Order because you

rescued the small helpless creature." Mox gestured to the small thing curled up near the girls' feet.

"Where I come from, it's just something we do. Thanks for the warning." Dana nodded at them, picked up her drink when Lalema placed it on the bar, and turned away, stepping out of earshot, Ari at her heels. "Ari, I need you to find the nearest communications terminal. We need to contact our ship and find out what's going on as soon as possible."

"There is a communications server close, but it appears to be hidden."

"Where?"

"It is in the back with the supplies and crates."

"Can you think of a reason to go back there?"

Ari's head tilted to one side, as if considering the question. "No, I cannot."

Dana huffed. She needed a reason to get back there, and for Ari to go with her. "Stay here." She turned and stepped back to the bar, putting her drink down once more. "I need the restroom."

Lalema shrugged. "It's in the back past the crates."

Dana thanked her and mode to leave, but Lalema called out again when she saw Ari following her.

"Hey, where's that thing going?"

"I don't know what's back there," Dana shot back. "I'm not going alone, especially at a time like this."

She put her hands on her hips, waiting for Lalema to protest. She blinked her large black eyes twice before she nodded.

"No pets near my produce. It stays in here," she said, glaring at the creature who had appeared next to Dana's boots and was now giving his version of a bark.

Dana held up a finger and commanded it to stay. It ran itself in a small circle before retreating back under her chair. Ari led Dana through the cafe, and they passed through an archway leading to a closed-door storeroom. The smell of whatever spices were in the stacked crates was so strong it made her eyes water.

"Are you all right, Captain?"

"It's pungent back here." Dana rubbed at her nose, eyes watering. "Where's the communications terminal?"

He pointed to the left. "It is just on the other side of these crates."

The bathroom was on the right. They'd have to be quick.

"Well, hook yourself up and find out what's going on with the *Hope*."

Once again, he removed the tip of his mechanical finger and inserted a nodule into the slot.

"Captain, the *Hope* has recalled all passengers and crew in the vicinity back to the ship. The docks are still locked down. They are prepared to leave the station on your orders."

"Send a direct message to Lieutenant Commander Valente with the locations of Wade, Maggie, Eartha, and myself, so they know we're all right and safe for the moment. They should leave whenever he deems it necessary."

"Done."

"Now let's get out of here before Lalema catches us."

"Too late," she shushed, slipping in behind them. "What do you think you're doing in here?"

"I didn't realize the communications terminal was off-limits," Dana replied carefully. "I needed to get a message to my ship."

"Why didn't you use your own personal comms?"

Dana frowned at her. "We don't have personal communications tech."

"You are from the beyond, aren't you?" Lalema shook her head and shushed again, then pointed a webbed hand at the door. "Stay away from my crates."

The girls were wide-eyed and curious when they returned. They'd moved from the table near the door and had found one closer to the bar. The hairy creature had stayed put under the chair, as Dana had commanded. Ari took his position behind her as Dana sat down to join the girls. She waved the little creature over, and it sat obediently at her side.

Before the girls could ask her what was going on, she gave a slight shake of her head. Lalema was still staring hard at her when she returned to the bar where Mox and Pak were waiting. When their attention was diverted again, she turned to Eartha.

"I got a message out to the *Hope*. Your parents are probably worried sick about you."

Eartha's eyes widened for a moment, but then her expression fell into one of bland indifference. She lifted one shoulder in a shrug.

"What?" Dana asked.

"I don't think they'll notice. They're too busy with the baby coming. They don't have time for me."

Dana sighed. She'd heard Eartha was struggling with things. She'd lost too many sets of parents, and no doubt was feeling anxious about her future.

"You know, I always wished I'd had a younger sibling."

"Why?" Eartha asked incredulously.

Dana shrugged. "I don't know. Being alone all the time as

a kid is rough. I would have liked someone to complain to about my parents. Someone to understand when I rolled my eyes at my mom or ignored my dad."

Eartha perked up, listening as if the idea had never occurred to her. But then she shook her head. "I don't know. He's going to be so much younger than me. We won't have anything in common."

"That's true. Being closer in age gives you a playmate, but this way you get the chance to teach them the things no one was around to show you growing up. Imagine what your life would have been like if you'd had an older sister looking out for you."

Eartha seemed to consider that for a moment. While she thought, Dana glanced at Bumi, who had a vein pulsing in the middle of her forehead. *Is she angry?*

"Something wrong?" Dana asked the girl.

She seemed to snap out of it, plastering a fake smile on her face.

I didn't think so, Dana said to herself. Whatever the girl was up to, she didn't like it. As soon as possible, she would have to get Eartha away from her.

"Maybe we shouldn't be here when the beetles come back," Bumi said, her eyes still on Dana in that unnerving way of hers.

"We should sit tight for now," Dana told them. "There's no point in putting ourselves in unnecessary danger. Bumi, why don't you go up to the bar and see if they've got another one of those pastries. We may be here for a while."

Eartha perked up, excited to change her mind just as Dana suspected she would be when offered the chance.

"Sure," Bumi said woodenly, standing and crossing over to the bar.

It wasn't far enough out of earshot for her to speak for very long, but Dana leaned over and whispered in Eartha's ear.

"I don't trust that girl. She's hiding something. If she tries to get us to split up for any reason, don't go with her alone."

When Dana leaned back, Eartha was staring wide-eyed at her, as if she'd told her she'd killed her pet turtle. There wasn't enough time to clarify herself though as Bumi returned, plopping down next to Eartha.

"All out," she said, holding up her hands in fake dismay.

Dana glanced back at the bar and saw Lalema staring after the girl with a look of confusion. She'd have bet a week's rations that she hadn't even asked for the dessert.

Eartha's eyes bounced between them, and she leaned in closer to her friend. "The captain isn't dumb. She knows," she said in a hiss to Bumi.

Dana's mouth fell open, not sure what she'd uncovered.

"She doesn't know anything," Bumi hissed back.

"I think you should tell us the truth," Eartha insisted.

Bumi looked Eartha dead in the eye. "Are you willing to do the same?"

Eartha's mouth clamped shut.

Dana watched the exchange with fascination, wondering what they were talking about. She'd obviously told Eartha something about herself that she was hiding from the rest of them.

Dana reached her hand over to lay it on top of Eartha's. "You know you can tell me anything. What exactly is going on? Who is this woman?"

Eartha glanced back at Bumi, her eyebrows drawing together. "You're not really a kid?"

Bumi's mouth opened to answer, but she closed it again when the scratching of claws against metal drew everyone's attention.

"Why are they trying to come in here?" Dana wondered aloud in dismay.

"There are over four hundred food vendors between the docks and this cafe," Ari replied. "The likelihood of them devouring everything, or pursuing this cafe in particular, is one in—"

Dana held up a hand. "Enough stats. The question is why?" She glanced back at Lalema and saw she and the other patrons were inching back toward the storeroom. Dana leaped up from her seat to join them. "They don't seem to use any kind of acid or venom to get inside, only their claws."

"They don't have an acid sac," Lalema countered. "The fluid inside of these will not burn through anything."

Dana frowned. "How do you know that?"

"Because if they were interested in getting inside, they would have melted the front door off the hinges already," Lalema confirmed with a brisk nod.

"So why are they trying to get in here?" Dana demanded.

Lalema shook her head, her large black eyes shifting from left to right. "I don't know," she stammered.

"That's not true," Bumi said from behind Dana.

But before she could confirm it, a large slice opened up in the metal door with a loud screech. A black leg with sharp hooks running down its length snaked inside. Dana was sure the beetles could sense their fear, and by the sounds of increased scrabbling, were growing even more excited.

"We need to get out of here, now!" Dana said.

Lalema led them all into the storeroom. Dana coughed again at the assault the spices had on her senses. Eartha gagged, covering her mouth. Bumi merely looked displeased.

"Hiding in here is going to be a problem," Dana said from behind her hand. "They can probably smell this place all the way to the docks."

"I believe you are correct, captain." Ari glanced around, as if seeing the crates for the first time. "The beetles seemed to be fixated on the smells in this storeroom."

"We need to hurry," Mox said. Pak stood at their side.

Lalema put a pale pink webbed hand to the wall. A panel light illuminated underneath it. She said something that the TMI translated as shushing, and a large durometal door four times as thick as the storefront slid open. Dana couldn't make anything out on the other side, and hesitated even as Lalema tried to usher them through.

"Where does this lead?"

"I'll explain, just go," she insisted, her high-pitched voice straining with the effort to watch her and her back at the same time.

Dana grabbed Eartha by the hand and stepped into the darkness. She looked back in time to see the beetle. It was as large as her transport vehicle on Zelenia and had four large, spiked legs. Its antennae reached out as if probing the air for something.

It let out a screech as Lalema stepped through into the dark corridor, letting the durometal door slam between them. Dana hadn't realized she was holding her breath until she couldn't hold it any longer. They all let out audible breaths, and Eartha, who'd plastered herself to Dana's back, finally peeked around her to make sure they were safe again.

On the other side of the door, the beetles continued to screech and scratch, but the durometal held up solidly against the assault. An answering screech from behind them had them all turning and clutching their chests. Lalema activated a light beam in her hand, and used it to scan the surrounding corridor.

"Are they in here, too?" Eartha squeaked in fear.

Dana didn't know the answer, and even if she did, she wouldn't tell the girl.

"Two levels down and to the right," Ari supplied.

"Thanks a lot," Dana said with sarcasm.

"You are welcome, Captain. Is there anything else I can do?"

"Be quiet."

Eartha had gone pale, and was gripping Dana's arm hard enough to hurt. The little hairy creature was at her side, panting from the effort of running with them. She was glad it hadn't gotten stuck on the wrong side of the door. Mox and Pak were shielding their eyes from the light beam. They didn't seem to need it to be able to see in the darkness, and Lalema lowered it to the floor when it was clear they were out of immediate danger.

The floor of the dark corridor was puddled with moisture, the air close and humid. It seemed to be outside of the general air filtration that existed on the public side of the Nexus. However, compared to the current condition of Lalema's cafe's storeroom, it was a welcome relief.

"We're okay for now. Let's find a way back to the ship." Dana turned to Lalema. "Which way to the docks?"

"Three levels down and to the left," Ari supplied instead.

"Are you crazy?" Mox glanced from her to Eartha. "You can't go down there! That's where they got loose. There may be more of them."

Lalema shook her head. "Not yet, but if there is a female among them, there could be babies. Though so far they seem to all be males," she said, the expression on her alien face unreadable.

Dana cringed as a ripple of fear crept up her back. "Babies?"

"Yes, the adults are large and can be captured, but the babies..." Lalema made a noise that was a cross between her shushing and a gurgle. "They'll tear through the walls of the space station. They're so dumb and so hungry they'll eat everything in their path."

"Captured?" Mox asked. "I think we need to be prepared to kill them."

Dana nodded, liking Mox's plan already.

"How do you know if they're going to have babies?" Eartha asked. Her wide-eyed question was directed at Lalema, who shrugged.

"You know all that screeching they're doing?" Lalema waited for her to nod. "That's their mating call. I'd say we're fine unless there is a female. If there is, their mating cycle doesn't take long, and within hours we could be in more trouble than we are now."

Not liking the sound of that, everyone in their small circle stiffened. Dana had no intention of waiting around for the beetles to capture them or for the possibility of babies. They needed to get back to the ship and defend themselves.

"Lalema, is there anyone nearby who might have weapons?" she asked.

"Weapons are not permitted on the space station," Mox said, quoting the rule book while Pak nodded in agreement.

"Yes, because we're not locals. But I think the locals are a little less compliant." Dana turned to Lalema. "Someone around here has to have a way to protect themselves. Please tell me you know of someone like that."

Lalema smacked her lips in thought. "There is someone, but he won't be happy I'm bringing you to see him. He may not give you anything either, and may damage you just for asking."

Dana drew back her shoulders. "I'll take that chance."

"We're not willing to take the risk," Mox argued. "This situation is out of control. If we follow you, we may end up dead, or worse. We will go in the opposite direction–away from the docks." Mox gave them each a nod, then took Pak by the hand and marched down the black corridor.

"I guess that means we're going this way," Dana said, jabbing her thumb to the right.

Lalema nodded doubtfully. "We will go visit the boss and see if he has anything to help you."

"Captain?" Eartha tugged at Dana's arm until she leaned down. She whispered, "We should not trust her."

Dana turned her mouth to Eartha's ear. "I'm getting that too. But for now, we stick together."

She took Eartha's hand and followed Lalema. Bumi seemed content to stay at their rear. Her following them in the dark made the hairs on the back of Dana's neck stand up, but she kept Eartha close.

CHAPTER 11

After they'd trailed Lalema down two corridors and followed a gradually curving third to the left, she pointed a webbed hand at the wall.

"There," Lalema said. "This guy has all the weapons we could possibly need."

Dana stared at the wall, the strange lettering marking it barely legible in the dark. She could barely make out her hand in front of her face. If it hadn't been for Lalema's palm light and Ari's finger light, she would have stumbled and fallen on her face already.

"It just looks like a wall," Eartha said, staring at it along with the rest of them.

"The appearance can deceive," Bumi said.

That's the truth, Dana thought, smirking in the dark. "How do we get inside?"

"He's got a backdoor, just like the rest of us. We just need to get his attention first and maybe he'll open up."

Dana felt along the wall, looking for some way to signal the door. Her hand ran into something.

"Ari, over here. Shine that light on this edge."

The small light illuminated a bit of the edging, along with a pulsing red thread when her hand had brushed against it.

"It's got a bio-reader, but it won't recognize us," Lalema said. "Can the android crack it?"

Dana looked at Ari, who shook his head.

"I do not have that capability. It seems that I have been less than useful so far."

"That's okay, Ari. This is a new place for all of us," Eartha said, reaching for his non-mechanical hand and letting go of Dana's.

"I guess we'll have to get his attention the old-fashioned way," Dana said. "Ari, please knock."

Ari pulled back the sleeve on his mechanical hand and hit his fist against the wall three times, the rock crumbling where he'd struck it. They waited less than a minute before the door slid to one side.

A tall creature with exaggerated facial features, no hair, and heavy, drawn together brows opened the door, peering down at them. His muscles bulged in odd places, but no doubt served him well. A brute was the best term Dana could use to describe him.

"What are you doing here?" he asked, staring at Lalema, who didn't seem frightened by him at all.

Eartha was at her back, but Dana stood tall as his gaze passed over each of them.

"Where's Mack?" Lalema asked.

"He's busy. We've got bugs all over the place." He spoke with a slower cadence, several decibels deeper than any human speech.

Dana wasn't sure if the brute meant they had beetles

inside, or if they were merely preparing to deal with them. Either way, she leaned back from the door.

Lalema shushed and placed her hands on her hips. "We need to see him."

He shrugged. "You want to get in his way, your funeral. Oh, and no pets," he added, peering down at the small creature by Dana's boots.

Dana knelt and, with one hand palm out, signaled for it to stay put.

The brute peered into the dark behind them before ushering them inside. He indicated with one hand they should wait as he stepped out of the room through a sliding door. In the short time that the door was open, Dana could hear the staccato beat of pulse fire, silenced again as the door closed behind him. Around them, the stockroom was filled top to bottom with crates. The markings on them were as unfamiliar as the ones that had been on the outer wall.

"Ari, what do these crates say?" Dana whispered.

"I am not familiar with this language. It is not based on the Common spoken on the space station."

They didn't have to wait long before the brute returned with another individual that she assumed was Mack, who must be the brains of the outfit. Built like an accountant, he was physically the opposite of the brute except for a pronounced brow. He had wiry arms and legs, but his green eyes were sharp as they took in their group. With no muscles to speak of, his clothes seemed to hang off his bones. He scowled at them before looking back at the brute, then lifted a weapon the size of a shock-glock from the front of his trousers and aimed the barrel at Eartha.

"What is this Gorgi?" he demanded with the voice of a

twelve-year-old-boy. "We're in the middle of a crisis. That's why I have you, so I don't have to deal with rats sneaking in my back door."

Before the brute, Gorgi, finished stumbling over his words, Lalema spoke up.

"Mack, we need weapons," she said, her voice less demanding and more pleading. "I brought credits. We can pay."

Dana stared at her. She had nothing to bring to this exchange. She'd already spent most of their earned credits on food, she doubted the twenty she had left would be much help. Dana wondered what they could get with whatever Lalema had.

Mack sneered back at them. "No."

As he turned to leave, Lalema spoke out. "Wait, if there are any of those beetles around, we're all in danger. You know that."

"Don't pretend to care, Lalema, it's annoying," Mack said, his features contorting into concern as a crash behind him drew his attention. Whatever was going on, he was doing his best to salvage the front of his shop. He turned back with a deep frown. "We're closed."

"Look," Dana said, stepping forward, her hands raised, "I don't know exactly what kind of business you're running, or why you've got a soundproof door to this room. But I'm going to guess it isn't legal, and you wouldn't want the IC to find out about it."

He turned to glare at her, waving the weapon in his hand toward her. "I knew you were an IC rat the moment I laid eyes on you. How dare you threaten me? I should shoot you down where you stand."

Another crash had him yelling something the TMI couldn't translate.

"The odds are better for all of us if you give us some weapons," Dana insisted. "I'm an excellent shot. I was at the top of my marksmanship class at the Space Fleet Academy. People are getting killed out there, so how about you loan us a few of your products, and we'll help keep the beetles we find off your shop?"

Mach groaned in frustration. "I don't know what a Space Fleet Academy is, but I'll make you a deal. I'll give you one of my weapons, but you're going to pay a fifty percent markup."

"Deal," Dana said, rubbing her hands together. When he didn't move to arm her, she stared at him, wondering what was wrong.

"Credits first."

Ah. Right.

"How much are they?" Dana asked.

"Two hundred credits each on a good day." Mack tilted his head. "Today they're three hundred."

Dana looked at Lalema, who shook her head and shrugged. It seemed to be more than she carried.

"We'll give you what we've got for a deposit and pay the rest later," Dana tried.

Mack shook his head. "That's not going to work. You'll be dead later. Credits upfront, or no deal."

Dana had very little to bargain with, but she had more than most.

"How about a shuttle?" she asked.

The smaller man paused, his eyes lighting up.

"I'll pay you later. If I get killed, then you can have one of our shuttles. That's more than fair since a shuttle is worth far more than a couple of weapons."

"Two weapons," Mack shot back.

"Six." Dana fought the grin that threatened to give her away. "Two weapons each. We won't be able to resupply ammunition."

The man rubbed his chin, a stalling tactic she knew well.

"Four, and I get paid by the end of the day."

"Five, or no deal."

He seemed to be considering that for a moment. "I'll get fifteen hundred credits by the end of today if you survive."

"And a shuttle if we don't."

"Deal." Mack narrowed his eyes at her. "How do I know you'll hold up your end of the bargain?"

"Ari, make a note of our transaction and store it in a readily accessible memory."

A panel in Ari's mechanical arm opened, and he removed a small chip. He handed it to Mack, who looked it over.

"That will get you past the ship's security and hold a record of our transaction, should something happen to me," Dana explained.

Mack spread his arms wide, pointing to the crates. "Take your five from any of these crates. Most of them are pulse weapons, but all of them will work on the beetles. Then go out the way you came in." He turned to Gorgi, who stood wringing his hands as if befuddled. "Make sure they take no more than five."

"Sure, boss." Gorgi stood with his arms crossed over his chest, a bit more confident as Mack went back to the front of his shop, leaving them alone.

"Let's get our weapons," Dana said.

Lalema handed a metallic card to her before she could step forward. "Here, take this and put it toward the weapons."

Dana returned the card with a shake of her head. "No, it's okay. It's our deal. We'll give you one of our weapons for helping us get these and leading us to our ship."

She nodded and reached into the nearest crate, choosing a smallish handgun.

"Ari, take the two biggest ones you can carry," Dana said as she dug into the same crate as Lalema for another small handgun, testing the safety and slipping it into her belt. She reached in and grabbed an arm's-length weapon double the size of the one Mack carried, a blue looking plasma loaded inside.

"Careful, those are powerful," Lalema warned.

Dana nodded. "Good."

"What about us?" Bumi asked.

"Children don't carry guns on our world, so stick close." Dana's lips quirked at the way Bumi huffed, crossing her arms.

"Don't need them anyway," she mumbled.

Once they had what they came for, Gorgi made a visual check on a small thermal readout of the corridor. When he was satisfied there was nothing on the other side, he pressed the button, and the wall slid to one side. Dana and her group filed back out the door.

A glance around out in the corridor showed that the little hairy creature was no longer there. Dana figured it had gotten bored and gone off to find its way back home.

"Hey little guy, where'd you go?" The silence of the corridor was her only response. *May the Majestic protect you.* She sighed. Then turned to the others, taking command.

"Okay, let's get back to the ship." Dana turned to Eartha. "You stay close to me. Ari, you'll be our first line of defense. Lalema, you stay in the rear and make sure nothing is creeping up on us." The last statement was meant as much for Bumi as it was for the beetles. Lalema nodded, and Ari started down the corridor toward the docks.

Strangely enough, they hadn't run into anyone else escaping through the back tunnels. In a structure like the Nexus space station, Dana found it odd.

"Do all the businesses have a back door like you do?" she asked Lalema.

Lalema smacked her lips. "No. Many of us put them in because we didn't want our cargo or products carried through our front entrance."

Dana thought of the offensive smell of Lalema's cargo and had to agree. Though Mack's reasons were much different. His room had two soundproof doors, a convenient feature when dealing with criminals. Dana had never considered herself on the wrong side of the law before, and now she'd twice gone against the IC's orders.

Ari, technically a weapon himself, was still roaming the ship with them, and now she was carrying even more illegal weapons. If she ran into any IC, she wondered if she would even get the chance to explain before they hauled her away.

A screeching from up ahead had them all stopping in their tracks. Not one beetle, but two slid over the wet floor in front of them, blocking their way. Up close, in the dimly lit corridor, Dana finally saw the beetles in their entirety for the first time, and couldn't hold back the gasp of shock that escaped her.

Their large talons sparked as they scratched at the walls,

as if doing their own hunt for secret passages. The six black orbs of their eyes reflected the light as they rolled around in the glossy carapace of their segmented bodies. Lalema had turned off her light, as had Ari, but it seemed too late. The beetle's antennae quivered in the air before another loud screech filled the tunnel.

Everything that followed registered in unyielding slow motion.

Eartha clapped her hands over her ears to block out the beetles' screeching as it echoed down the corridor. Bumi pulled her away from Dana as they charged straight for them. Ari managed to aim and fire off a shot with the pulse cannon, one beetle exploding in a splash of green viscera before he was knocked to the floor by the other.

The second beetle ignoring Ari, leaped into the air to attack. Dana lifted her pulse rifle and aimed, blowing it into a million pieces before it landed on top of her. The green guts of the thing rained down on her, the sulphuric stench of rotten eggs and dead fish filling the tunnel. She spat, trying desperately to remove the taste from her tongue.

A slurping sound made her turn. She watched as Lalema licked the green goo from her fingers one by one, moaning in delight.

"Ugh!" Dana shouted, unable to keep back the wave of disgust.

Lalema eyed her. "You weren't saying that when you were having my Buk To. It's even better in its raw form."

Dana wasn't sure she'd heard right. "Are you saying these giant beetles are... are Buk To?"

"Yes." Lalema tilted her head. "What did you think it was?"

Dana gagged. She looked down and startled when she found the little hairy creature had reappeared, licking the goo off her boots.

"Where did you come from?" Dana asked the little beast, looking all around for a place he could have popped out from.

"Are you all right, Captain?" Ari asked, bumping her with the weapon dangling from a strap around his neck.

"I'm fine. Let's get this green goo off me before it stains my uniform." Dana turned around. "Wait, where's Eartha?"

Ari tilted his head to listen before he straightened and turned back to her. "She's in the ventilation system."

"How the *sou* do you know that?"

Ari pointed to the open ventilation shaft along the edge of the wall. It was too small for anyone other than the creature and the girls to fit into. Eartha may have been safe from the beetles, but whatever Bumi had planned, Dana was sure it wouldn't be good.

CHAPTER 12

WADE

The next time Wade opened his eyes, he was burning up. He tried to swallow, but there wasn't enough moisture in his mouth. Maggie was at his side in seconds. He must have moaned because she was talking to him in a tight, high-pitched voice. Wade tried to tell her to slow down, but the words didn't reach his tongue, stuck burning in his head.

"I'm going to help you, sweetheart, I promise," he heard her say.

He felt her cool lips on his forehead, then a brush of air as she moved away from him. Wade realized with the part of his brain that was still working that he was fighting an infection. He must be delirious. If he didn't stay hydrated, he might die of it.

Where is she? He needed to tell her to keep the fire going and bring him water.

Wade didn't know how long he waited, but at some point he felt something cool on his forehead and lips. He opened his mouth to it and water rushed in. He gulped it down and groaned when it disappeared. It returned, and he swallowed through the burning in his throat, making him choke. His whole body felt like it was on fire, and he slipped back into the darkness, waiting for the next cool touch.

HE CAME TO A LONG WHILE LATER. A COOL BREEZE BRUSHED HIS skin, and he shivered. He took inventory of his body with his eyes still closed. His chest ached as if something had hit him. He tried to pull his blanket up under his chin, but his arms were leaden and refused to obey.

Memories were slow to return. He and Maggie had crash-landed on this planet. His leg was broken. Was Maggie still hanging from the tree root? No, he'd have heard her screaming by now. Instead, he heard the crackle of a fire. It was close. The air smelled of ash and a hint of something else. Something savory.

He wasn't alone. Maggie was humming to herself nearby, and he pried his eyes open to see what had put her in such a good mood.

The sun stung his eyes and he blinked against it as the blobs and colors around him came into focus. He struggled to make sense of Maggie's silhouette against the backdrop of the sun's rays, pouring through the trees outside the cave where he lay. His throat was dry, but he swallowed a few times and then, when he was sure he could get the words out, spoke.

"I hope some of that is for me." His voice was a raspy croak, barely above a whisper, but it startled her.

"Wade!" Maggie dropped what she was doing and crawled over to him. "Oh, thank the stars you're alive."

Up close, he could see she looked different. She wasn't wearing the tattered yellow sundress anymore. Her red mane was tied in a topknot, and she smelled fresh.

"What happened?"

"You came down with a fever, that's what. The infection in your leg was so bad I thought I might have to cut it off to save your life."

If she had, he couldn't be sure. He didn't have the strength to ask the question, but he raised an eyebrow, which made her giggle.

"Of course I didn't. I cleaned you up and found the infected wound on your knee. As soon as it was cleaned and cauterized, you were on the way to being fine. Your fever broke yesterday, and I knew you'd be out until you were ready to wake up. I thought I was going to go crazy all by myself."

Wade licked his lips, working up to interrupting her, but she interpreted his need before he said it, and brought a small bowl of cool water to his lips, helping him drink it down. He looked over the wooden bowl with some surprise.

"I didn't make it. It was a piece of bark that broke off just so, and I fashioned it into a bowl. Another piece I use for a plate and that's all for the dishes. I found some other things you'll be interested in hearing about, but I don't want to talk your ears off."

Wade smiled as she rambled and shook his head. "No, tell me everything. How long have I been out?"

Maggie's eyes turned glassy, and she reached out to touch him. He wasn't sure if it was meant to reassure him, or her.

"You've been out for a month."

"A month?" he echoed, voice cracking.

"Well, technically it's been two of our weeks, but on this planet, the sun goes up and down so fast I had to switch to the local time. Right now, it's eight or ten o'clock in the morning. A couple of days ago the temperature dropped. I'm starting to wonder what kind of seasons this place has."

Maggie moved around the space as she rattled on. He saw her pick up a thin stick and poke at the fire before bringing over the 'plate'. She tested whatever it was that she'd been cooking with one finger and found it cooled enough she could tear off a piece and feed it to him. Wade opened his mouth, no questions asked, and accepted it. It was smooth in texture, and it slid down his throat with little effort.

"That's good."

"I found a bird's nest in a nearby tree. She had three eggs this morning. I'm so excited. The first time I found it I got two eggs, but I knocked the whole nest down and she and her lovebird had to start over."

Maggie popped some of the egg into her mouth as she waited for him to chew between bites. He shook his head after several more bites. He didn't have much of an appetite. Wade was only eating because he needed it for strength.

"Are you sure?" she asked with a frown.

He nodded. "It was good, but I'm still worn out. You said you found some other stuff?"

"After you fell into a fever, it took me a while to do more than gather wood and look for eggs. I was afraid of running into one of those giant wolves."

"Giant wolves?" Wade asked, perking up in interest.

"That thing that tried to attack me when I went for wood the first day, remember?" She continued on as if he'd answered. "Well, we were both getting pretty funky in here, and I needed something to wear on my feet, so I ventured a little further away up the ridge. I found another pod."

"There are other survivors?" Wade blurted out, but Maggie shook her head.

She held up a finger to signal she needed a minute to finish chewing and swallowing. Then she drew out the suspense even more by taking a drink from the bowl. When she spoke again, her voice was soft and serious.

"There was blood everywhere. Inside the pod, outside the pod, on the ground." Maggie gulped as her eyes filled. "If they'd only made it back inside the pod in time..."

"They?"

Maggie turned around, picking something up off the ground. She slowly turned, cradling a pair of child's shoes in her hands. "It took me almost the whole day to get the blood off their clothes and shoes."

Wade sucked in a breath and shook his head. Not the little girl and her mother from the station. The ones he'd thought he'd saved, putting them in their pod together.

Maggie let the tears fall when she saw Wade understood.

"I was angry with them for taking that pod until I saw them. It took me two days, but I buried their remains and salvaged what I could from them and their pod."

That's where she'd found the clothes. The boots on her feet had belonged to the dead mother. The child's shoes were still in her hands.

"I saved these in case they came to rescue us," she said softly. "I wanted something to give to the girl's family."

"Rescue?"

She nodded. "The beacon on their pod works. I turned it on and secured the pod, then left the marks on the ground directing them to the cave if they find it."

Wade lifted his hand until he could reach her leg. She clasped one in hers and smiled.

"You did good, Mags."

She nodded. "Thanks. I'm learning. There's still more we can strip off the pod, but I figured we could do it together once you were feeling better."

"Good idea. I don't want you going back there alone. The smell may still bring predators around. But you found water?"

"There's a stream about half a mile away. I haul water back every day so we have something to drink. I bathe there, and I'm sorry, but I've only had the energy to bathe you once. It was more because I needed your clothes than anything."

Wade's neck and cheeks grew hot as he realized he was naked under the coverings. Maggie's cheeks were flushed as well.

"It wasn't anything I hadn't seen before. I didn't take advantage of you or anything."

"No, I'm just embarrassed. I hadn't had a shower since rationing energy back on the *Hope*. I was probably pretty disgusting."

Maggie smiled. "Don't worry about it. You can make it up to me by getting better and going down to the river yourself."

He couldn't help smiling with her. "You saved my life," he said with wonder as his eyes fluttered with exhaustion. He'd pushed it, and now he was so tired he could barely focus on her.

"Yeah," she said softly. "Now we're even."

CHAPTER 13

Maggie's Diary
Day 30

Wade woke up yesterday. I'm conflicted. His eyes are free of the brightness of fever, and when he looks at me, there's something soft that wasn't there before. It grates on me. It reminds me too much of how things were between us. I miss him dreadfully, and like a nervous bird, I'm afraid of making any sudden movements for fear he'll fly away and never come back.

I know things can't go back to the way they were, but something inside me wants to believe they can. It's been so long, and there's been no contact from our ship or the Nexus space station.

In the commotion, they'll have declared us dead, in which case it will take them a lot longer to find us. Though, if she cares for him as much as he cares for her, she'll come.

For now I guess I'll do what I can to keep him placated and easy going. There will be no mention of what was between us, and *we'll continue to side-step any subjects leaning toward dangerous relationship mines that would turn our civility into an all-out war.*

We need each other for survival, and I'm willing to hold on to that tether with all I have. If someone ever finds my journals, I want to be honest. The man with whom I shared my last days was one that I once loved, and could very well love again, if only he'd let me.

CHAPTER 14

EARTHA

Bumi nudged Eartha through the tight ventilation shaft, giving her non-verbal instructions until they reached a junction, where she stopped. It smelled just as bad as the corridor had after the first beetle had exploded, and her hands and knees felt just as grimy. However, at least the junction was big enough that she could sit, giving her knees a rest.

When the beetles had attacked, she hadn't thought twice. Bumi had pushed her into the vents, and she'd followed. It was a safe place for more reasons than one. Eartha had spent her first two weeks on the *Hope* in the ventilation system, though compared to the Nexus, the *Hope's* system was pristine. She'd felt safe there. This was nothing like it.

Bumi situated herself to one side of the vent while Eartha waited on the other.

"Why did we leave the Captain and Ari?" Eartha asked.

"It's not safe with them." Bumi's eyes shifted, and her left ear twitched, as if she were listening to something Eartha couldn't hear. "Do you hear that?"

"I don't hear anything. What do you mean it's not safe with them?"

Bumi crossed her legs and held up a hand. "Wait. Just breathe, focus, and listen."

Eartha sucked in a large gulp of stale air and closed her eyes. Then she heard it.

An army of beetles, the sound of their large legs clicking against the metal of the station's floor getting louder.

"They're coming this way," Eartha gasped.

"Yes, and your captain and the android won't be able to protect you."

Eartha scoffed. "And *you* can?"

Bumi lifted one sculpted eyebrow. A smile quirked at the edge of her mouth. "Don't you get it, yet? You and I are from the same world, Eartha. We're able to do things the people who raised you can't."

Eartha shook her head. She wasn't sure she understood. How could they be from the same world? Did she know Eartha's parents? "What do you mean?"

"I'm from Trellis, like I told you, but I'm not as young as you." Bumi's smirk was bemused. "Your captain was right about that part. However, she doesn't understand our people or our race. She doesn't trust me. I had to get you away from them to help you into the next phase of your development and determine if you're ready to return home."

Eartha perked up. What if this girl knew her family? Did they miss her? Was she their only child? What would they think of her? She had too many questions to keep the hope out of her voice. "Do you know my parents?"

Bumi nodded. "I do. But before we go down memory lane, there's something you need to learn about your abilities."

"You mean when I see things or have dreams?"

"Those are not predictive dreams," Bumi said, shaking her head. "You can hear thoughts and intentions. Sometimes they come to you very clearly, and sometimes they are hidden, and you have to look for them. You can even direct the thoughts or intentions of others, but this takes much practice."

"You can do it, too?"

"Not exactly. I can listen, as you do, but I cannot change the intentions of those around me. There is something else I can do, and I'll share it with you later, but for now, you have to trust me. I know what's best for you, and right now, this challenge is the perfect way to hone your skills."

"You mean when I saw my teacher in the car accident, and the vines from planet 2396, that was me 'listening'?"

"Yes. At that moment, their thoughts were strong enough for you to reach with little trouble. Of course, your abilities have been growing stronger, and are much affected by your emotions. When you have anxiety, they heighten, and sometimes are not fully within your control."

Eartha nodded, trying to understand. She wasn't sure she could control it even if she tried.

"You've been able to use your gift before to influence others' actions." It wasn't a question, but Bumi waited, eyebrows raised, for an answer.

Eartha nodded slowly. "When the ship was infected with

an alien virus. People were violent and out of control. I made them go to sleep, but it made me tired, too."

"That is an effect of the extreme use of a new power. It weakens you because you have to draw on the strength from within, and you hadn't used it before, so it took a lot out of you. The more you use it, the easier it will become. Though, not all species are as easy to influence as your people are." Bumi frowned. "The beetles, for example, will be difficult.They only listen to the voice of their queen."

"You want me to put them to sleep?" Eartha asked.

"Not exactly, but for you to help your people, you're going to have to do something you've never done before." Bumi held out one slender hand. "Are you ready to try?"

Eartha wasn't sure she understood her role, but Bumi knew about her ability. She'd called them gifts. She wasn't afraid of them. To her, they were normal, and something to improve on with practice.

Eartha reached out and took her hand. "I'm not sure. What are we going to do now?"

"We're going to go to the docks. But we're not looking for your ship."

Bumi turned down one of the adjoining ventilation shafts and started crawling.

"Can you tell me more about Trellis and our people?" Eartha asked as she filed in behind her.

"Of course," Bumi said. "Our world is unique in the universe. Before the five stars came from heaven, it had no life. The five stars are the queens that rule our worlds, now populating much of our galaxy."

"How many planets are there?"

"The Trellis control twenty-five planets in our system."

"Does everyone have gifts?"

"No. The gifts are only granted to the children of the stars." Bumi shimmied through a tight bend into a new section of the vent. "Be silent through this area. We are close to where the beasts are traveling, and we don't want to draw attention to ourselves."

Eartha's nose wrinkled as she recognized the stink of the beetles, so strong she clamped her mouth closed to keep the smell from coalescing on her tongue. The two inched along the ventilation shaft, and when Eartha came to a section of grating, she couldn't resist looking down at them.

Even with their attention on something else, the beetles were terrifying. The scratching noise of their segmented legs on the metal flooring was too much. Eartha shivered, moving out of view of the grate as soon as she could.

Once they'd turned to the left and away from the hold where the beetles had gathered, Bumi spoke again, continuing the story where she'd left off.

"The five stars rule our people as queens and have brought peace for centuries. It is their duty to serve the people and bear the future rulers of our world."

"So, you don't have one person in charge? That's good, right?"

"The five bring balance because the five are perfectly balanced within themselves. It is their fair judgments and rule that have improved our people. We are not made up of one race. We have continued to add variety to ourselves. Though our culture and beliefs are dominant, each new assimilated species adds their uniqueness to ours, creating an improved version of ourselves."

Eartha thought about that for a moment, letting the idea

of what life would be like living around beings who were so different from herself play out in her mind. When they reached the next junction, Bumi stopped again, allowing time for Eartha to catch up. In the dark, Eartha met her eyes, though with no light. She couldn't remember which was blue and which was green.

"Who are you really?" Eartha asked. "How did you know I was from Trellis, too?"

Bumi's smile was coy. "That will take a little longer to explain, and we don't have much time. We need to hurry if we're going to get to where we will be most able to help the station and your captain."

"Help them?"

Bumi nodded. "You're going to help save them all, but traveling this way is slow."

"But you know my real parents,"Eartha said, mind still sticking on that fact, catching on it over and over. "Are they still alive?"

Bumi bit down on her lower lip. For the first time since they'd been together, she didn't appear to have it all together.

"I shouldn't tell you too much of anything too fast. First, I need to help you tap into your abilities on a different level. Then we'll see."

"Like a test?"

"An evaluation of a sort, yes." Bumi paused for a moment, meeting her gaze. "Your mother and father are not as you imagine. They will not look like your lost parents on Zelenia. However, they care for you very much. They are the ones that sent me to find you."

Eartha's heart lightened for the first time since learning the truth about her people. They cared about her. They wanted her despite how she'd been feeling. They might have been searching for her all the time, not knowing that Zelenia had been destroyed.

"When did they send you?"

"As soon as we heard of the destruction of your planet. We went there to see if you were one of those left behind. When we did not find you, we assumed you were with the survivors on one of the ships."

"Wait, what do you mean?" Eartha asked, dropping her voice to a whisper when she heard a beetle skitter by. "There are more ships from Zelenia?"

"Yours was not the only one. The others were sent in opposite directions, all looking for a new planet."

"How many? Who's on the other ships?"

When Eartha's questions grew too loud, Bumi held up a hand.

"We must be quiet," she whispered. "I promise to tell you everything I can, but it is too dangerous here. We need to keep moving."

Eartha nodded her assent, but couldn't help asking just one more question. "How many other ships?"

"Two."

Eartha's heart leaped with joy. What if her mom and dad were on one of the other ships? They'd be reunited, and she would find out the truth. Maybe there were others she knew who had survived as well!

She couldn't wait to tell the Captain. Everyone would be so excited when they found out they weren't the last Zelenians alive.

CHAPTER 15

"Happiness is a full belly and a full ocean."
- From *A Tale of Happiness* an Ostea poem

DANA

Bumi had taken Eartha. Dana paced the sticky green floor, furious with herself for having taken her eyes off the girl for even a minute.

"If you would like me to retrieve Eartha, Captain, I can track them."

Ari was eager for an android, but despite his close bond with Eartha, Dana needed him with her. She and Lalema wouldn't be able to hold off more than one beetle at a time.

Dana shook her head. "No, I need you here. The vents are too small for us to follow, so the beetles don't have a chance at reaching them. She's safe, for now."

"The babies will be able to fit," Lalema said between smacks of her tongue in her mouth.

"Thank you for that bit of knowledge," Dana said dryly, rolling her eyes to the ceiling. She let out a weary sigh. "Ari, are they headed for the docks?"

Ari turned his head, listening. "I believe so. The ventilation shaft is not the most direct route. Like these corridors, it follows the shape of the space station. However, I believe they went in the direction most likely to lead to the docks."

"Are you sure?"

"There is a seventy-eight percent probability based on their direction and speed."

A high, vibrating screeching ahead of them got their attention.

"Good enough. Let's keep going." Dana picked up the little hairy creature and tucked it inside the ventilation shaft. "You're safer with them, little guy. Go!"

The beast stared up at her and whined. The little thing was starting to grow on her. Better she get rid of it before it got any ideas about following her home.

"Ari, replace the grate so the little guy can't follow us. It's too dangerous. Either he'll catch up with the girls, or someone will find him."

"Yes, Captain." Ari did as she told him, replacing the grate. There was more whining, and some scratching at first, but before long, she heard his little paws scampering through the tunnels.

Dana nodded to Lalema and started down the corridor, the others trailing behind her.

"Does this happen a lot?" Dana asked.

Lalema shook her head. "No, this is the first time since I

opened the cafe that there's been a lockdown of the entire station."

"These space beetles though. You must know a lot about them. Where do they come from?"

"They're from the Ming Fa system. The planet where they originated is still there. They are shipped in for Buk To." Lalema stopped abruptly when they heard a distant screech.

Then there was an eruption of pulse fire ahead of them and on the right.

"Come on!" Dana called, running toward the sound. When she turned the corner of the corridor she was standing behind three beetles who had three IC agents cornered. Dana recognized them from their uniforms and helmets. A fourth beetle was already immobile on the ground, and the agents continued to fire on the other three.

Ari stepped in and finished off two by himself while Lalema and Dana took care of the third, who had leaped on top of one agent. The green goo of the destroyed beetles covered the small contingent, the agents panting as they got to their feet.

As Dana reached out to help one stand, there was a moment of recognition.

"I thought I told you to return to the Major," said the man Dana recognized as the leader of the six agents who'd been charged with escorting her back to her ship. "I thought I told you to escort her straight up to the IC?" He swiveled around to look at the agent who was on the ground.

She shrugged, and Dana cleared her throat.

"Are you going to worry about protocol, or thank me for saving your butts?" Dana asked.

"I gave you a direct order to go up to the IC office," he said to Dana.

She pulled her shoulders back and faced him down despite the disparity of their heights. "I don't do well with orders."

He lifted his helmet visor for the first time, and Dana got a good look at the man's face. Bright green eyes glared down at her. His pale skin was smooth other than the thick, dark brows over his eyes. Human in every sense of the word, and, if she was being honest with herself, attractive.

"Fair enough. You're right. We can't really stand on protocol at a time like this," he said, looking around at the damage they'd caused. He let out a sharp breath through his nose, then stuck out a hand to shake Dana's in thanks. "Thank you, Captain. Agent Vandermann. And I need to insist you return to the fifth ring and wait in our offices. These beetles are running amok, and there's no way to protect the entire station. The locals are being picked off like flies."

"I'm afraid I'm going to have to disagree," Dana countered. "You need us right now. As you can see, my android can carry twice the firepower I can on my own and we've enlisted some help." She met the agent's eyes, lifting a brow. "If you don't ask us any questions, we'll proceed to my ship as planned."

The man considered her rag-tag little crew for a moment, then his head tilted to one side as if he were listening to something. Dana listened for the sound of the space beetles, but didn't hear anything. Vandermann shook his head. "It's not a good idea."

"But it is an idea," another agent said from behind him.

Dana recognized her as the one who'd been trying to telepath her way into her mind.

"Do you mind sharing your thoughts with the rest of the class?" Dana asked, tapping a foot with impatience.

The other agent lifted her helmet visor. The familiar face of Agent Sorel smirked back at her. "I was just saying that a little help might not be a bad idea."

"I think it's the smartest suggestion you've had all day," Dana said, readjusting her pulse rifle over her shoulder.

"It's not the best plan, but it might be all we've got. We could use the help."

"I was just waiting for you to make me an offer," Dana said, her mouth lifting to one side.

"An offer?" Sorel echoed indignantly, turning on Dana in a flash.

Dana's nostrils flared in response. "Yes. We are, as you know, in a tight spot. We need credits to get off this space station and pay for the weapons that just saved you from certain death. I'm sure the IC can find a way to reward us for our efforts."

"We don't have time for this," the third agent said. His voice was rough with exhaustion, and he looked barely able to stand. He had nothing in his hands.

Had he been fighting the beetles with his bare hands?

"There's something you don't know," Vandermann said.

"No–"

Vandermann raised a hand, cutting Sorel's protest short.

"They need to know all the facts if we're going to nego- tiate a deal," he said, turning his green eyes on Dana.

Sorel backed down, dropping her eyes to the floor. Dana

waited at attention. What more could there be than a bunch of rogue beetles rampant on the Nexus?

"The Nexus power generator is offline."

Only then did Dana realize that the faint buzz that had been under her boots for that past seven hours was gone. No wonder it had been so easy to hear the beetles coming. Indeed, the familiar rumble had stopped, along with the general commotion of the space station. There was nothing but eerie silence. The emergency lighting was still active, though.

Vandermann must have noticed her looking up at the lights, because he shook his head. "You don't understand. The generator is stopped. That means if there's a power build-up in the core, the entire station will blow. All we have left are the backups, and they won't last forever. Not with the size of the Nexus and the number of species on it that need to breathe."

Dana looked at Ari, who seemed to process the information silently.

"What do we do?" she asked.

"You need to get to your ship and get off the Nexus," Vandermann said firmly. "We're on our way to the generator to stop the explosion."

Torn between helping them and helping her people, Dana thought through the consequences of each choice within seconds.

"Captain, I'll make you a deal," he added. "Help us get to the generator, and then not only are you free to return to your ship, I'll plead your case to ensure you have enough credits to get yourselves off the Nexus. I can't promise you enough pay to cover illegal weapons, though."

Vandermann held out a hand to shake.

Dana took it without preamble. "You've got a deal, Agent Vandermann."

He gave her a tight nod. "Agent Sorel, take point. Captain, you and your friend flank the rest of us from the rear. I'll need the android to help me with Agent Hoffman."

Lalema stood looking confused until Dana signaled for her to stay in the back with her as they followed the others. Vandermann used Ari as a crutch for his injured man while he kept his weapons at the ready.

At first, Dana wasn't sure why Agent Sorel was in the lead until she remembered she could communicate with a thought. Her voice broke into her thoughts, and she assumed those of the others as well.

"Wait, something's coming this way."

Everyone halted except for Lalema. Dana grabbed her sleeve, stopping her. It was then that Dana realized Lalema couldn't hear Agent Sorel. She'd have to relay the messages to her as they came. She wondered how often that happened to Agent Sorel, if there were many other species that she couldn't read or hear.

Agent Sorel raised a hand and they waited. Dana held her breath as she strained to hear whatever had stopped them in their tracks. Then she waved them forward and they were racing through the dark tunnels again, only to stop fifty meters ahead.

They found two crumpled bodies, shaped wrongly, as though they had been drained from the inside. The distinctive copper pants and matching green shirts identified them as the two beings who had split off from Dana's original cafe crew, Mox and Pak.

"The Frakmanans," Lalema said. She whispered some-thing Dana couldn't understand. Lalema's only interpretation for the words was, "They were of The Order of the Prophet Dasha. They didn't make it."

"No," Dana said, taking a steadying breath, "but we will."

Lalema shook her head. "If Dasha didn't protect them, what chance do we have?"

"We don't need The Prophet right now, we need you," Agent Sorel said, her brown eyes intense as she looked between Dana and Lalema. "It's not far now. We need to hurry. They're coming."

Agent Sorel ran ahead. Dana could only go as fast as the injured man in front of her could move, but Vandermann stuck close to Sorel's back.

They stopped again when they reached a door with a secure access panel.

"I tried that on our first pass," Sorel said. "It didn't work,"

"Now what?" Dana asked as she faced the rear. She heard the distant scraping of space beetle legs on metal. "Ari, get us through that door."

Ari leaned the injured agent against the wall and proceeded to the panel. He opened the tip of his finger and attached it to the coded keypad. Small wires from within him spread out through the circuitry. It took less than a minute and the door whisked open, revealing a much larger room where the station's generator must be located.

"Well, he's handy," Sorel said as she entered the spacious room.

"I want one," Vandermann added with a smile as he waved the rest of them inside.

Dana noted the platform extended to the middle of the

cavernous room, running all the way around to encircle its edges. A small guide rail kept anyone from walking off the edge, but the gaps between the railing's supports were easy enough to fall through. She imagined there had to have been accidents.

As Vandermann had said, the entire generator was off, and with nothing churning, there was no way to stop the steady build-up of energy.

"We've got five minutes to get this thing under control," the injured agent told them. He had managed to make it over to one of the information panels. He must have been their tech officer.

"I do not wish to alarm you all, but I believe we have less than five minutes," Ari said, looking up.

Dana's mouth fell open and Lalema let out a small squeak. Above them was a space-beetle like nothing she'd seen so far. Where the others had been a glossy black, these were jewel-toned, iridescent blues and greens shimmering over their carapaces.

And they were nearly triple the other beetle's size.

"What the *sou* are *they*?" Dana asked tightly.

"Those are the princes," Lalema said, shuddering as they let out loud screeches. "They are looking to mate with the queen."

"What queen?" Vandermann asked.

Sorel gave her partner a look. "We were told the escaped beetles were all male."

Lalema shrugged. Dana knew she was holding something back. There was something in the shifting of her large black eyes that didn't sit right with her.

Sorel saw it, too. Her eyes flew to Dana. She must have

sensed her doubt about Lalema. There was more going on than met the eye, and Lalema might just be in the middle of it.

"Sorel, hurry," Vandermann called out as the beetles shifted their attention toward them, beginning to skitter down the sides of the room's domed ceiling.

Whatever Lalema was hiding, they wouldn't learn what it was now. There were more than a dozen of the beetle princes making their way towards them, all of them shimmering beautifully. Dana squinted her eyes against the assault on her ears. Their screeching was giving her a headache, and their legs scraping against the metal of the station like nails on a chalkboard weren't helping matters.

"We need to move!" Dana said. She snatched up the arm of the tech agent, who'd been left to fend for himself at the monitoring station, and threw it over her shoulders. The two of them backed up and out of the door, back into the corridors.

Ari fired on the nearest beetle, but that only made the others angrier, charging the platform toward them.

Sorel had her eyes on a beetle in front of her. Dana realized too late she didn't see the one behind her. Sorel aimed her weapon at the same time a beetle lunged for her.

Vandermann shouted as soon as he saw it. "Got it!"

He shot at it at the same time Sorel flattened herself to the floor. The beetle sailed over her and into the oblivion below the generator. It was then Dana realized there was an active one-way force-field at the bottom of the cavernous room, allowing things to pass through without exposing the entire area to the vacuum of space. The beetle froze instantly as it passed through, curling in on itself and growing smaller and smaller.

Dana marveled at the coordination of the IC team. They were so in sync. It was like watching a dance.

The rumbling of the generator suddenly grew louder. The beetle princes screeched in a way that felt like ice picks digging into Dana's brain. Then they turned and raced back up the room's walls, away from the sound.

"The rumbling must be on a frequency that they don't like," Dana said as Vandermann and Sorel joined her, both lifting their visors again so she could read their faces.

"That explains what happened," Vandermann said, frowning to himself. "They must have figured out a way to turn it off."

There was a silent look between him and Sorel. Dana knew they were still communicating, but waited patiently for them to explain.

Sorel nodded and took up a position on the platform as if preparing to guard the generator.

"We have to stay here," Vandermann told Dana, turning their way. "If we lose the station, everyone will die. It's just not an option."

Dana looked them over. They had two small pulse guns and one injured member. They might not make it without more help. She couldn't spare Lalema, who was her guide, and Ari would stick by her to get to Eartha no matter what.

"Ari," she decided, "give them one of your pulse rifles."

Vandermann shook his head. "Captain, where you're going, you're going to need them as much as us."

"Yeah. But like you said, if we lose the generator, we lose the station. It's not an option."

Dana nodded to Ari, who handed over one of his large rifles to Vandermann. He grunted at the weight, and gave her a tight smile before lowering his visor.

"Stand ready," he called out to his team. To Dana, he added, "I owe you one."

"Don't you dare forget it. I'll be back for those credits."

"With all speed, Captain," Sorel said, with her back to the door and her eyes on the ceiling. "They're preparing to release the ships from the dock. If they do, you won't have a ship to go to when you get there."

Dana nodded. "If something should happen to you three, how long before we lose the entire station?"

"A matter of minutes," Vandermann said. "But you'll make it, and so will we."

Dana turned to her group. "Lalema, Ari, let's go get my ship."

THEY SET OUT, FOLLOWING LALEMA. THE CORRIDORS BEHIND the shops seemed even more humid than they'd been before. When they reached a junction, Lalema paused, smacking her lips as if tasting the air.

"Do you know which way to go?" Dana asked, sniffing the air but getting nothing but the musk of dank tunnels and the faint reek of beetle goo on her clothes. She took several steps forward, then stopped when she heard something like a firearm powering up behind her.

"Down!"

Dana pushed Lalema to one side. Before she could think, Ari had grabbed hold of her, pressing her against the wall and squeezing the air out of her lungs.

A bolt of red flashed down the corridor, hitting a beetle they hadn't seen clinging to the ceiling above them. It dropped to the ground and lay on its back, legs twitching, but still alive. Lalema reached for her weapon, preparing to finish it, but the creature who'd fired the weapon was already at her ear, holding a pulse weapon to her neck. She shushed in distress, the short pink tendrils on her head whirling as if waving for help.

"You kill that Buk To, and I'll separate that ugly pink head from your little Nerimisa body."

CHAPTER 16

WADE

It took two months for Wade's femur to heal enough where he could put weight on it. Four for him to realize their second beacon might not be working again.

"I thought you said you fixed it," Maggie said. Her whining was getting on his nerves again.

"I told you," he said, wiping his brow with the back of his hand. "I turned it on over a month ago, and I know the signal was getting out. Whatever the problem is, I'm checking it now."

Maggie's voice quivered. "What if they've already gone? Maybe they're not coming for us."

Wade's face felt hot and tight, half from the midday sun and half from Maggie's complaining. "They're coming. How many times do I have to tell you? They wouldn't leave us."

Maggie huffed, turning away from him and picking up

their waste bucket. He let out the breath he was holding as she stomped away. He shouldn't be so short with her. If it hadn't been for her, he'd have never survived this long. She'd nursed him back to health, and had continued to do the major foraging while he'd recovered—though he was tiring of eggs and small game.

At night, he dreamed of hunting down one of the howling creatures and roasting it over a spit. As soon as he could do more than shuffle along, he was going after one of them.

Of course, he didn't want to be stuck on the planet long enough for that either. If he'd had modern medicine, his leg would have been healed already. His patch job and Maggie's ministrations had saved his leg, but it would never be the same. He was going to have a permanent limp until he was back onboard the ship and Dr. Jabar could repair the damage.

Between the two of them, they were doing okay, but Wade could feel himself losing muscle mass in the recovery, and Maggie could only do so much on her own. She'd had a few close calls already with the larger beasts. In Wade's mind, it was clearly time he made it clear who was at the top of the food chain here.

Maggie returned and plopped down on the ground with an armful of sticks. From the look of them, he was going to need to chop some more wood. The air was steadily getting colder. They'd suffered through a couple of chilly nights already. Another reason to go after the howling beasts. They had fur, and that was something they would need if they were going to survive a winter.

Wade had spent the last few months half-sick and heart-sick. The days were going by too quickly, and there had been no sign of other survivors, pods, or search parties. He tried not to imagine the worst, but it was difficult when they were struggling with the barest supplies, living like their ancient ancestors had back on Blue Earth.

He'd finished taking the beacon apart and putting it back together. He threw down his tools and stood up.

"Well, what's wrong with it?" she asked.

Wade whirled around on her. "Nothing. That's just it. There's *nothing* wrong with it, so where are our people?"

Maggie's bottom lip poked out in a pout as she continued stacking their meager supply of firewood. Wade picked up the hatchet he'd made from the durometal of the pod and a thick, sturdy branch he'd sanded down for a handle, and stormed off into the woods.

"Where are you going?" Maggie called after him.

Wade ground his teeth together, ignoring her. He needed to get away from all things Maggie and their shared campsite. It was feeling more like home, which made his stomach churn. He didn't want to be comfortable on this no-named planet with his ex-fiancé.

Wade made off for the woodpile he'd started and began chopping. He was about to take off his shirt when he heard a low growl. He'd warned Maggie that the wolf-like beasts were growing more daring, coming closer every day, but they usually stuck to the shadows until nightfall. It was still late afternoon. The sun would dip low soon enough on their twelve-hour day, and then it would be night. He'd worn out his limited energy chopping, but he prepared himself to go toe-to-toe with the beast anyway. He wanted meat and fur more than he cared about the pain in his left leg.

Wade squared himself with the wolf-like beast. The

matted hair still stood up on its neck. The large yellow and brown teeth bared at him. It was preparing to strike when Maggie rounded the corner.

"I just don't understand why—" Maggie's mouth fell open with a squeak. She raised her bare hands out in front of her as if to stop the beast from charging.

The next moment happened so fast, Wade barely had time to think. The beast decided that Maggie was the easier target between the two of them, and rotated its body toward her. Wade pulled the ax from the woodblock and ran toward the wolf-thing, which crouched before rearing up on its hind legs to lunge at Maggie.

The beating of Wade's heart in his ears muffled Maggie's scream as he focused on the animal. He lifted the ax high over his head, bringing it down on the beast's back, sinking the blade between its shoulders. Its pained howl pierced the sky before it rolled, snapping its jaws at Wade. The blade remained stuck in its back, and Wade held on to the handle with all he had, along for the ride as it ran in crazy circles, trying to reach him.

Wade held fast until it slowed, then he jerked the ax free again and planted it in the wolf-thing's neck, cutting off its cries. Maggie was still screaming as she lay on the ground. Wade lifted the ax again, the beast's blood dripping from the blade as he moved to check on Maggie. Her shoulder had a large gash in it, blood seeping down her arm.

"Let's get you cleaned up. Can you walk?"

She nodded distantly, and Wade reached down with his free hand to help her on her feet. She winced, but the gash wasn't very deep. He could see she was going to need stitches to close it though. That posed a bit of a problem, as they didn't have much in the way of medical supplies.

Maggie was still staring at the wolf-thing as it bled out in the grass between them and the woodpile.

"Maggie?"

Her eyes couldn't focus on him for more than a second before shifting back to the beast's corpse. He pulled her toward him, and she stumbled to keep up.

"It's going to be alright," he told her. "He won't hurt you anymore. Do we still have some water left?"

Maggie nodded, her eyes on the ax. Wade put it down at the entrance of their cave and eased Maggie down on one of the pod chairs they'd collected. She fell into it, wincing when the pain hit her again, and then she was sobbing.

"It hurts," she said, tears falling freely down her pale cheeks.

"I know." Wade worked to clean the wound with a bit of water and a rag that had once been part of Maggie's yellow sundress. She sobbed throughout. He knew nothing of the planet or its wildlife, if a scratch or bite from the wolf-thing was poisonous or not. He didn't trouble Maggie with his worries as he checked the wound for any odd coloring or odor, but he wasn't a doctor. The best they could do out here was field medicine.

Wade put his small knife to the fire. Without the supplies for stitches, he needed to cauterize the wound and stop the bleeding. Maggie's face was growing more and more pale as he worked. She didn't protest when he eased her to the ground, facing away from the fire, leaving her shoulder exposed and dripping into the dirt behind her.

When the knife was hot, he lifted it with a bit of wet rag.

Wade braced himself against her arm, pinning it down, and used his free hand to hold the other down. The knife sizzled against her skin, and Maggie bucked and cried out before she passed out. When the bleeding had all but stopped, he wrapped the wound with the remaining clean cloth, then lifted her into their cave, wrapping her in a blanket to rest.

Wade tended to the meat for the rest of the evening. He hung the carcass to bleed out from a nearby tree. He enjoyed tying the thing up, thinking of it as a warning to any other beasts that today was not the day to try to come after him. Wade was contemplating how much meat they would have, and the amount of fur. He'd finally have the energy to hunt for another, and then they'd have two furs to keep them warm until rescue came.

It was hard for Wade to believe they'd already been on the planet for two months. Four if they were counting in local time. Too long already, and with the nights getting colder, they would soon have to worry about feeding themselves over the winter. He had no idea how long winter on this world could last. From the vegetation, he assumed it was an equal four-season kind of climate. That meant at least two more months of watching the leaves change as the temperature dropped. During that time, their protein sources would diminish.

He stared up at the dead wolf-thing, hanging by its hindquarters. He needed to figure out how to dry out the meat and store it for the lean times. Its sharp claws and teeth would probably make good carving tools as well, should they need them.

Yes, one more was all he needed. Then they would have something to get them through whatever was coming.

WINTER CAME WITH AN OVERNIGHT COLD SNAP A MONTH later, a month earlier than Wade had been expecting. Snow fell in large flakes, piling up quickly as Wade and Maggie prepared to hunker down in their cave home. Wade noticed the way she moved with resolve now. Maggie had complained about the lack of amenities almost from the moment he'd saved her from the edge of the cliff. Now she went about her daily chores in silence, her head hung, her shoulder curved with defeat.

It was the first time he'd ever seen her looking so depressed.

"We knew this was coming," Wade said, as if that would resolve her feelings.

Maggie didn't answer. She piled up the furs they'd collected and sat down with one over her shoulders, her white face and bright red hair the only thing showing underneath the dull, matted fur. Even without the layer of make-up and shine, she was stunning. Hard work and a daily routine had only enhanced her beauty.

She glanced up, green eyes focusing on him when she caught him staring. Wade dropped his gaze and went back to tending the fire. They'd piled the wood up along both sides of the cave's wall, and at a glance, he knew it still wouldn't be enough.

He slipped into his boots and pulled a fur over his shoulders, preparing to go. She didn't call out after him, so he turned to explain.

"We need more firewood." The words come out as more of a grunt than anything comforting.

Wade grabbed his ax at the cave's entrance and marched off into the cold toward the felled trees he'd gathered a week ago. His back still ached from dropping them, but they'd be no good to him frozen and wet. He lifted the ax and swung. He tried not to daydream about Dana while chopping. The last time he'd been thinking of kissing her, he'd almost sliced open his leg. But she would be a welcome distraction on this frosty morning, and now more than ever, he wanted to visualize her face.

Dana hadn't answered their beacon. No one had. There was an ache in his chest whenever he thought of her, which was far more often than he wanted to admit. Every day, week, and month that passed they marked inside the back of the cave. With every mark, he grew more and more worried that she hadn't made it. Dana had recruited him for the *Hope* mission personally when he'd declined the first invitation. She'd known his life was at stake, and regardless of her feelings, she'd wanted him to survive the destruction of their home planet.

He knew her too well. Dana wouldn't leave without him, just like he would never leave without her.

There was a thick dusting of snow covering everything around him by the time he'd completed his task. It took two trips to gather up all the wood he'd chopped, and he stacked them in neat rows just on the inside of the cave and on the outer edge. When the winds picked up, they'd be grateful for the parachute they'd positioned at the front of the cave to keep the cold air out.

His muscles aching and Dana on his mind, Wade did his best to keep to himself as he moved around, tending to the fire again.

"There's enough wood on the fire. You'll feel warmer once you've eaten something," Maggie said, her tone bitter.

Wade looked up at her. "What's gotten into you?"

She stared back, eyes dull. "What do you mean? I'm not the one walking around like there's a chip on my shoulder."

"No, you're just moping around like you're about to break into tears," he shot back. When her eyes filled, he immediately regretted the remark. He hadn't meant to snap at her, but he was in a snappy mood, and there wasn't anything he could do about it.

"I hate you," Maggie muttered.

"Well, that makes two of us, because I hate me too right now." He ran a hand over his face, letting out a sigh. "I'm sorry, Mags. I'm not in a great mood is all."

Maggie swiped at her eyes, huffing out a humorless chuckle. "You're never in a great mood. There was a time you could make me laugh about anything." Maggie stared over the fire, avoiding his gaze. "That's the nicest thing you've said to me since..." Her voice faded as she realized what she was about to say. "In a long time."

Before he could bluster, she leaned over and stoked the fire some more.

"You know, I should still be angry with you," she added after a long stretch of silence.

"Angry with me?" Wade wondered what she had to be angry about.

"If it weren't for you and Dana going at it like a couple of dogs in heat during the virus, I wouldn't have considered leaving the ship."

Wade shook his head. "Dana and I are just friends."

"Not because that's what you want." Maggie shook her

head and waited for him to deny it. He didn't. "Let's not pretend like you don't want more."

Dana was the one that got away, and Wade was determined to have her in his life again. He looked down at the ground. He'd been writing Dana's name with a stick in the dirt. Wade often did that when she was on his mind.

"I'm not mad about that anymore," Maggie said. "I'm not mad about anything. Hanging off the edge of a cliff sort of puts things in perspective."

She poked at the fire. The snow falling outside deafened the sounds of the forest. Even the wolf-things had gone into hibernation. Wade hadn't killed one in over a week. Maggie was sitting on two furs, and had one over her shoulders, like him. He'd killed four, and it looked like they'd have enough meat to last them a while. She'd preserved berries, drying them and keeping them sealed inside the medi-cases they'd found in the pods. There were only three medical shots left. If they were careful, they wouldn't need them. Maybe they were going to be alright.

"I would have only been second best," she said eventually, breaking into his thoughts. "No matter what I did, I would have never lived up to the legend of what Dana Pinet was to you."

Wade rolled his eyes and met her glare. "Says the woman who was dating two men."

"At least I was honest about my feelings," Maggie snapped. She stood up and stomped around the fire, throwing the fur off her back.

"To yourself!" he yelled. "You let me believe I was the only one in your life!" He stood to face her, grabbing her hand and forcing her to look at him when she tried to turn away. "I may have had some unresolved feelings for Dana, but you were the only love in my life."

"We can't go back," Maggie said, yanking her hand out of his grasp, looking up at him, her eyes almost pleading.

"I guess we'll never know, since you didn't give us a fighting chance to begin with. I didn't even know I still had feelings for Dana until that virus took over. In my mind, I'd moved on. I wasn't looking back at her, I was looking forward to what you and I could be!" He said pacing back and forth. "Then you ruined it by being in love with someone else. It was only then that I realized why it hurt so bad."

Maggie's head dropped, her eyes on the floor. "Why?" she asked as she took a tentative step toward him.

"It wasn't because you were dating the two of us," he said. "It was because I knew in my heart it was possible to be in love with two people at the same time."

Wade wasn't looking at Maggie, and so he didn't notice she was crying until she spoke.

"Because you were already in love with two people, and didn't realize it."

Maggie's face was wet with tears. He had to look away before he spoke again.

"After I found out the truth, I realized you had followed your heart and tried to have us both." He shook his head. "I couldn't do that to both of you. Even after I knew what you'd done, I was in love with you and what our future could have been. But at the same time, I was in love with my past and what I might have lost."

Maggie sniffed, using the back of her hand to wipe her nose.

"Well, at least you know someone who understands what

that's like," Maggie said. She lifted a hand and placed it on his shoulder. It wasn't demanding, or even flirtatious. It was an olive branch of friendship, and he took it.

He lifted her hand to his lips, kissing the back of it. "Thanks, Mags. For everything. We had a good run, and I don't regret what we had. I swear."

"I don't either. I wasn't fair to you, and I am sorry for that. But I'm not sorry for loving you. I never will be." She pulled away, wiping her face. "Now, go to bed. You look like death frozen over."

"I'm sick of these short days and nights," he said, easing himself down to his furs with a smile. Maggie hadn't moved. "Night, Mags."

"Night," she said. Her voice had a hint of bewilderment.

CHAPTER 17

Eat, mate, serve the queen.
- The Buk To life cycle

DANA

Dana lifted her pulse rifle and focused it on the alien with his gun to Lalema's neck. He wore a brown utility vest with more pockets than she thought any piece of clothing would deem necessary. His head was sloped back, and he had two sets of eyes, the second set horizontal and further off to the sides of his head, no doubt aiding in his peripheral vision. She saw the second set of eyes blink as she took a step forward.

"I don't think so," she said, watching him as she aimed. "Why don't we start with introductions, and then we can put our weapons down and play nice."

He grunted before taking a step back, keeping his weapon raised.

"Lalema," Dana tried instead, "tell the nice man with the gun you're not going to kill the Buk To."

"But it's—"

"Just do it."

Lalema made a smacking noise of protest, but put her weapon away and crossed her arms.

"Now," Dana said, turning to the new alien. "My name is Captain Dana Pinet of the Starship *Hope*. Our planet Zelenia was destroyed, and we're in search of a new home. Who are you?"

"Your name and planet mean nothing to me, as I'm sure mine would mean nothing to you," the being replied roughly. "If you're killing the Buk To, you're in dangerous company with this one. I don't recognize the other with you. Are you with the IC?"

"No." Dana tapped her foot with impatience. "And I'm still waiting to hear who *you* are."

The being snorted in irritation, but assented. "I'm Kob Suthfari, an Arudite of Arus. I am an animal wrangler. My assignment is to bring the Buk To in for shipment. Unharmed. Perhaps your species is ignorant of the Buk To's origins. I will be glad to educate you."

He lowered his weapon, and Dana did the same, her arms aching from the stand-off. She handed the weapon off to Ari and took a step forward, giving Kob a respectful greeting. He gave her an odd look, then seemed to understand. He presented two fingers forward, then pressed them to his chest before pointing them at her. She inclined her head in recognition.

"To your first point," Dana continued, "yes, Lalema is a new acquaintance, but she has saved my life once today already. You are a stranger. Though, to your second point, I was not aware anyone could capture these space beetles."

Kob let out a deep laugh and then smiled, showing off thick, blunt teeth behind his thin lips.

"What's so funny?" Dana asked.

"You call them space-beetles. Not very accurate. However, they've reached distant locations because of those like your friend here, who insist on eating them." He shrugged. "Of course, they have substantial healing properties as well. However, we are running out of time to gather them. Their adult cycle is complete, and I suspect there is a female somewhere on the station, as the males seem to be using the mating call."

"I thought they were all males," Dana said.

"They should be," Kob agreed. "However, I believe there is a female here."

"How could you possibly know that?"

"The Buk To didn't escape. You've seen what they can do, and the containers I searched had no damage. They were released, I suspect, because someone is interested in breeding them without paying the fees." Kob glanced all four eyes around as if he'd heard something, then continued. "By now, she could be ready to lay eggs, or already doing so. It won't be long after until they hatch, and her young will tear through this place like a dinner buffet. Tagging them will no longer be an option."

"Killing them is much faster, anyway," Lalema said, lifting her small mouth in challenge.

"Yes, as would killing you rather than waiting for you to betray us," Kob said, turning all four eyes on her.

Dana raised her hands placatingly. "I think in this case we would be wise to work together. I'm trying to get back to where my ship is docked. What do you do with them once they're like this?" Dana asked, pointing to the one still twitching on its back.

"These are tagged and prepared for transport. In this state, they cannot harm anyone." Kob inclined his head. "What is that?"

Dana glanced in the direction he was looking, and realized she had yet to introduce Ari.

"This is ARI Three. He is an android."

Kob's eyes narrowed. "Those are not legal on the space station."

"Neither are you, it seems," Dana said with a smirk, giving a nod toward his mechanical arm.

"This is a cybernetic enhancement. I purchased it a few years ago for a year's wages, and it earned that much back in a month." He smiled as he looked down at his right arm with pride. "The rest of me is all organic."

"So what are you doing here?" Dana asked. "How did you know about the beetles?"

"I was contacted by the IC. Major Adams said there was an escaped cargo of Buk To. I entered the system and stationed my ship beside the Nexus, then entered through a hatch on this level." He gestured to the prone beetle. "I've been tagging all the creatures I've come across until I ran into you."

"So, you don't have a ship docked?" Dana asked.

"That wouldn't be wise. The adult Buk To can tear

through anything if it smells like there might be food on the other side, and the newborns are worse."

Dana nodded, thinking of her ship. How long would they wait for her? Had Eartha made it back yet? Her parents would be extremely anxious...

"Then we need to hurry and get to the docks. Are you coming?"

Kob stared at Dana for a moment, then blinked. "Yes. I think I'll join you, if for nothing else than to watch your back from this one." He jerked a thumb at Lalema, who shushed in annoyance.

"Her? She seems harmless enough," Dana said.

"Yeah, well, there's a saying on my world. If you perceive another by their clothing, you won't know the truth that lies at the skin."

Dana huffed in amusement. "We have a similar saying. You can't judge a book by its cover."

Kob cocked his head. "What is a book?"

"It's a tablet made of parchment. It usually tells a story and is written in our script."

"Sounds interesting, and a bit inconvenient."

Dana smiled, thinking of the books her father had kept. One in particular was always on his desk. They'd already twice restored it, but he still handled it with care. A book about a man named Horacio.

"Do all of your species look like Agents?" Kob asked, breaking into her thoughts. He'd turned his head so he could stare at her with both sets of eyes.

"We come in a variety of shades of brown and cream, but yes. I am of the same species as the Agents of the IC, though my people originate from another world. Zelenia." Dana turned to him, looking up at his sloped head and noting the brown color of his eyes. "What about your people? Are they all in this basic form?"

"Yes and no. The females are smaller, more graceful. They are not permitted to take cybernetics."

"Why is that?"

"They bear our young." He didn't elaborate, and the matter seemed to be closed.

Dana glanced at Ari. He had a stiff-legged march, and tilted his head in odd ways when he was processing something new. He'd been oddly quiet since meeting Kob. No doubt their conversation fascinated him.

Kob seemed to like Lalema out front, so she walked along with Ari while Dana fell into step with him behind.

"You like your hair?" he asked. Kob's fingers twitched as if he wanted to reach out and touch it. Dana remembered that the IC Agents, regardless of gender, shaved their heads.

"We do not generally remove the hair on our heads," she explained. "Among my people, it is something else that makes us distinct from one another. Does your species grow hair?"

"We do not," he said, as if he found the idea repulsive. "Though it is unique. Do your mates also have the hair?"

"Mates?"

"Those with whom you have an intimate bond. The word for them in my language carries the similar meaning as a mate. They bear your children and provide physical comfort. I thought your species also had a similar practice."

"Ah. I understand the concept," she said. "I have no mate. However, we are usually paired rather than in multiples. Is it customary for you to have more than one mate?"

"Most have multiple," Kob replied, "and each of them has one or more. Living in the same dwelling is not required, though some have tried. I have two mates in my home, and one who has a home of her own with another."

Dana's mind reeled with the idea of caring for and loving so many. She had a million questions, and he seemed open to talking as they scanned the tunnels, so she asked, "Do you have any offspring?"

Kob smiled as he looked down at her. "I have eight children. One is nearing the age of maturity. However, I believe I will have at least twenty, like my father."

Dana's head dropped as she cast her eyes down in front of her. "You must love children."

"You do not have any offspring, but you want them?" Kob asked.

Dana glanced around uneasily. She didn't exactly want to discuss her issues with a complete stranger in front of Ari.

"What if you were mated to one who could not bear you any children?" Dana asked.

Kob thought about it for a moment. "There is more to the mating than the birthing of offspring. There's also the coupling. A mate can give much satisfaction even without having children." He shrugged. "Though all of mine have borne offspring."

Dana nodded. She wondered if Wade would feel the same.

"Have you ever considered mating with another species?" Kob asked.

Dana realized with some surprise he was gazing at her with a new intensity. She tripped, and he reached out and caught her with his biological left hand. His grip was firm, but gentle.

"Um, no," she stammered out. "I hadn't considered it."

"You should. I think you would find it fascinating to be bonded to someone who would appreciate your talents." He looked her up and down. "You seem old enough to be mated. Are you too young among your species?"

"I–no, not that young." Dana sighed as they turned another corner and found it empty of beetles, trying to think of how to explain her culture and her own beliefs within a few sentences.

"Our planet was destroyed recently," she started slowly. "My people are the survivors, currently looking for a new home. As the captain of my ship, it's my duty to see that we arrive. It's not exactly the right time for me to be waiting around to be swept off my feet."

"Swept off your feet," Kob repeated with wonder. "Is this an expression that means to bond with another?"

"We compare loving someone with falling uncontrollable. As inevitable as gravity."

Kob nodded. "Yet some gravity is artificial."

Dana laughed. "Yes, love can also be compared to floating or flying without wings, defying gravity."

Kob seemed to take that in a moment when he stopped suddenly, throwing his mechanical arm in front of her so that his body was between her and the wall.

"Hold!"

Ari and Lalema stopped, their eyes also scanning the dark.

"Do none of you hear that?"

Dana strained, trying to listen, but it was clear Kob's

hearing could do something hers couldn't. She wondered just where his ears were located.

"The sound has been getting louder the closer we get to the docks," Ari said.

"What is it?" Dana asked.

Lalema's large eyes grew even wider, and she made a shushing sound. "The mating calls. They've stopped."

"Isn't that a good thing?" Dana asked, wondering what she was missing.

"No," Kob said grimly. "That means the mating is over and the babies are being born. We need to run!"

CHAPTER 18

ERIC

Chancellor Jeremiah barged onto the bridge without stopping, and approached the captain's chair as if to sit down. "Who's in charge here?"

Adrian was there before he could get a step within range of it. "Technically, the duty falls to me when the Captain and First Officer are not on board." Adrian squared his shoulders, preparing for a fight.

Esme stepped forward, but Eric grabbed her arm and shook his head. This wasn't their fight. They had other things to worry about, like getting their ship out of the docks.

"Contact the dockmaster," Eric said.

"He's already left the docks." Esme's eyebrows were drawn together, her hand slowly rubbing her swollen belly.

"I know, but I think the only way off the station is with

help. Remember, they could tether us and guide us in. We might make it with some help."

Esme nodded, understanding his plan. She contacted the dockmaster as Eric moved to Adrian's side. It seemed the Chancellor wasn't taking the hint.

"I'll have you know I was ruling a country before you could walk!" The Chancellor's eyes bulged, and his chin quivered as he spoke. The man's brown skin had gone ashen with the time in space, but he still moved with the quick ease of a young man.

"You cannot have control of a military run vessel," Adrian replied stonily.

"We're under attack. By the Majestic! How long are you going to do nothing?"

"I know, and the more time I spend defending my position to you, the less time I have to resolve our current dilemma. If you'll excuse me Chancellor, your presence is no longer going to be tolerated on my bridge." The Commander gave a slight nod of his head, and Eric knew it was up to him to escort the Chancellor off the bridge.

"Sir," Eric said, holding his arm out toward the door.

Chancellor Jeremiah balked at him. "I will not be dragged off the bridge like common rabble."

"We wouldn't think of it, sir," Eric said, still leading him lightly by the shoulder to the lift. "As soon as the Captain returns, you can take it up with her, but for now, we've got to get our ship out of the docks before we're torn apart by those beetle things."

The Chancellor blustered, but conceded his position and left the bridge. The atmosphere went from one of hostility back to urgency in the space of a breath. Adrian in command was like watching a boulder slowly moving downhill, picking up speed as it went.

Esme called out from her station. "He's refusing to tow us off the docks."

"Let me have a crack at him," Eric said with a look to Adrian.

"Put him on the main viewer," Adrian said, stepping aside so Eric would be seen standing in front of the captain's chair.

"Oh, it's you again," Fazil said with a glance at the screen and a wave of his left upper arm. The other three seemed to be multitasking. "Like I told your wife, we're busy, and I've got a fleet of ships to look after. You should have abandoned your ship when you had the chance."

"There are over two hundred and eighty people on board this ship. You can't be serious," Esme called out from behind them.

Fazil ignored the outburst. "You're more trouble than you're worth."

Eric cleared his throat and waited for Fazil to meet his eyes via the screen. "Fazil, we still owe you half a day's work, and we're better than you expected. How are we supposed to make good on our deal without a little help here? We've got our suspended cables, but they're not going to do us any good without propulsion systems. Surely you can spare a couple of towing transports to get us off the station."

Fazil rubbed his chin with his free hand. "Add another day on to your time, and you've got a deal."

Eric looked back at Esme, who rolled her eyes, but nodded.

"Fine," Eric agreed. "But that includes a tow back into the station when this is all over."

"What a waste of fuel," Fazil muttered.

"That's two excellent engineers for another day and a half. You can't tell me that's not a value trade."

Fazil threw two hands up. "Fine. But not one more thing out of you two until your debt is paid."

"You have our solemn promise," Eric said. The screen went black as Fazil was giving the order for the tow ships.

Eric flinched as the scraping sound of the beetles carving into the side of the ship reached them on the bridge.

"They're attempting to breach decks four and five, sir," Ensign Harding said.

"Evacuate those decks," Adrian ordered. "Do we have any shielding to reinforce those decks?"

Esme's hands were already moving over the console. "I think I can get us a work around. It won't keep them out for long, though."

"Incoming," Harding announced. "I believe the tows have arrived, sir. Two ships on port and starboard sides."

The ship shifted and keeled as the tows locked onto them with their tethering technology. Once the ship had stabilized, they were pulled through the dock's force-field barrier and out into space. Any of the beetles that had been attached at the time froze as they passed through, dropping off and fading away into the black.

"Well, they don't like the cold," Adrian said with a sigh as he sat back in the captain's chair. "That's good for us. Let's get started on repairing the damage to decks four and five. Chief, I'm going to need to see if what repairs you can do on our ship before you're loaned out to the dockmaster."

"Of course," Eric replied. "Our daughter is on that dock. We'll get her back."

Esme's chin wobbled as if she were fighting back tears. The pregnancy had made her much more emotional than normal, not to mention the short time she'd spent under the effect of the alien truth virus. Eric thought she'd never forgive him for some of the things he'd said. They'd both regretted their words and actions, and had fought enough during those days for a lifetime.

Eric took his wife's hand and led her off the bridge. "You need to rest."

"We have so much to do," she said, but her hand remained in his, a sign that she was as exhausted as she looked.

"We're not used to working on this space station's time. I want you to rest so we can work in shifts while we're out here. We'll be no good to anyone if we're exhausted from lack of sleep. Go and see Dr. Jabar."

She nodded. "What about you?"

"I'll sleep on the next shift. You first, for the baby," he added with a look down at her stomach.

She sighed, and he saw her shift in her boots. Her feet were swelling by the day. Soon she wouldn't be able to get the boots on at all.

"Fine, but wake me when it's my turn. Don't let me oversleep."

Eric nodded without saying a word. He had no intention of overworking his pregnant wife. There was no such thing as oversleep in her condition. He gave her a peck on the cheek, and she boarded the lift. He turned back to the bridge.

"Chief," Adrian called out as he stepped back on the bridge, "I need you down in the engine room."

"Sir," Eric said in acknowledgement. "I'm not sure there's much I can do, but I'll at least be able to assess the damage."

"Good, and thank you for your assistance earlier with the Chancellor."

"My pleasure," Eric said with a smile. He had enjoyed throwing him off the bridge. The corner of Adrian's mouth lifted in a way that made Eric think he'd enjoyed it, too.

CHAPTER 19

EARTHA

After an hour spent crawling around in the ventilation shafts, Eartha's knees ached. Bumi had led Eartha to a grate leading out onto the docks. She held up a finger and pointed up.

Everything was so quiet. Before, there had been all kinds of aliens bustling in and out of the place. Now there was nothing, not even the sounds of ships being worked on. Eartha wasn't sure what Bumi was pointing at until she saw the long legs of one of the beetles scurry into view.

Eartha sucked in a breath and waited while Bumi watched the creature move off.

"I think we're clear," Bumi whispered.

"What if it's still out there?" Eartha was already inching back, not sure what her new friend had planned for them.

"We need to go now." Bumi moved the grate and climbed

out. She didn't wait for Eartha to follow, trusting that she would.

Eartha's heart was pounding in her chest. She'd heard what the beetles could do, and she'd seen them attack the Captain and Ari. She wasn't sure it was worth the risk.

"Hurry!" Bumi hissed.

Eartha climbed out of the shaft and crept along behind Bumi. They hid behind crates and eased their way through the docks, dodging the few beetles that seemed to patrol the area. Eartha wondered what they were doing here while the others were out feasting.

Then, to her horror, she saw what she'd missed while they'd been too busy running from the beetles.

"Oh no," she breathed, the words slipping out in a rush of defeat as tears welled in her eyes.

"What?" Bumi said, grabbing her and pulling her behind another set of large crates.

"We're too late. The *Hope*... it's gone." Eartha pointed to the place where the ship had been docked. There were no other ships in the dock. That should have been her first clue that the *Hope* would have left too, but now they were truly alone, and the captain was somewhere behind them, racing through the tunnels, avoiding beetles.

"It doesn't matter," Bumi said with a wave of her hand. "That's not why we're here."

"What?" Eartha asked, looking at her friend in wonder. It was clear now that Bumi had plans of her own, and that she hadn't shared them. Though they were both Trellis, Eartha wasn't sure that was enough of a reason to trust her. "Then why are we here?"

"You need much more practice with your powers. This is the perfect place for it."

"I don't understand," Eartha said, shaking her head. Bumi sounded crazy. Eartha thought if she hurried, she might make it back to the ventilation shaft before the beetles noticed them creeping around.

"Eartha," Bumi said sharply, mismatched eyes catching her own, "you have the ability within you to control these simple beasts. You only have to wield it the way I showed you in the shop."

"I can't," Eartha said, gasping when two of the beetles took notice of them and begin to move their way.

Bumi glanced at them, then caught Eartha's eyes again, her face resolute. "You must. It's the only way we're getting out of this."

Eartha pulled away from Bumi and started running, but the creatures followed her. They turned away from Bumi and focused on her, running frantically for the ventilation grate.

Then, out of nowhere, Peter Barnes was standing in front of her, an enormous weapon pointed at her face. Eartha skidded to a halt. Before she could ask him what he was doing, he grabbed hold of her arm, swinging her around behind him.

"Get down!"

He blasted the first beetle to bits, and the second one froze, flipping onto its back. Peter shot it, and it died there, leaking all over the platform. Eartha's knees were still shaking when she stood. A man who was dressed like someone going to war, with a sloped head and skin that looked like the colors you'd need to blend into trees, appeared. He had his right mechanical arm weapon and two sets of eyes aimed at Peter.

"What do you think you're doing?" the man asked.

"Saving these girls' lives, what does it look like?" Peter sneered at the man, keeping his arms outstretched and his weapons trained on him.

"We didn't need saving," Bumi said. She moved in as if to help her, but Eartha inched away, toward Peter. He was familiar. He would get her home.

"You cost me more cargo than I think you can afford, alien," the war man said.

"Barnes! What did you do?" Dana asked, appearing behind the odd man with Ari and the pink cafe owner in tow.

"Like I was telling this woodland man, I was protecting the girls," he shot back, pointing their way.

The Captain's eyes finally found hers. "Eartha!" She ran toward her, and Eartha sobbed as she was folded into her chest. She didn't know why she felt like crying, only that she'd been so scared, and if it hadn't been for Peter, she might already be beetle food.

"Miss Eartha, have you been harmed?" Ari asked, looking from her to Bumi and back again.

She felt bad that they'd been so worried about her. "No, it's just I couldn't do it. I couldn't save us. I don't know how."

Bumi rolled her eyes. "That's becoming more and more obvious."

The Captain straightened, and with one hand still on her, Eartha could feel the heat of anger rolling off her. "Don't you ever take one of mine again, or you'll have more to deal with than just one child."

"She is of my people, the Trellis," Bumi shot back just as angrily. "You're the one who is harming her."

"Look, I hate to break up your reunion," Peter interrupted, "but this commando still has a gun on me, and we've got more beetles headed this way."

"No, they're not," the commando replied. "These were not dangerous to you in any way. They are trained to listen to my commands, which is why I came here. It was the only leverage I had left in dealing with the infants."

Peter frowned in confusion. "Infants?"

"There is a female on the space station, and it seems she is spawning more eggs," Ari explained. "They will hatch soon, according to Kob. He is An Arudite of Arus, an animal wrangler, who has been helping us get here."

"Thanks for the update, Tin Man." Peter slapped Ari on the back as if they were friends. "I'm not sticking around for *space beetles attack part two*. Captain, it's been... well, I was going to say a pleasure, but I think we both know that's not true. I'll be seeing you."

"I hope not," Captain Pinet said.

"Aren't you going to ask me where I got all these nifty toys?" He pointed to his ear, where he had his own TMI, and hefted his weapon.

"No, and I don't care. Kob is with us, and he's the only one who knows anything about these space beetles."

The man known as Kob leaned over to speak to Captain Pinet. "Is he one of your options?"

"Ew! No," she said in disgust. It made Eartha wonder what kind of 'options' they'd been talking about before.

"We need to get down to the next level where the queen is

located," Kob continued, eyeing Peter. "If we don't remove the males, she'll continue to produce."

"Is anyone else bothered by the fact that this one is licking the remains of a dead insect?" Peter asked, looking at Lalema, who was sucking beetle guts off her pink webbed fingers.

Eartha wanted to gag, but turned her face away instead. When she heard scuffling, she looked back and saw Kob had a thick hand wrapped around Lalema's neck. He'd hauled her up against the nearest wall, her thin legs dangling.

"Kob, wait!" Captain Pinet let go of Eartha to run after him.

"This is the guy that's with you?" Peter yelled after her. "He hurts little girls, and nothing. I save them, and I get yelled at. This doesn't make a lick of sense!"

"Put her down," the Captain said, ignoring Peter. "If she knows anything, she won't talk with her air cut off."

"She can breathe through the gills," Kob replied easily. "This isn't cutting off her breathing."

Eartha leaned forward and noted the small slits in Lalema's skin on either side of her cheeks near where her ears might be, if she had any.

"I think she knows exactly what's going on, and where the queen came from when there were only supposed to be males here."

Lalema sputtered. "I make the best Buk To on the space station, but there is a lot of competition for fresh ingredients. I needed more. All of us do."

"You made this happen?" Captain Pinet asked, her voice thick with emotion.

Eartha wondered why she sounded like she might cry.

Peter spoke up. "Fine, so we know who started all this. Doesn't get us out of this mess," he said, waving a hand around the docking bay.

"You are as slow as you are red," Kob said. "If we know how and why it began, we know how to stop it."

Peter was about to protest, but Kob cut him off.

"Where exactly is the queen?" He had not let go of Lalema or dropped her. Though she didn't struggle, she seemed to be slowly turning from pastel pink to purple.

"She's in the sewage ducts," Lalema gritted out. "We released her where it would be easiest for her to have the babies. There is a team collecting the eggs now."

"How long do we have?" Captain Pinet asked him.

"Minutes." Kob dropped Lalema to the floor. "I hope it was worth it. We're going to be swarming with beetles any minute."

"The queen can be subdued," Lalema said, rubbing at his throat. "There is another female. We were planning to use her to divide the males so we could capture them."

"Where is she?" Kob demanded.

"She is also below, but she is in a cage on the other end. They cannot hurt her," Lalema said, thin lips smacking together.

"We need to hurry. She may be our only chance."

"No, Eartha, you are our only chance," Bumi said, taking one of her hands.

Eartha wanted to pull away, but Bumi looked so sincere. She focused her blue and green eyes on her as if pleading.

"You have to do this. You can give them a suggestion the way you did on your ship."

"How?" Eartha asked. "How did you know that?"

"I know everything I need to know about you. This is part of your heritage, your purpose."

Eartha shook her head. "I don't know how."

"Eartha, this is your heritage," Bumi repeated. "You must do this."

Captain Pinet hadn't heard what Bumi said, but when she saw her speaking to Eartha, she came over and divided them. It was clear she didn't trust Bumi anymore. Eartha wasn't sure she did either. Bumi wanted her to do something that she'd only done once, and she'd been plenty scared, but the beetles were terrifying. The thought of them paralyzed her.

"This fear, you need to overcome it if you're going to survive," Bumi called out from behind the captain.

"Eartha, stick with me," Dana told her. "Don't leave my side. Understand?"

Eartha nodded.

"Let's go find the queen," Dana said.

"For the record, I think this plan is crazy," Peter said.

Dana turned his way. "For the record, you weren't invited."

CHAPTER 20

"Everything has its purpose under the stars. Do not crush underfoot the thing that could save your 'morrow."
- Wisdom of Arus
(Pages from the Oracle's Handbook)

DANA

"This Peter, I do not like him," Kob whispered to Dana.

Peter walked behind them with Ari. Dana glanced down at Eartha, who'd befriended him, and whispered back, "I don't either."

"He is reckless and destructive."

He was talking about Peter killing his pet beetles. The strange thing was, she hadn't even known Kob had brought pet beetles. Things had gone from wild to out of control. Peter had managed to get off the ship before they'd left, procured a translator module implant, and gotten a weapon that had taken down two beetles. Peter was resourceful, she'd give him that, but she wasn't about to think she could trust him again.

This plan of dividing up the colony with two queens instead of one was risky. The first queen's babies would begin hatching if they didn't hurry, and the infants would tear through the metal on the space station like hungry termites.

Dana watched Lalema ahead of them. She never would have thought her the mastermind behind this whole thing. She'd planned the beetles' escape with her friends so they could get free meat for their stew. Even saying it to herself it sounded ludicrous. Lalema had even gone along with them, pretending to help them when she was just helping herself to the free buffet, though there seemed to be something more to it.

"What is making you shake your head in this way?" Kob asked as he glanced over at her.

"I was just thinking how strange it is that Lalema was in on the whole thing, and I had no idea. I think we'd have been in trouble if we hadn't found you."

"I agree. It is good that I was here to assist you, though I doubt she was working alone."

Dana looked his way. "You think she was working with someone else?"

Kob nodded. "And whoever they are, they want the entire space station crippled."

"What good would that do to anyone?"

"The Nexus is the hub of the financial district for this region," he explained. "Access to it and the wormhole would mean complete control. There are few who wouldn't make the attempt."

"I'm still learning about the value of this space station and what goes on here. Who do you think is behind it all?"

Kob considered that for a moment. "If I had to guess, I would say it's one of the Syndicate."

"What kind of group are they?" Dana asked.

Kob scratched his narrow chin. "Mostly mercenaries and pirates. But when the Syndicate fell, they became the Syndicate of Three and went to battle. They fight for planets, trade routes, and ships. The Nexus would put one of them leaps ahead of the rest."

"Dissolving the Triad would also have some political benefits as well."

Kob gave her another sidelong glance. "You are also very capable. I understand why they chose you. You are very quick."

That took Dana aback. She'd been feeling a lot like someone who had no idea what they were doing, and making poor decisions was becoming a regular thing.

"Thank you. It's been a long time since anyone else has acknowledged that fact," Dana said, smiling at him.

He grinned back at her, his two sets of eyes squinting in pleasure. "The compliment pleased you. I should give you more. There are lots to choose from."

Dana felt her face warm. There was a twinkle in his eye that reminded her of Wade.

"I'm not sure how to respond to that one."

"Like you, I've learned to hide my emotions down deep where those I lead, and my enemies, are not able to see them. It's only when I am home among my mates and my children that I'm allowed to share my deepest fears." He nodded to himself. "I think this is something you will need, Captain Dana Pinet, if you're going to survive."

Dana's mouth fell open, and she tried not to trip as she scurried to catch up when he started into a slow jog after Ari and Lalema.

"There's something wrong," Kob said, rushing after Lalema when she let out a squeak of horror.

"Where's the queen?" Dana asked, looking around.

Lalema pointed to the corner of the cage where the queen was supposed to be. Dana's eyes adjusted, and she saw the small queen on her back, stiff legs sticking up at odd angles.

Kob tilted his head. "We're too late."

The scurrying of legs hitting the water all at once carried to where they stood. A chill ran down Dana's back. The last thing she wanted was to deal with hundreds more of the space beetles.

"What now?" she asked quickly.

Kob shook his head. The reality of their situation seemed to sink into all of them.

"They're coming," Lalema said, inching herself toward the bars or the little queen's cage.

"Is there another way out?" Dana asked, eyes on the dark ceiling above them.

"In here." Lalema slipped through the bars and pointed to the ventilation shaft above the dead queen.

Bumi followed her into the shaft, but Dana held Eartha back from following them. It was clear no one larger than a twelve-year-old could get through the bars. Dana wasn't going to let Bumi separate them again.

"No." Dana held on to Eartha and looked around. "We'll find another way so we can all stay together."

"You'd sacrifice her rather than let her be safe with me?" Bumi asked. She looked as if she'd grown two inches just by squaring her shoulders.

"She's not safe with you," Dana said stonily. "Eartha stays with her people for now. If you feel safer going with Lalema, go ahead and follow her."

Lalema was already out of sight. The sound of her making her way through the ventilation shaft was fading as she got further away. The sound of the scurrying beetles was getting louder as Dana and Bumi stared each other down.

"Now can I shoot them?" Peter asked, lifting his weapon in the direction of the sound.

"Kob?" Dana looked to him, not sure if she should make the call.

"We're cornered here," he said grimly. "There's not much else we can do."

"Captain, may I?" Ari asked, stepping forward and moving toward the metal bars of the cage. He lifted the tip off of his pointer finger and it rotated until a small jet of blue flame sparked. He used the tiny torch to cut through the bars. It was going to take time they didn't have to spare, but then the rest of them could fit through the bars.

"This isn't going to work." Bumi said, slipping back through the bars. "The babies can already get through the bars and up into the ventilation shaft. If they see us, getting through the bars won't matter." She ran ahead of them, unarmed, calling back, "Eartha, you know what you need to do."

Eartha clung to Dana and shook her head.

"Then I guess it's up to me for now. Go!" Bumi raced down the tunnel toward the sound of the beetles.

Eartha reached out a hand toward her friend's back. "Bumi!"

"Ari?" Dana asked.

He didn't have to guess at what her tone was asking. "Eight seconds, Captain."

Once the last bar was free, the others climbed inside the cage, using the queen's carcass to boost them toward the opening above them. Dana cringed at the way the soft underbelly gave a little when she climbed up toward the grate. Thankfully, Eartha was already inside, crawling fast.

"Ari?" Eartha called out.

"It will be snug, but I will make it."

"Wait, where's Kob?" Dana asked as Ari looked up at her from the floor of the cage. Kob was still standing on the other side of the bars. He hadn't followed them. "Kob!"

"I won't fit in the ventilation shaft," he said simply. "But like the girl, I can give you more time to get away." Kob lifted his weapon, preparing to fire. He wasn't wrong. He was almost twice the width of Ari, and he carried so much equipment he'd have to strip down to fit.

"No." The word was a plea. Dana's chest ached, the sound of the infant beetles scurrying toward them growing louder with each passing second.

Kob looked up at her. "It was a pleasure meeting you. In another time, I would have asked you to be my mate, offspring or none." He winked the two eyes on his left side at her before dashing out of view.

Dana stared after him, her heart in her throat. She didn't have time to process the sudden revelation of his intimate feelings. He'd certainly left an impression on her, but to be mated to an alien was a different matter altogether.

She pushed the complicated thoughts of Kob to the back of her mind where she kept Wade and Rido, and focused on the task in front of her.

Ari weighed a ton, and getting him up into the shaft wasn't the only issue. He just barely fit, so he had to drag himself along with both elbows. Thankfully, the beetles wouldn't mistake him for food.

The crawl through the ventilation shaft without Lalema as a guide meant Eartha was in front of them. Dana had lost her bearings after the third turn. When they came to a junction, Eartha paused.

"Which way should I go?"

Dana tried to place a map of the space station in her mind over their current location, but she couldn't figure out which would be more correct. "Ari? Do you know where we are?"

"I do. However, the tunnel system is not in my memory files. I can tell you that the docks are above us and to the left. I do not have the precise path to our destination."

"Okay," Eartha said, and she turned to the left, exactly what Dana would have done in the same position. Dana noted the defeat in her voice though, and knew it was because she'd lost her friend. Despite being afraid of Bumi, it was clear she had some hold on Eartha. But Dana was dealing with the loss of Kob, trying not to think of what it took for him to sacrifice himself. He had a family. Multiple families and mates who would mourn him once they learned what had happened to him.

The three of them made it up a level and found themselves inside the docks. It was quiet. The unnatural kind that waited just before a storm. Eartha crawled out and Dana behind her. They both waited for Ari to join them.

"Captain?" the android asked.

Dana shrugged. "Do you hear that?"

"You will need to be more specific," Ari said.

"The Nexus core. It's no longer running. There's no rumble below our feet." Dread crept up her spine. "The Agents couldn't keep it running. The male beetles may have attacked them. Whatever happened, the entire space station may lose backup power. We're out of our depth here."

"I believe a location that is unappealing to the creatures might be our best option," Ari suggested.

"I agree, but where?"

Ari's head shifted to one side. "Space."

CHAPTER 21

WADE

One day he hated Maggie, and the next month they were friends. The next year Wade was fighting the feelings growing inside him for her. He'd loved her once, and it was becoming harder and harder to hold a grudge against her for loving two people when he was fighting the same fight.

The last thing he wanted was for Dana to arrive with a rescue party and find him in the arms of his ex.

So why couldn't he get the thought out of his head that he and Maggie could be together again, at least for now? Would that be enough for her? Would Dana resent him for finding comfort in the arms of another woman while they spent unknown years apart?

Maggie was an independent woman, and he didn't want to mislead her. He knew in his heart it would only take the sight of Dana to convince him to leave her. But the sight of him with Maggie might be enough to turn Dana away forever as well. It wasn't fair to either of them, and that was the endless loop his mind played on repeat throughout the following days, weeks, and months.

The cold weather had forced them inside again, where he couldn't avoid her any longer. Maggie was everywhere he turned. It was their second time braving winter on this planet. As predicted, the rotation of the planet was about half of what they were used to, though they were becoming more and more accustomed to the days. That they'd been on the planet for three summers and two winters now seemed unbelievable.

Forced back inside the cave while the winter weather raged only made things worse. They'd learned how to preserve their food and store all their supplies in the back of the cave, safe from predators, but it meant there was barely enough room to turn around without bumping into one another.

Currently Maggie's clean clothes were drying on a clothesline she'd created beside the fire. Her body was within the furs he'd caught, keeping warm beside him. The meat he'd hunted himself, but she'd gathered and dried the berries and nuts. She'd also dried the herbs they'd found and used to season the meat. She had worked so hard, striving to survive, and Wade was losing the battle of hating her with every day that passed.

Maggie must have sensed that shift, because she'd grown testy with him. Nagging him about cleaning his own clothes and watching every bite he ate, counting the servings to be sure they'd have enough to last through winter. Wade had already done the calculations. He didn't need her confirmation or reminders.

Wade's stomach growled, and he knew he needed to eat. He reached over and grabbed a piece of dried meat and a handful of nuts. As if on cue, she smacked her lips together and rolled her eyes, but her passive aggression was tired.

He sighed. "What?"

"You're going to eat through all of our rations. We don't know how long this winter is going to last."

"I've already calculated what we'll need," he shot back. "Even if it lasts a year, we'll have enough."

She groaned as she shifted under the furs, near naked as she waited for her clothes to dry. "Not the way you're eating. If I recall, last year I wound up foraging in the snow."

Wade turned away from her, not wanting to think about the last time they'd been together and happy, but unable to push down the memory.

They'd been planning for their wedding. He'd been blissfully ignorant of the truth about her past, and he hadn't even considered getting back together with Dana.

"Are my clothes dry yet?" Maggie asked, the bite still in her tone.

"Not unless they've completely dried in the five minutes since I last checked," Wade said between clenched teeth.

Maggie huffed, but she wasn't through nagging him yet. "Maybe you could go out and see if the weather is breaking yet."

"I can still hear the wind howling. What do you want me to do, die out there?"

She mumbled something he couldn't hear. He stood up to throttle her or kiss her, he wasn't sure which. When he realized what he was doing, he sat back down on his own furs and turned his body away from her. It was obvious they were going to continue to snap at each other unless one of them attempted to be civil or leave. The angrier she got, the more color came into her cheeks, making her even more stunning than usual.

The cave just wasn't big enough for them anymore.

"That's it. I can't take any more of your complaining," Wade said. He stood up, and this time he slipped into the boots he'd made for himself to trudge through the snow. He tugged on the rest of his layers, another shirt and jacket, then he wrapped furs around himself and stormed out of the cave. As soon as the icy wind hit his face, he felt some of the anger recede, and was grateful for it. He'd needed the cold air to calm him down.

Wade had marched half a mile from the cave when he realized his mistake. It was freezing, and with the wind blowing, it didn't take long for him to realize he'd overestimated his ability to navigate in all the white. The cave had been on his left, but now a rock face on his right was the closest landmark, and he moved to follow it around. His boots crunched through the layer of ice over the fallen snow as he continued forward, still not ready to turn around. Then something dark caught his eye, a misshapen rock—no, an entrance. He'd found another cave.

How they'd missed it after all this time, he wasn't sure, but here it lay. It could hold double the capacity of the other. Despite being unable to see to the back, there were no indicators that there were animals inside at the moment. Perhaps he'd already killed the beast who'd lived here.

He crept to the edge of the hole and looked inside. It was

filthy. He squatted down and gathered some dry twigs from the ground a few feet inside the cave, then ripped a bit of fur from his skins. Using his hand axe, he sparked a small fire, lighting his makeshift torch.

A puddle in the heart of the cave indicated a hole in the ceiling. If cleared of snow, it might lead to the outside. The smoke from their fire would ascend, leaving the cave warm below.

Wade's mind was working overtime to figure out how to move their things over to the new cave. He needed to find more wood first. He wanted to keep a fire going long enough to be able to use its smoke to find his way back. Snow covered everything outside the cave though, and the dormant trees wouldn't be of any use to him.

All the wood they'd gathered was still at the other cave, where Maggie was waiting. How long had he been gone? Thirty minutes? An hour? He wasn't sure, but despite her blustering, she'd be getting antsy for his return.

He swept the twigs and dried detritus that had fallen into the entrance into a pile, lighting it with the stub of his torch. The small fire he'd started wouldn't last, and he didn't have anything more to keep it going. Decision made, he ventured back to their original cave. He needed the supplies they kept there, and Maggie could help him start transporting some of their things.

Wade raced back, bubbling with excitement to tell Maggie what he'd found. He half slid on the snow outside of the entrance, slipping through the thick parachute that still covered it.

Inside, against the far wall, Maggie was standing with a fur around her shoulders, facing the mouth of the cave. In front of Wade, a ragged beast on four legs prepared to attack. The beast was far from where Wade had last seen the predator's pack. He could imagine the trajectory of this lone beast, which meant it had been cast it out. In the middle of winter, with its ribs sharply protruding from its sides, it must have exhausted its food sources and come in search of more. It had found Maggie, no doubt looking a lot like one of its kind, draped in the fur, but her scent would have been all wrong. Now it was prepared to fight Maggie for the food she appeared to be guarding.

From behind, Wade could see the beast had lost half of an ear on the side that faced the cave's entrance. No doubt that was the reason it had yet to turn on him, fixated as it growled and panted at Maggie.

Maggie's eyes pleaded with Wade to do something, but she didn't dare speak or move for fear that the thing would charge. She wasn't wrong, and in the next breath it was rearing up on its hind legs. Wade scanned the entrance of the cave and, to his annoyance, saw that all their weapons and heavy sticks were closest to the animal, out of reach for both him and Maggie. Though, if he could lure the beast further out...

Wade had an idea that had only worked one other time, when they'd come across two much younger versions of the animal.

"Hey!" Wade kept his tone loud and angry as it turned to face the new threat. "Get away from my house, you mongrel!"

He used the fur on his back to make himself appear bigger, continuing to shout curses at the wild thing. With his hands in the air, he signaled for Maggie to grab one of their weapons. She shook her head. The last time they'd done the maneuver, she'd attacked the beast but instead of piercing its hide, had only made it angrier.

"Maggie, give it all you've got!" Wade yelled, keeping the animal's attention on him.

There wasn't much time. Either she'd have to stab it, or Wade would be attacked, and despite his healed leg, he wasn't able to take down the beast with his bare hands.

"High and hard!"

Maggie nodded, grabbing their fishing spear, a long durometal tube that they'd scavenged from the found pod with a sharp piece of the hull lashed to one end. The animal lunged for Wade and he turned, preparing for the claws of the animal to sink through the fur and pierce his back, but the beast howled before plowing into him, tumbling the both of them through the parachute and out into the snow.

Maggie repeated her death strike three more times before she heard Wade calling her name.

"You got it! Now help me get out from under it!"

Together, they rolled the beast over, its fatal wounds bleeding into the snow beneath it. Maggie's arms were shaking. It was in that moment that he realized she'd discarded the fur that had been covering her, standing barefoot and bare skinned in the snow. The adrenaline was fading, and she was going into shock. Wade whipped the fur off his own shoulders and wrapped it around her, scooping her up into his arms.

"I dropped the spear," she said numbly.

"It doesn't matter," Wade told her, carrying her back into the cavern and putting her down on the fur that acted as a rug. Wade gently ran his hands over the fur at her arms, trying to stop her teeth from chattering. He stoked the fire with more wood, then lay on the fur rug, tugging on her elbow to ease her down beside him. She did, keeping her arms tight around her body. Wade found her discarded fur and pulled it over them both, then pulled her close, determined to warm her up with his own body heat.

Maggie let go of the edges of the fur she clutched around herself, allowing Wade inside. Sometime later, her body stopped shaking and her breathing evened. He thought Maggie might be asleep, but then she shifted, rolling over so they fit together like spoons. It was the way they'd slept most nights when they'd been together. When he pressed his body against her, she let out a breath she'd been holding.

"Wade?"

"Yes."

"Thank you."

"For what?"

"For saving me. Again. You let me in. For everything."

Wade nodded. He needed to get his mind off her body pressed against his and back onto household business.

"I found another cave."

Maggie whirled around so she could look over her shoulder. The movement let in a rush of cold air, which was both good and bad.

"You're leaving me here alone?"

She'd misunderstood. He pulled her back down against him and readjusted the fur overtop of them.

"No, it's much bigger than this one. It will do for another year or so, but I think it's time we prepare to move into something a little more permanent."

Silence slipped in between them for a moment as they

both considered his words. Maggie's voice was almost a whisper.

"You want to build a house here." The words were a statement, not a question, but Wade answered it as if she'd asked.

"We need a place with a door, not just a parachute sheet. I don't like the idea that every time we leave our cave, we have to worry about finding something in here when we return." He sighed, and after a moment added, "Also, I'm tired of hating you."

Maggie went quiet again.

Wade gave up wondering what she was thinking after a long handful of minutes had passed and asked, "Are you okay with that?"

There was no hesitation in her answer. "Yes."

She rolled over so she was facing him. Their bodies were no longer touching, but they were both still warm.

"I'm tired of hating you, too."

Her hand closed the gap between them, reaching for his face. He hadn't bothered shaving since their arrival almost two years ago. The beard growing on his face had gone soft with its length. He did his best to keep it from reaching his chest with regular trims. Maggie's hand crept along his chin to the back of neck. Then she raised herself up on one elbow and kissed him hard on the mouth. Wade tasted the cold and the salt of her lips before he lost himself in her touch.

CHAPTER 22

Maggie's Diary
Day 2,556

We've been married for five years and still I see that faraway look he gets when she crosses his mind. I'm not angry about it the way I once was, when our love was fragile and new. Now, after everything, I know nothing would ever tear him away from me.

The child growing in my belly will be our second, and he's as excited for her as I am. Our first child was a boy, as predicted, and this one is so unlike her older brother, it must be a girl.

My frequent urination and unquenchable thirst withstanding, there are subtle differences that give me the feeling that this child might be her mother's daughter. For one, she refuses to keep a sleep schedule, and often wakes me in the middle of the night. We're going to have a difficult time keeping her on a decent sleep shift. Wade was so kind with our first, helping me almost every day to get little Wade Jr. tired enough to sleep through the short nights.

It's a wonder they're both on our original sleep schedule despite being born on this strange planet. *Wade believes our signals are being blocked by the density of the atmosphere and the spin of the planet's natural rotation or some such. I don't know enough about it to weigh in with an opinion, but it seems feasible. Either way, no one has received our distress call, though we continue to wait for a passing ship to pick it up.*

However, it's obvious to us both that after so many years, we've got very little chance of anyone hearing it. This planet isn't on any major trade routes, and has no resources that would garner attention.

As I stare down at my belly, watching my son sleeping near the hearth, I wonder what they'd think of the old Maggie, the one who could be found in front of a camera more times than not. She had no intention of settling down to have children so soon.

I'm not that woman anymore, but I miss the life I might have had. If things hadn't turned out the way they did, I'm sure I would have preferred chasing stories to chasing babies. Even as I record this, though, I'm smiling. I wouldn't trade this life with Wade and our babies for anything.

I do wonder where his lost love went. If she died in the accident on the Nexus. It seems they must all be gone. If they weren't, someone would have come looking for the Commander.

It's a world and a life our children will never really comprehend. They will learn to check the escape pod for signals, but they'll never have to grow up on a ship. Instead, they'll enjoy the life of most land-dwellers, with the open sky above them and the stars far out of reach.

I never believed in the Majestic before, but I've learned to pray the signal never comes. I don't want anything to take away the family and the life we've built here.

CHAPTER 23

WADE

The day the signaler went off at the pods, Wade used his walking stick to race behind their three children and listen to the message. Every day he seemed to grow weaker, but his children were strong, and helped him care for the needs of their family as he and Maggie got older. His oldest son, Wade, was an adept hunter, while Marcus, the second, would prepare their meals with the flair of a chef. Their daughter, Elizabeth, had learned the plants and natural fruit that grew in the area, and she and Maggie created remedies for when they were sick and salves when they were injured.

They'd built a life on the planet that he was proud of, but leaving meant his children would have a future.

"It's an automated message, dad. They're coming for us," Marcus announced.

"Who?"

"A ship called the Persephone," Wade Jr. confirmed.

"Did they say when?"

"They estimate it will take some time," Wade Jr. continued. "They gave us the calculations, but they're using metrics that don't make any sense to me."

"That's still good news," Wade said.

"We're getting off this planet. We're going to see space!" his daughter said, then squealed with delight.

His middle child, Marcus, was jumping up and down. "Can you believe it?"

Wade felt relief wash over him. He knew they would all be cared for and rescued, no matter what happened to him and Maggie. They'd get to meet others their own age. They would find partners, maybe have families of their own, maybe even travel the stars.

THE SHIP DIDN'T COME THAT WEEK, OR THAT MONTH. THE automated signal of their rescue continued to beep for a full year, mocking them. Wade grew anxious with every month that passed.

Maggie was losing her memory. She'd forgotten little things at first. He'd paid little attention to her lack of details or her forgetfulness. Then one day she'd looked at him with a confused expression, unable to place his face.

It broke his heart. He knew that if the ship didn't come soon, it would be too late to reverse any of the effects that old age was having on her. Most days she went about them like any other, gardening, exploring with him, but the days where she couldn't remember her children were growing far too often. Even their marriage was a blur most of the time. Some days she'd be calm and want to know more, other days she'd be frustrated and angry. Today was the former.

"Tell me about the *Hope*," she said while they walked along in the forest.

"I was commander, and you were our official record keeper. Your reporter background gave you a lot of experience telling stories and getting to the truth of things. You're a much better storyteller than me."

She looked astonished at the thought. "I was?"

He nodded, gently patting her hand, clasped in his own. "Maggie Brooker could interview anyone and get answers. You were one of the few reporters permitted to interview members of the CAH when we were on Zelenia."

"CAH?"

"The Coalition Against Hope."

She frowned. "Why would anyone be against hope?"

"They were against the ship called *Hope*. Many of them already suspected that the government was covering something up. They didn't know it was the end of the world."

"Yes, our world. What was the name of it again?"

"Zelenia. It was so beautiful and green, we called it the Green Earth."

"Earth?"

"Earth was the home of our race before Zelenia."

She nodded, but still looked troubled. "You're a member of the CAH?"

"I was." Wade took a breath. It surprised him she still remembered that, of all things. "But as soon as I realized it was our only chance at the survival of humanity, my goals realigned to match that of the Captain."

"You changed. I don't remember any of that," Maggie said as she rubbed her temples. "The captain and I, were we friends?"

"We named our daughter after her, Elizabeth Dana."

Maggie's face remained scrunched up in confusion.

"It was a long time ago, and that's a lot of history to remember. Don't worry. Let's pick some of these flowers for the table," Wade said, leaning down to pick the white petaled flowers with the thick green stems. They were her favorites.

"I love these," Maggie said as she helped gather them up.

"I thought you might. Let's turn back, the suns are going down." He put out his arm for her.

"Okay," Maggie said, taking it.

FOUR YEARS LATER, THE SHIP ARRIVED. MAGGIE WAS TOO FAR gone by then, but Wade refused to leave her.

"But the ship is here, Dad. We've got to pack up our things and go." His daughter's blue eyes were intense as she pleaded. She was only just eighteen, and was the most affected by Maggie's memory loss. "We're not going to leave you both here alone."

"I don't know why we're having this discussion. We can all leave," Wade Jr. said with a shrug of his shoulders.

"Your mother needs to be in her own home, in a place that's familiar. We'll be fine on our own. We've done it before."

"That was when you were both young," Marcus chimed in.

"You don't think I can handle myself, boy?" Wade's face

was stern. "Go and live your lives off this planet, in the stars. We're staying put."

"But, what if she...?" Wade Junior's voice trailed off as he looked at Maggie.

Maggie was blissfully unaware of the situation, continuing to work on a new hat she'd started. It was her third that week. She hadn't finished one yet.

Wade put a hand on his son's arm. "I'll be here for her."

"But you?" Dana asked. "You'll be here all by yourself when she's gone,"

"Yes, and I'll be happy to live out my days here."

His children looked from one another, then back to him. They walked outside to confer together. It was clear his children were in doubt as to his sanity. They each came by individually with the same questions, trying to convince him to change his mind. Wade assured them all the same thing. He wouldn't leave their mother's side. He'd be fine on his own after her death.

When they were all packed and ready, he waved them off and watched the ship leave orbit. Its crew were generous enough to leave him enough supplies to last another lifetime. They stacked the blue and gray crates in a pile on one side of the house. They'd even found a way to cut through the atmospheric interference using a special communications device that he could use to contact his children.

Maggie enjoyed some of the new flavors he added to their meals. They had plenty to entertain themselves. His children vowed to check in on him, and if he wanted to change his mind, he could just answer the rescue beacon.

As she grew worse, Wade found he couldn't leave her side. If left alone too long, she wandered off. Maggie didn't remember about the cliffs or the beasts that prowled the night. She needed his protection all the time. Sometimes she'd be so focused on something, she'd forget who he was and what he was doing there.

A few months later, the communication's beacon went off, signaling another ship in the vicinity, but Wade ignored it. Maggie wasn't doing well, and he sat at her bedside as the end came.

"Oh Mags... don't leave me."

CHAPTER 24

"I cannot convey the depths of which my soul longs to be with yours. You're the breath between the beats of my heart. How my fingers itch to play along your soft skin and be entangled in your limbs. I will be incomplete and unsatisfied until we're together again, as one."
- A communication from Kob to his first wife.

DANA

Even as they suited up, she didn't like it. However, she still had people on the station, including Kob. After revealing his desire to make her one of his mates, she'd been so shocked that she hadn't known what to say. Now she replayed the conversation over in her head, imagining herself giving him an answer, though she hadn't liked anything that had come to mind so far. The idea was so foreign, and yet so endearing, she couldn't find anything that sounded appropriate.

Then there was Lalema, who'd crawled into the ventilation shaft and disappeared. Had she been planning to get away from them all along? Maybe she had a ship or transport of her own and had no intention of helping them further. Whatever her reasons, she hadn't shared them with Dana and the others.

They were on their own.

The queen and the babies seemed to move around the space station in unison, though she wasn't sure how long that would last. It was both an advantage and disadvantage, as the queen was far more mobile and deadly than Dana liked. Kob was the only one of them who understood their behavioral patterns well enough to make a decent call on what to do next, and he'd taken Peter with him.

What about Wade and Maggie? Are they as protected as Magnus claims? There was no way to find out.

"Space?" Dana repeated.

"It will be safer for you there, as they can only feed off organic material," Ari said.

If they lured most of the beetles out in space, there would be less of a chance they'd take over the entire space station.

"What about you?" Eartha asked. She'd seemed to have noticed his very particular phrasing as well.

"They are not interested in me." His eyes focused on Dana as he spoke, as if not wanting Eartha to see the truth. Though, even to Dana, his intentions were clear. "I can help encourage their exit."

"You're not meant for space," Dana said. "If you're

exposed, you could be permanently damaged. It's not like we can go to the local shop and replace you."

"No," Eartha said. "You shouldn't go alone."

Eartha's concern came from a different place, but Dana had to agree.

"It is the most reasonable solution to our current dilemma," Ari insisted. "My primary function is to protect and serve the crew and passengers of the *Hope*. This is my duty and purpose."

"Wait," Dana said, holding up her hands. "The ship is out there. Maybe we can get their attention. Is there a way to call them back for a pickup?"

Ari's head tilted to one side as he considered the question. "Perhaps if I was attached to a kiosk."

"You'll need to hurry."

"I suggest you and the others get behind the decompression doors so that I can turn off the shielding and they'll be pulled into space," Ari said, moving with purpose.

"They're afraid of being cold," Eartha said, her voice far away.

Ari moved to one of the mechanic's workstations and found the tools he needed to open the device. He lifted the tip of his pointer finger and attached several lines to the device, working with his eyes open, shifting from side to side as if speed reading a view screen.

"Someone is coming," Eartha said, grabbing ahold of Dana's hand and pulling her back toward the decompression doors.

"Who?"

Eartha shook her head. "The queen, she's here."

"You almost done with that communicator, Ari?" Dana called.

He didn't answer her, as he was still scanning.

"We need to go, now! I'm shutting the doors with or without you," Lalema yelled in a voice louder than Dana had heard her use in all the time they'd been with her.

Even through her surprise at Lalema's reappearance, Dana didn't need to be told twice. She grabbed ahold of Eartha and was already retreating toward the sealed doors.

"Captain," Ari said, returning to himself and tossing her the communicator. It landed in the palm of Dana's outstretched hand, and she raced for the doors at the sound of the first claw scratching against the bulkhead. Eartha was right. They were coming, and fast.

"Ari, you should tie yourself to something so you're not thrown out with them."

"A wise and logical idea, Captain. I will secure myself before I deactivate the shielding."

"We're not going to make it," Eartha said as Dana dragged her along.

The large door came down. Dana and the others watched behind the duroglass as the beetles skittered into the room, covering every surface with their dark bodies. Even Ari had several babies on him, but they soon lost interest when they realized he wasn't the kind of food they were looking for. The queen, however, caught up to their location with more speed than expected. One of her long talons poked at the glass, leaving a spider web of cracks.

"Ari, hurry! Open the doors!"

On her command, the alarm sounded. The air in the room shifted as every piece of loose debris and tool lifted.

With the shielding down, larger items shifted around the docks, flying out into open space. The vacuum cast hundreds of baby beetles out along with them.

There was a loud screech from the queen as she moved to the back of the room, furthest from the doors. She held on even as the babies around her were hurled into space. Her screeching call continued, and Dana watched as hundreds of babies attached themselves to her legs and then to each other, forming a long chain of resistance against the pull of space.

"It's not working. The queen won't let go," Dana said under her breath.

"She's too strong," Eartha said. "She'll hold on, and the babies will hold on to her."

Even as the cold took the ones closest to the door, the others covered the queen. An orange glow emanated from her. More and more of the babies climbed on, then they too glowed orange. The queen was generating enough heat for their combined body heat to keep them from freezing.

"By the majestic," Dana swore. "What's it going to take to kill these things?"

It wasn't long before Ari was freezing, the epidermis of his synthetic skin hardening and crusting over with frost. He couldn't keep the doors open any longer. Eartha's hands flew to the glass as she willed him to close the shielding. His movements were stiff, but he reactivated the shielding and the entire room re-pressurized. Once he'd given the final signal, Ari dropped to the ground, stiff as a board, his eyes open and his arms firm at his sides.

"Ari!" Eartha cried out behind the glass. Dana pulled her back, but the girl resisted. "We have to help him!"

"There's nothing more we can do for him," Dana told her. "Help is on the way, though I'm not sure what they'll be able to do once they get here and discover all these beetles still inside the docking bay."

The queen, more determined and probably angry that they'd pushed her babies out into space, returned with a renewed effort to break the glass. Four of her six legs reared up, the sharp talons on their ends slamming into and poking through the glass.

"Eartha, you need to get behind me," Dana said, trying to push the girl behind her, but she refused to budge.

"No. You can't protect me, and I need to help you."

Eartha stood in front of Dana, her hands held up in front of her. She was saying something under her breath that Dana couldn't hear, repeating it over and over.

The babies were the first to react. They fell to the floor, curling up with their small legs in the air, and then, shockingly, the queen. She resisted whatever Eartha was doing to her at first, but then she pulled away from the glass as if running to escape before she, too, flipped over onto her back, her legs curled.

Eartha's knees gave out, and Dana had to catch her before she collapsed to the ground.

"Are they dead?" Dana asked.

Eartha's eyes fluttered closed before she answered. "No. Asleep." Eartha smiled with her eyes closed, still limp in Dana's arms. At the sound of boots running toward her, she let out a groan.

"What are you still doing here?" Peter asked, running into the room and looking over everything.

"I thought you were dead," Dana said with a roll of her eyes. "You're like a cat. How many lives do you have left?"

"Yeah. What a coincidence, right?"

It was not a coincidence, but there were no words to explain what had just happened. If Eartha hadn't put the beasts to sleep, they'd all be dead.

Dana shook her head, deflecting. "Where's Kob?"

Peter looked back, concern on his face as his hand readjusted around his weapon. "He was right behind me..."

The sound of pounding boots drew closer, and Kob burst into the room behind Peter. "We've got incoming!"

Dana couldn't hide the relief she felt at seeing him. "How did you get out of the tunnels?"

Kob was about to answer when Bumi appeared behind him.

"I may have had a hand in his survival," she said, rushing to catch up and put herself next to Eartha.

Dana looked from her to the others, but before she could ask another question, Bumi knelt in front of Eartha.

"Good girl. You did well." Bumi brushed Eartha's hair from her face, and, for the first time, Dana noticed the change in color at the roots. Her dark hair had gone from black to purple, and now her roots were lavender.

"I did?" Eartha asked, her voice weak.

"You put them all to sleep."

"Not all," Kob interjected. "Did I mention there are more coming?"

Bumi pressed her lips to Eartha's and breathed something into her. Eartha's eyes fluttered open, and she looked stronger, though she didn't move from Dana's arms.

"You'll feel better soon." Bumi stood up and faced Kob

and Peter. "The queen called her army back to her. They're coming here now." Bumi looked back at Dana. "Get back."

Dana looked around, wondering exactly what she meant by that, even as she lifted Eartha and moved them behind the last of the heavy machinery that hadn't been blown out into space. Peter stood with his guns alongside Kob, who took flanking positions around Dana and Eartha.

Bumi, on the other hand, straightened her back and marched out into the middle of the sleeping beetles, determination in her eyes. She raised her hands and let out a sound very similar to that of the beetle queen. Male beetles soon filled the docking area, climbing up the walls and around the edges, taking over everything but not moving in to strike.

Then the small girl with the pixie-like features did something that Dana never thought she'd live to see.

Bumi's entire body changed before their eyes, morphing into a queen beetle. She made several calls that reminded Dana of a general shouting commands. Then, one by one, the male beetles turned over onto their backs. Though not asleep, they were no longer a threat to them.

"What in the *sou* is that?" Peter's face had scrunched up in disgust.

"I don't know," Dana said. "But show a little respect. She just saved your life."

Dana stared down at Eartha, wondering what this recent change in her meant. Bumi had been right. She and Eartha seemed to have similar abilities. Would she be able to return to common life trapped onboard the *Hope* after what had happened here? Dana couldn't fathom what the limits of Bumi's abilities were if she could transform herself into something as different as a space beetle queen.

The rumble of the Nexus' core returned, and Dana realized she was shivering from cold. It hadn't been just the open door to space, it had been the generators being off that made the station feel so frigid. Someone had managed to get the core going again, and she wondered, not for the first time, who hadn't survived their encounter with the beetles. The memory of Mox and Pak lying crumpled on the floor, their bodies emptied of their contents, made her ill.

She needed to get her ship back and track down her people, now.

CHAPTER 25

The dockmaster, Fazil, was the first to return, docking his small ship. He kicked several of the beetles out of his way as he made his way to his station before storming over toward Dana and the others. She stood up and squared her shoulders, waiting for the assault.

"What in the biscuit were you and these other screwdrivers playing at on my dock?" He spat on a nearby beetle as he met them, one set of his arms crossed over his chest.

Dana held up her hands, trying not to grin at the TMI's flawed translations. "As you can see, the bug wrangler cleaned up. Looks like you owe us for saving the place."

"Saving the place?" Fazil echoed angrily. "More like you threw half my gear out into space and the rest you damaged! I'll be speaking to the local authorities about this."

He scoffed as Kob approached.

"Well, what are you waiting for, an invitation? Clean up your pets and go."

Kob stood next to Dana, looking down at Fazil like he was about to scoop him up with the remaining beetles. "Ignore him. He's a small man, and is not so tough without his arms. A word from you, and I would tear them off."

Dana turned, surprised at his tone, and stared up at him. She caught the slight lift of one side of his mouth.

She let out a laugh. "For a second, I thought you were serious. Do you need any help with all of this?" Dana waved a hand over the beetles.

"I don't trust anyone else to do it. They're helpless, and there are enough creatures here who'd rather take them for their soups than help me."

"There are enough in space for them to pick up if they need them," Dana said, "but I'll be sure to let the Agents know that Lalema and her chef pals were up to something shady."

Dana felt the thrum of generators turning back on under her feet, and soon the advertisements and local announcements were reengaged.

"ATTENTION NEXUS VISITORS. PLEASE SECURE YOUR BELONGINGS *and report any missing people or losses to the local Inter-Galactic Authority. On behalf of the Nexus, we offer our sincerest apologies for the disruption.*"

"NOW THAT YOU'VE HELPED ME AND YOU'VE HELPED THE Agents, they'll owe you. What will you do now?" Kob asked.

Dana shrugged. "I don't know. We're still looking for our people. They were here not that long ago. Someone must know where they're headed. Preferably someone who doesn't want to overcharge us."

Kob nodded in agreement, and added, "After the Nexus, avoid the Syndicate of Three. You are closely aligned with the IG, and they won't like your kind invading their territory."

"I think we have enough enemies for now, but thanks for the tip. And uh, about your offer," Dana said, clearing her throat. "If my heart was not already engaged elsewhere, it would be an honor to join your family, Kob Suthfari." Dana inclined her head while keeping her eyes on him.

Kob's four eyes blinked in surprise. "The honor would have been mine. Let me offer you another piece of advice. If your heart is already engaged, then you should start a family of your own. Don't wait. Your species doesn't live forever."

Kob clutched a fist to his heart and bowed, and then he was off, collecting the beetles for transport. By the time he'd finished in the docking bay, many of the previously docked ships were returning, including the *Hope*. Dana watched the towing transports bring her back into position on the docks. A few steps from her, Eartha and Bumi, seemed to be in the middle of an intense conversation. At the moment, they were all safe.

Then she remembered Wade and Maggie.

"Ari, I want to know what's going on with Wade and Maggie. Are they still in that virtual room, or was it attacked?"

Ari nodded and inserted himself into the nearest communication kiosk. After a few moments, he disconnected himself and returned to her side.

"Wade and Maggie are still inside the program, and the location is secure. Would you like me to retrieve them?"

"How long is the program going to last?"

"According to the feed countdown, it ends in two hours."

Dana wasn't sure why that rankled. They were safe. She should be happy the space beetles neither killed nor injured any of her crew. Instead, she was debating whether or not to end the program early. It seemed they were in no real danger, but she still wanted to give the proprietor a piece of her mind about his establishment tricking people into situations they didn't choose and couldn't control. Luckily for him, she had her hands full with collecting her people.

Dana glanced around and noticed Peter wasn't standing with them.

"Where's Peter?"

"It seems he has disappeared again," Ari said. "Do you want me to run a search for him?"

Dana rolled her eyes. Of course he'd be in the wind. The whole point had been for him to get away. "He won't be on their grid yet, and as long as he's off my ship, I'm happy. Let's go assess the damage."

Once the ship was docked, Dana called for Eartha to board.

"Captain, wait," Bumi said, then she whispered to Eartha, who shook her head and bit down on her lip as if she were holding back tears.

"What's going on here?" Dana asked, her eyes darting between them.

"Eartha cannot go with you," Bumi said.

Dana scoffed. "What do you mean she can't come with me?"

"Mom! Dad!" Eartha called out as Eric and Esme ran down to the docks to meet her. The three hugged fiercely before Eartha came up for air, explaining everything that had happened to her in one breath. A glance at Bumi's tapping foot and Dana knew their conversation wasn't over. Bumi was going to have a fight on her hands if she thought she could just leave with Eartha. Dana didn't care what planet she came from.

Adrian arrived with the latest report on the ship, and Dana took it without turning her gaze from the family in front of her.

"You'll see from the report the biggest concern is our engines," he explained. "We had to put our engines to the test. If it wasn't for the Rogans, we never would have made it off the dock."

"You don't understand," Bumi said, looking up at them, and then back to Eartha.

"You're not taking our daughter anywhere," Eric said, standing between Eartha and Bumi.

That was her cue. Dana knew without her intervention, things would only escalate from here.

"We've all been through a harrowing situation. There's no need to argue out here on the docks." As if they understood, several aliens passing by paused to watch what all the commotion was about. Dana lowered her voice. "Why don't we gather ourselves, and have this conversation in the conference room onboard the ship."

"Your ship. Of course," Bumi huffed, crossing her arms over her chest.

"It is our home, the place where Eartha feels the most comfortable," Dana challenged. "I think for her sake, we should not have this discussion here."

"Fine," Bumi relented stubbornly. "But I'll need to change."

"We're not going anywhere, and I'm sure Eartha would

like to shower and rest as well. Come by in a couple of hours and we'll receive you on board. Adrian, make sure Bumi is escorted to my conference room."

Adrian looked at Bumi from head to toe and nodded. "Done."

"In the meantime, I owe some people credits, and there are others who owe me. Ari, you're with me. The rest of you, return to the ship. Esme and Eric, I know you owe Fazil some more hours on the dock, but that'll have to wait until we've assessed our damages and Eartha's situation is settled."

"As far as we're concerned, the matter of Eartha is settled," Esme said. Her lips pressed together firmly. She looked close to tears.

Dana admired her determination despite the circumstances. "Regardless, I gave Bumi my word. We have to hear her out. It's not just what we want, but what Eartha wants that needs to be considered." She stepped closer to the Rogans, lowering her voice again. "I realize this may surprise you, but you didn't see them together. You're going to want to hear what Bumi has to say."

Esme looked to her husband, and Eric nodded, but he wouldn't let go of Eartha. The young girl met Dana's eye before her parents dragged her off.

Dana wasn't sure if she was pleading for Eartha to go or to stay anymore. Eartha had done things that were humanly impossible. Bumi was more powerful than the Rogans knew, and it wouldn't do any of them any good to be on her bad side. Eartha might need the guidance that could only come from being among her own people, but Dana wouldn't just hand the child over to Bumi on her say so. The conversation needed to play out, and onboard her ship was the only safe place she could think to do it.

"Captain," Ari began as he walked at Dana's side, keeping pace with her, "if you recall, my presence on the station is unacceptable."

"I'm aware of how they feel about you, and I don't care. You saved this station as much as the rest of us. They'll just have to deal with it while they're paying us what they owe."

Dana reached the Ring and noticed the change in activity. There were even more beings out and about than the last time she'd entered, and almost every moving billboard had images of Wade and Maggie playing on them. Dana hadn't forgotten she'd sent her first officer off with his ex, but didn't need the constant reminder.

"It appears that they are doing well in the virtual world," Ari remarked.

Dana glanced up and saw Wade and Maggie working side by side on what looked to be their shared home. Every smile they shared was like a dagger in Dana's heart. She wondered how they would feel when they exited the world and realized that what they'd experienced was a simulated reality.

She was about to make her way to the fifth level when the door of one of the financial buildings near them opened. An alien about the size of the Fashin Teku came running out.

"Captain Dana Pinet!" The creature had two black eyes, a squat nose, a small mouth, and what she thought of as a male tone of voice. The most notable difference between him and a human was his stature and the purple scaled skin that glistened like jewelry and covered every inch of visible skin.

"Can I help you?" Dana looked down and tried not to let his excited manner throw her. The financial aliens had unceremoniously ignored her when she'd applied for a loan earlier. She couldn't imagine what they wanted with her now.

"My name is Zdunek with Financial Freedom. We have graciously accepted your transferred funds. Here is your bank card. We linked it to your prints, and the credits upon this are transferable with the use of your bank chip."

He handed her what looked like a blank white square. There was no visible identifier along either side. She turned it over between her fingers, wondering what he was talking about.

"I don't understand."

"You recently applied for a loan at our bank. However, because your print is now on file, we could open an account for you the moment your funds became available from the VFA." At the look of confusion on her face, he continued, "There is another sizable amount of credits coming in from Virtual Fantasy Adventures once your program is finished."

Understanding dawned, and she watched his expression relax. "One square is all I'm allowed?"

The small man laughed as if she'd made the most ridiculous joke. "Of course not. You may approve any of your people for cards of their own once you've approved them. Their prints will be added, and a biometric card will be created for them as well."

She nodded absently. "Thank you, I guess."

"It's our pleasure to be doing business with you. Please come back to Financial Freedom for any future financial needs," Zdunek said, racing off back into the building.

Dana's brow furrowed, wondering if he'd been standing in the entryway waiting for her to pass by. The Nexus had an interesting way of doing business, but with the card in her hand, she could pay off some old debts before she headed upstairs to retrieve the Fashin Teku.

The first stop on her list was a visit to Mack. She owed him for the weapons she'd taken, and if he'd survived, he might have something else she could use.

The Third level was a shambles. Broken glass and shredded durometal littered the floor of the corridor. Dana found the front of Mack's shop in a state of intense cleanup. The beetles had ripped the front door off from the outside, and there were angry black burn marks covering what was left of the storefront. Several cases of items had been blown open, and there were sharp shards of glass glittering over the floor.

"Clear out the product and then pick up the glass, you moron!" Mack yelled to one of the other larger creatures working for him. When he saw Dana, he rolled his eyes. "So you're still alive. I hope you've got my credits, or this day is just going to get a lot messier."

"Wow, thanks for your concern," Dana replied with as much sarcasm as she could muster before reaching into her pocket. "I repay my debts," she said, holding up her shiny new white bank card.

Mack's eyes went to the card, then back to hers. A small smile crept over his lips as he turned from her. "Come with me and we'll settle your account."

It was Dana's turn to smile as she and Ari followed Mack into the back. They proceeded carefully over and around the debris until they were standing in an undamaged, though cramped office. Mack sat down at a small desk and pulled out a card reader. He entered an amount, then showed it to Dana. She nodded, remembering to do the math, but when she held out her card, he put down the reader.

"You know, you're not like the others."

"The others?" she echoed.

"The others of your race. The humans," he clarified, looking at her strangely. "Most of them are connected to the Intergalactic Authorities. You don't operate like them."

Dana recalled her last conversation with Major Adams and had to agree with him. "We're the same species, but we're from very different worlds."

"I noticed you don't carry comms. Are they broken?"

She shook her head. "We've only recently become acquainted with the tech," she said with a glance at Ari. He'd collected all the information he could, though, and they might one day create their own version.

"What if I told you I could offer you a special deal on comms?"

Dana raised a skeptical brow at him. "I'd ask how special."

Mack smiled as he lifted his small arms to reference his office walls. "You've seen what those beetles did to my place. I'm at a bit of a disadvantage, what with my shop being closed until we can clean things up. How about I give you a crate of my finest comms for a mere twenty-thousand credits?"

Dana laughed as if he'd told a joke, then let her face fall back into place. "No."

His face had no actual eyebrows, but the muscle where the hair would be lifted as he waited. "No counter offer?"

"I can afford five."

He shook his head. "Are you trying to rob me? I couldn't let them go for less than fifteen."

"Ten, or I walk and never look back," Dana said, pulling back toward the door as if she was ready to do just that.

"Fine!" he called out hastily. "Your crate will be delivered directly to your ship."

He reached a hand for her card, and she started to give it to him, then pulled it back at the last second. Mack was not the kind of being to let go of something he could keep, so she shook her head. "Actually, I'll have Ari collect our crate now. I'd hate for something to happen to it before it gets delivered."

Mack's look this time was almost one of respect. "You're good, Captain. I believe we'll have an excellent working relationship. And should you need any more fire power," he tipped his head at her, "call first and make an appointment. Don't use the back door."

Dana nodded and collected her card before she turned to Ari. "Check the contents of our new purchase, and then bring it directly to the ship. I can visit the IC on my own."

"As you wish, Captain."

CHAPTER 26

EARTHA

Eartha's return to her cabin with the Rogans was a quiet affair, but once inside, within minutes, they were smothering her. Eric wanted to make her something to eat, even though she said she wasn't hungry. Eric wanted to help her redesign her room. Now that she knew they wanted her, the feelings of jealousy for the baby were gone. She wanted them all to just get back to normal.

She made an excuse about needing to check up on Luke since she hadn't seen him since they'd gotten separated during the emergency. It was strange walking down the corridor of the ship again. The *Hope* had been her home since losing her first family, and now she was considering leaving it to find her birth parents.

Bumi had been very careful not to identify who her parents were, only telling her that they came from Trellis, and that her mother was one of the five queens. There was so much she didn't know, but leaving everything she did know behind felt wrong somehow.

Eartha rang the chime at Luke's cabin and waited. When his father answered, he had a surprised look on his face, and then he reached out and hugged her without a word.

"We were so worried," he said against the top of her head. "Come in."

He pulled her inside, where Luke's family surrounded her. They showered her with hugs and touches of concern. His mother waddled to the couch and held out her hands for her. Eartha walked over and fell into them. Luke's mom smelled of sugar almost always, and the sweetness of her made Eartha miss her own mother, the one who'd raised her on Zelenia, Sarah MacLaren.

"We thought we'd lost you," she said, easing back to stroke a hand over her hair. Luke's twin sisters both climbed up on the couch next to their mother, staring at Eartha as if she'd grown another head. "Telling the Rogans we didn't know where you were was the worst moment of our lives."

"Why is your hair pink?" one of the twins asked, pointing to her head. Eartha couldn't remember their names, not that it mattered when she couldn't even tell them apart.

Eartha had forgotten that her hair was changing from dark purple to pink now. She officially had three colors, as the ends of her tight curls were still black.

"Are you okay?" James, Luke's younger brother, asked, coming to stand beside her.

His question was as much about now as it was about before. Eartha had long forgiven him for his actions under the influence of the alien virus, but he still gave her strange looks. It was as if he were worried she would bring it back up. She wanted to ease his anxiety, so she reached out and took his hand as she spoke.

"I'm fine. I swear. A kind alien man helped me to the other side of the emergency bay door before it closed. I even found Captain Pinet."

James looked down at their joined hands, and in an instant, his adorable dimples returned. She hadn't seen that kind of smile from him in a long time, and it warmed her to see it again. Though she relaxed her hand, he didn't let go, which only made the zing she felt up her arm intensify.

"Did you see the bugs up close?" the other twin asked.

The question distracted her from the sensation. "Yes, and they were really gross. But they didn't hurt me or the Captain. It's nice that they're back where they belong."

"We're so glad you're alright," Luke's dad said. "How are your parents?"

If it had been any other day, she'd have answered in a blink. Now, though, she thought of her parents a galaxy away, waiting for her to join them.

"Eartha?"

"They're fine," she said, remembering why she'd come and glad for a reason to change the subject. "Where's Luke? I came to ask him something."

Eartha felt the rush of cold air as James let go of her hand and crossed his arms over his chest. "He's probably playing with the old man," he said, sounding annoyed.

"Oh right. Mr. Franklin will be in the Commons, too. I'd better find them." Eartha turned to go, then remembered her manners. "Thanks for being worried about me."

They all waved except for James, who'd suddenly turned angry. Why did it always seem like he was mad at her?

Eartha found Luke and Franklin at their usual table playing their game, just as James had said. Instead of interrupting them right away, she sat down next to Franklin and waited for Luke to look up. He did, losing his concentration as he scooted closer to her across the table.

"You're okay!" he said, relief softening his face. "I mean, I heard you were okay, but seeing you in person is a whole other matter."

"Yeah, thanks," she said. Her face heated with the embarrassment of having his undivided attention. "I'm fine."

"What happened on the other side?" Luke's eyes bore into hers, a million more questions on his face, but there wasn't much time before Bumi returned, and she needed help.

"It's a long story. That's why I came here. I don't have a lot of time, and I need your help. Both of you," she said, looking to Franklin, who sat back with interest.

"Go on," the old man said.

Eartha told them of how she'd met Bumi and shortened the story of how they defeated the space beetles to get to her question.

"Bumi is from Trellis, and she wants to bring me back to my home world."

Luke's face scrunched up in confusion. "Your home world?"

She nodded. "I have some kind of destiny there. I don't completely understand it, but it's far away, and I can't decide if I should go or stay here with everything and everyone I know."

Franklin rubbed his chin and held up a finger before Luke could speak up. "Where do you think you belong?"

Eartha thought about it for a moment. "I think I belong with my own kind. I know you haven't seen it, but I can do things. Things that other humans can't do. Bumi says that I'm communicating on such a high frequency that I can hear people's intentions." She looked down at the table. "She's worried I won't reach my potential here, or be able to help my world, who needs me."

"When would you leave?" Luke asked, his voice softer than she'd ever heard it before. He also looked down, hair falling into his eyes. Eartha imagined reaching up and brushing it away from his face before she answered.

"Right away. Probably today."

"I suspect the Rogans aren't thrilled with the idea either," Luke said.

"No, they would fight for me, I think. If it came to that. Though I don't believe Bumi would hurt any of our people, she is powerful."

"Don't be intimidated by her abilities," Franklin said gently. "Think about what you need."

Eartha stared at her palms as if they held the answers she was looking for. "I don't know. I'm only thirteen. What do I know about anything?"

Franklin leaned over and put a hand to his heart. "It's not what you know, it's what you feel, here."

Luke's worried expression hadn't changed.

Eartha took in a deep breath, letting it out slowly. "Okay..." She nodded to herself. "I think I know what to do."

"Will you go?" Luke asked softly.

"I think so. If I don't, I'll never know who I truly am. The

Rogans have a baby to worry about, and..." She left the rest unsaid. She doubted they would forget her, but they'd be too busy to mourn her loss for long.

"So, this is the last time I'll see you."

"I... I think so." Eartha's heart suddenly ached. Luke was sixteen now, and though he still thought of her as a kid, she couldn't help but wonder if he'd miss her a little.

"Whatever choice you make, you've got support," Franklin said. "If you need anything else, you know where to find me." He reached out, and Eartha gave him a hug. He was the closest thing to a grandfather she had on board the *Hope*. Her grandparents and parents on Zelenia had never been very close which meant she rarely saw them. Suddenly, she realized that if she left, he might be long gone before she returned, and her eyes filled with tears.

"I'm scared," she whispered into his shoulder.

He hugged her even tighter. "It's okay. You've got a big decision to make. Know your friends are here for you."

Luke sat speechless as she got up to go. Eartha wanted to hug him, too, but it felt weird when he was still sitting down and she was now standing. Instead, she put a hand on his shoulder and wiped her eyes before walking away.

CHAPTER 27

DANA

Dana reached the IC on the fifth level without incident. She reveled in taking a private lift now that she was carrying credits, but didn't have time to enjoy the experience. Advertisements for the Virtual Adventure that Wade and Maggie were experiencing played on every screen.

The latest scene was the two of them getting married, happy, and celebrating. Dana gulped down the sadness and jealousy at the sight of the ad. Ari had translated the numbers for her earlier. He explained that the countdown of numbers was to indicate the end of the show. It was coming to an end. Then it showed a picture of a four-armed female holding up her white financial card to get into the theater.

It would be her last stop, and Dana wasn't sure if it was because she didn't want to see them, or if it was because they didn't seem to be in any physical danger. Either way, she turned to the IC first to get the Fashin Teku back.

When she arrived, the receptionist, her hair pulled tightly back from her face, looked her over, then gestured for Dana to wait on one of the uncomfortable-looking chairs that lined the wall.

Dana shook her head. "Captain Dana Pinet. I'm in a hurry."

The woman gave Dana a nonchalant shrug before she contacted the major's office via a small earpiece. After a brief conference, she looked back up. "The Major will see you right away."

As she said it, a uniformed Agent came to bring Dana back. From the size of him, it was someone she hadn't seen before. She assumed the rest of the Agents would be in some form of recovery after their encounter with the beetles. Agents Sorel and Vandermann would have called her out by name.

The Major seemed only slightly less enthusiastic to see her again.

"Captain," he sighed wearily, "what can I do for you?"

"I'm here to get the Fashin Teku out of holding. All four of them."

He frowned. "Are you sure about that? In my experience, they tend to get themselves into a lot of trouble when allowed to roam free, and your people don't need much more of that."

"We need a home, and the Fashin Teku have been far more help than you," Dana said, not bothering to hide her annoyance.

The Major's eyes flashed up to her face before he nodded stiffly.

"Suit yourself. I'll release them into your custody, but I'll warn you. They should not be allowed to roam the space station. Surely they'll be picked up again, and there are no discounts for frequent admissions."

"I'll see to it."

"And if you're looking for a nearby planet to settle," he reached across his desk, picking up a square drive the width of her finger and handing it to her, "there may be one located in the sector."

Dana took the drive. "What is this?"

"It's a map of the entire quadrant. There's not much in the way of vacant locations, but there is a planet nearby that is currently under dispute. If you can convince the neighbors that you'd be a good fit, your people might settle sooner rather than later."

Dana stared at the drive in her hand, and then back up at the man. A home for her people. It was what they'd been searching for all this time. That this man, of her species, had seen that she got what she needed made something shake loose inside of her. She didn't imagine it would be an easy path, but it was the closest thing to a chance at resettling than they'd seen since the destruction of Zelenia.

The tears stinging her eyes threatened to betray her feelings, so she gave Adams her finest salute before she completely broke down.

The Major gave her a rare smile before getting back to business. "One other thing. We captured most of the culprits responsible for opening those Buk To cages. There's one who claims to have aided you during the attack—a Lalema. She owns a cafe down on Three?"

"Yes, she provided some assistance." Dana shook her

head, wiping at her eyes. "What were they thinking, releasing those beetles? It couldn't have been just for the cafe."

"It wasn't. We believe someone was trying to take down the station. My agents barely made it out alive, and we nearly lost the entire Nexus."

"Did Agents Vandermann and Sorel make it back with their team?"

The major raised an eyebrow, seeming surprised at her interest. "As a matter of fact, they did. It was their glowing report of your help that convinced me we might have been wrong about you." He rubbed at his chin. "This Nexus assignment has proven to be more dangerous than we expected."

"Do you know who would want to take down the Nexus?"

"There are some unsavory characters in the region who believe they should control all access to the Arch. With the Nexus out of the way, they could swoop in and take over, giving them control over the entire region." He shrugged. "Though who specifically was behind the attack, we still don't know."

"Contact me if there's anything more me or my people can do to help," Dana told him. "Your Agents in the field were remarkable. I would be proud to assist in any way I can."

The Major nodded. "I'll keep that in mind, Captain. However, if you're taking the Fashin Teku with you, I wish you a speedy farewell." He nodded to the door in dismissal. "The Agent outside will take you to retrieve them. Good day, Captain."

THE FASHIN TEKU WERE ALL SEATED ON THE FLOOR WHEN
Dana arrived. She followed the guard until she was standing
in front of Ashwin's cell. It wasn't until he opened the locks
that their heads snapped to attention.

Ashwin's face lit up and his son, still shy of her, stepped
behind his father and peeked out to look at her. "Captain, you
came back."

She nodded. "You're all being released into my custody."

"This place doesn't welcome us," Ashwin told her.

"No. It doesn't."

The Agent led them out to the Ring, and when the door
closed behind them, Dana spoke again.

"I have more business to settle. You need to return
directly to the ship. We will transport you to another planet."

"This is very kind, Captain, very generous." Ashwin
bowed low, and the others did the same.

"Don't make me regret this. Go straight to the ship," she
repeated for emphasis. "If something else happens to you
after this, I won't have the credits to save you."

"Yes, Captain." Ashwin held out a hand for his son, and
the four of them hurried along in the direction of the docks.

*By the Majestic! If they could just get back to the ship without
incident this time.*

Dana turned toward the large marquee advertising the
Fantasy Adventure with Maggie and Wade. The line forming
outside of the building was already wrapping around the
Ring. From the looks of things, they would be getting another
sizable deposit from Fantasy Adventures.

She ignored the line and the racing of her heartbeat and
stepped up to the closed window.

"Oh, it's you again," the man with the pink tentacles

called out when he caught sight of her. "Do you want to catch the end of the show? It's almost done. Then you can go back and see Magnus and your people. I promise you they're still safe." He rattled off instructions while walking her to the door, keeping the others anxious attendees outside. "Next show in an hour, just wait your turn."

Dana slipped inside the building and found it looked very much like a multilevel theater house. There were four levels filled with seats from end to end, and creatures large and small occupied every one. A large screen lining the wall of the space station from floor to ceiling showed the virtual world from multiple angles as they watched.

"There's not much more left to play out," the attendant told her. "Just wait here, and when the house lights go up, enter that door at the end of the hall."

Dana's eyes followed where he pointed and she nodded. The screen had already arrested her attention, and she didn't hear when the young man left her alone.

Wade and Maggie were on the screen, but not as she knew them. They were old, frail. Maggie's once thick, luxurious red hair had thinned and gone white, as had Wade's. They were outside in the sun, and Dana could feel the tension ripple through the room as the audience leaned forward to catch their words. A light beeping sound played in the distance, insistent, and yet far off from where they were lying in the grass.

"Go," the older Maggie said in a dry croak. "They've come for you at last."

A young man and young woman knelt beside them, younger versions of Wade and Maggie. Dana caught her breath when she realized they must be their children.

"I'm not leaving you, ever," the older Wade insisted. "I didn't settle, Maggie. I love you. I always will."

The raw emotion in his gray eyes as a single tear fell made Dana's chest ache. Then Maggie's wrinkled, shriveled hand came into view, reaching for Wade's face. Her hand held him there for a long moment, and then it slipped away as the life slipped from her body. The audience erupted in cheers as a bright light filled the screen, whiting out their faces. Something scrawled across the screen as the lights in the theater house came up, but the crowd was already streaming out the doors. Several species rushed past her, speaking excitedly about the show.

Dana saw a light on the other side of the door where the man had pointed, and she wiped the tears from her own eyes before she entered. The room she found herself in was very much like an office. The desk in front of her was empty, and there were two chairs waiting before it. She wondered if she should sit down or just go through the next door. Dana wasn't one for waiting around, so she went through the next set of doors and found a room full of screens.

A woman with the same gray skin and pink tentacles as the attendant was placing something on the desk when she entered.

"Excuse me, you can't be in here," she said, her sharp teeth clicking together as she spoke.

"You are holding my people, and I want them back, now."

Her face scrunched in confusion before realization seemed to dawn, an excited smile lighting up her features. "Oh, you're Dana. Oh my goodness, I can't believe it's really you! I should have realized. Magnus is going to be so pleased to see you."

As if speaking his name brought him to life, a door on the opposite end of the room opened, and in walked the man himself, followed by Wade and Maggie.

The large man looked her over and rubbed his hands together. "Perfect timing, Captain. You've received your first payment, and you're wondering when you'll get the next. Don't you worry, it's all automatic. You'll get the next install-ment tomorrow. I couldn't be more pleased. Couldn't be more pleased at all."

Wade and Maggie both looked shaken, and when she glanced down, she saw their hands tightly clasped together as if they needed each other to stand.

Dana put on her most serious commander voice and pushed down the conflicted feelings that swam in her chest. "Are you two all right?"

Wade nodded and looked at Maggie, who had tears in her eyes.

"It felt so real," she whispered.

Magnus clasped his hands together, then ran over to his desk. It was strange to hear the large man giggle with glee. "Look at those numbers! You were right, Aggy. You know what I like."

"Excuse me, Mr. Magnus?" Dana said insistently, trying to get his attention again.

"It's just Magnus, and I look forward to entertaining you and your crew for years to come. This one alone is going to keep us in business for the year! It's been some time since we've had some first-timers."

"You took my people without their consent," Dana pressed.

"Not true, not true," he said, shaking his head. "They

agreed to participate, and I monitored them the entire time. You're very welcome to try out our virtual worlds yourself. Perfectly safe. Perfectly."

His assistant nodded to him discreetly, seeing herself out of the room as if nothing was amiss. Dana was close to strangling the man, but she held herself back when Wade took a step forward.

"You told us it was an interview," he said, voice tight. "Then the entire world came crashing down on us. We could have died in there."

"You could not have died inside," Magnus assured him, continuing to miss the point. "Everything is designed to feel as real as this world. The only difference is we keep the safety settings high enough to keep your species alive. The game provided you with everything you needed." He turned away from him and motioned to several screens with scrolling numbers. "Have you seen the numbers?"

Dana and the others stared at screens, but didn't understand what they meant.

"Everyone is loving you two on screen together," Magnus explained. "If only Dana had made an appearance." He moved around the desk as if to take her hand, but she pulled away from him, glaring at his hand as if it were made of rotten meat. He quickly aborted the move, gesturing instead between her and Wade hopefully. "Perhaps I could convince you two to try it out together. A quiet beach, perhaps. A secluded area where you can raise a family or just live. We can populate it with more people, if that's your thing. The people at home would love to be part of the world you design."

Wade shook his head. "No. No more games. You got what

you wanted out of us. Come on, Mags, let's go. Captain, we're done here." He was resolute, and it hurt that he'd addressed Dana so formally. There was a wall between them now. She didn't know how it had happened, but she could never have predicted this when she'd sent him after Maggie the day before.

"Come back anytime," Magnus insisted. "We pay handsomely. Maggie Brooker, you'll be hearing from your adoring fans soon enough. You can thank me later."

Maggie didn't even look at him.

They stepped out of the building and onto the Ring. Wade let go of Maggie's hand and turned her to him. There was something invisible passing between them that Dana couldn't understand.

"Let's head back home," he said. Maggie remained quiet.

"What exactly happened in there?" Dana asked, not sure she wanted the answer.

"The way they explained it, we just lived sixty years in a matter of hours," Wade said. There was a scowl on his face as he marched through the crowd, Maggie's hand once again in his. Dana wondered if he even realized he hadn't let go of her for more than a minute since they'd exited the game.

"Have Dr. Jabar look you both over before you get too settled," Dana told them. "I don't know what kind of operation Magnus is running, but I want to make sure neither of you were damaged."

"Yes, Captain," he said. Maggie only nodded, as if she couldn't speak for herself.

When they reached the ship, Dana watched them board together, her heart in her stomach. She couldn't blame them for finding a connection again considering the circumstances.

They'd lived a lifetime together. They'd had a family. She'd seen the way Wade looked at his children, and it had been like a knife in her gut. He'd gotten something with Maggie she could never give him.

Dana shook off the loss and resolved to let Wade make up his own mind. If he wanted Maggie back, there was nothing wrong with that.

Before she could board herself, she noticed an elegant woman dressed in long pink robes approaching alongside a taller woman with green skin who appeared to be her guard from the length of her staff. There was something familiar about the woman in pink she couldn't place. The other woman paused in front of Dana, tall and green, her eyes a brilliant violet as she took in everything around her and looked her over.

"Captain, I'm ready to join you now."

That voice...

Dana looked her up and down as recognition struck her between the eyes. "*Bumi?*"

"Yes." The response was simple. She motioned to the being standing in front of her. "This is one of my guards, Zehra. She will not speak to you as she is deaf."

"When you said you needed to change, I didn't realize how much you meant." Dana shook her head, still taking her new form in. "I didn't even recognize you."

"Eartha will know me. That is all that matters."

There was something behind her tone that Dana didn't like, but she cleared them through security and escorted them to the conference room. It felt like she hadn't seen the place in days. She ignored the flashing message light on her monitor. There would be so many reports on the ship she was sure she'd be wading through paperwork for days. There was also still the matter of settling up with the dockmaster, Fazil, but she was sure that could wait until the matter with Eartha was done.

She used the comms to locate the Rogans and asked them to bring Eartha to the conference room. They'd balked at the idea of Eartha being the deciding voice on such a large matter, but Dana believed the girl to be more than capable of deciding her own fate. Besides that, she wasn't sure Bumi would take no for an answer unless it came from Eartha herself.

Dana wasn't sure the girl would say no, though. The chance to know her own people had to be a powerful pull, and the girl deserved to know the truth.

According to Bumi's cryptic comments, Eartha's presence on their world was paramount. Would Eartha see it that way, or would she want to continue her development onboard the *Hope*?

CHAPTER 28

The Rogans arrived with Eartha in tow, and Dana caught the look of confusion on her face when she saw Bumi in her adult form. When Ari arrived, it was her turn to be confused.

"Ari asked to be present," Eric said, giving Dana a look. "I trust that's all right with you, Captain."

Dana wondered if he was expecting trouble. They trusted no one more than Ari to protect Eartha. Though, for the life of the scientist who'd created him, they couldn't figure out why. His attachment to Eartha went beyond his programming. Though Dana had interacted with him in her own way, it was nothing compared to how he was with Eartha.

"Of course he's welcome. Please, everyone, have a seat at the table," Dana said. She gestured to the remaining chairs as she sat down at its head. "Now, let's begin. Bumi, I believe you have a request to make."

"Yes. I request you allow Eartha to accompany me back to our home world."

"No," Eric said with finality. "Now that we've got that

settled, if you'll excuse us, we've got work to attend to." He snatched his wife's hand and Eartha's, preparing to leave the table. Eartha's eyes darted around the room with concern.

"Not so fast Eric, Esme." Dana kept her tone even and calm. "I know you have some strong feelings about your adopted daughter, but this is the time to keep an open mind. Please listen to what Bumi has to say."

Dana gestured for Bumi to continue. Instead, the woman smiled at Eartha and spoke to her in a language that their translation devices couldn't follow.

Eartha's head tilted to one side, and then her eyes grew wide. She smiled as she took in the woman's words and responded in the same language.

"What is she saying?" Esme asked.

"I'm just demonstrating what you already know," Bumi replied in English. "Eartha differs from the rest of you. She has a promised future as a future queen to her people, and she cannot fulfill it living here with you. As it is, her skills are nowhere near where they should be for a young princess her age. You cannot teach her what she needs to know."

"All she needs to know is what any mother would want for her child," Esme said, her eyes steady on the other woman's face. "She needs to learn how to take care of herself and be happy."

"She's learning that here, with us," Eric added.

"No, she's not," Bumi said, steel in her tone. "She's not human. She is of Trellis, and despite your limited under-standing of the universe, she will continue to grow and become a target for our enemies."

"You have enemies?" Eric's voice was filled with sarcasm, eyes rolling to the ceiling.

"As do you," Bumi snapped. "Eartha has told me of her time with you, and she's saved you more than once, including what she did for the entire space station today. You cannot train her for her duties ahead. Only we can do that."

"Why now?" Esme demanded. "Where were you when our planet was being destroyed? When her parents were killed?"

Bumi shook her head. "That was the fault of the Crankus. We thought we had more time, but they found her before we could get to you."

"Who are the Crankus?" Dana interrupted.

Bumi's face darkened. "A race of aliens with the power to move heavenly bodies like the ones that destroyed your world."

"Are you saying the Crankus, or whoever, targeted our planet with asteroids to destroy a little girl?" Eric asked.

"Not a little girl. A future queen."

Dana watched them bicker back and forth a moment, Eartha's eyes dropping to the table in front of her. "Everyone, please," she said, holding up her hands for quiet. "Let's table the discussion of the Crankus in front of Eartha. She's got enough to handle." Dana gave everyone at the table a significant look and they eased back, realizing too late what they'd done as Eartha had curled in on herself.

"Is it true?" Eartha asked, her voice barely above a whisper. "Is it my fault Zelenia was destroyed?"

"Oh honey." Esme reached around her husband and pulled Eartha to her side.

Bumi, too, seemed to understand the effect her words were having on the young girl. "I apologize for my bluntness, but she should know the origin of her people and their issues with the Crankus, among others. They destroyed your planet to get to her and they won't be the last to come looking for her. She is a target, and only we can keep her safe." She turned her attention back to Eartha. "You are not to blame, little one. These enemies go back before even my birth, but I want your friends to understand why it's so important we take you with us to Trellis."

Dana didn't like that they'd talked of the destruction of Zelenia in the context of Eartha's origins. If others came to believe that, there would be no shortage of people blaming Eartha for their losses; or worse, the girl blaming herself. She needed to get the room under control again. There was one person they hadn't heard from yet.

"A young girl's life is at stake, and I think there's one person we haven't yet heard from." Dana gestured for Eartha to come and join her at the head of the table so that she was between the Rogans and the Trellis queen.

Eartha stood with her eyes on the floor. Dana could see the rich lavender color growing in at the roots on top of the purple curls with the black tips. It was stunning, and just another example of how different the young girl was from the rest of them. But that didn't mean she had to leave.

"Eartha," Dana tilted her chin up to meet her eyes, "everyone here at this table loves you. There's no doubt about that. No matter what you decide, that won't change. Do you understand?"

Eartha glanced at the Rogans and then Bumi before turning back to her. "But what if I make the wrong choice?"

Dana lifted a shoulder. "Mistakes are a part of life. We all make choices we wish we could go back and fix. However, this decision doesn't have to be a permanent one. You can change your mind later. No matter what, you're always welcome here, and if you need more time, the Trellis people will wait for you."

Eartha nodded, but her eyes went back to the floor. Dana decided it was time to put her own words to the test and see how flexible the people at the table would be.

"Bumi, if Eartha went with you for a year and then changed her mind, would she be able to return?"

Bumi bit her lip in thought. "It's highly unusual. No one ever has."

"But if she decided she didn't want to be one of the queens of Trellis," Dana pressed. "Could she return?"

Bumi shook her head and sighed. "Yes, I'll allow it."

Bumi's guard, Zehra, looked over and stared at the queen, the concern in her eyes clear. Bumi raised a hand as if Zehra were yelling at her, but nothing but her expression had changed.

Dana continued. "Eric, Esme, if Eartha changed her mind, and one year from now she decided to go to Trellis, would you allow it?"

Eric and Esme clutched hands as they looked over at Dana.

"We would allow her to go any time she feels ready," Esme said.

Dana saw Eric's eyes fill, swallowing hard as he nodded once.

Eartha had watched them answer and turned back to Dana. There was more determination in her eyes this time.

"So you see, there's really no wrong answer here," Dana said. "You will disappoint someone, but they're all going to love you, and as the Captain of this ship, I will personally ensure your safety while you're with us."

Dana gave Bumi a look of challenge, but she nodded as they all waited for Eartha to decide. It was an impossible situation, and Dana could feel the girl vacillating between them. The desire to know her people would be strong, but there was the familiarity of the Rogans and home that she couldn't ignore.

Eartha bit her bottom lip and looked around the room before speaking. "I need to know something first. I left the ship in the first place because I wanted to ask the Rogans something."

"You can ask us anything, sweetheart," Eric said.

Eartha squared her shoulders as if preparing for a blow. "Were you ever going to adopt me?"

The Rogans looked at each other, then back to Dana, and smiled.

"Yes," Esme said. "We've already put in the request to the captain. We just wanted to talk with you about it before we made it official." She struggled with what to do with her hands, as if wanting to reach out to Eartha, and yet stayed seated.

Eartha nodded, relaxing as relief flowed over her. It seemed to be the answer she had been looking for. She turned back to Bumi. "I don't want to leave."

"This isn't even your home world," Bumi said, her hands hitting the table. "These people may take you in, but you'll never grow up to be like them. On Trellis, you will have everything your heart desires and more. It's a world of your own where you will be surrounded by those that love and adore you. Let us make you ready to be queen!"

"I don't need a home world," Eartha said simply. "I need my people."

The words rang in Dana's ears. Her people needed each other, not a planet. Kob had said the same thing. That's what the passengers and the crew of the *Hope* needed, time with each other to enjoy themselves without the stresses of duty and responsibility. She'd been in such a rush to leave the space station she'd lost sight of what her people needed most.

"Bumi is from my planet. I don't doubt that," Eartha continued. "She makes me feel different in a way that's good. I don't know if I can understand what's happening to me without her." Eartha looked down at her hands as if they were foreign objects. In some ways, they must seem different to her after what she had done with the space beetles. She then looked over at Eric and Esme and smiled. "But my life is here. My family and friends. I'm not ready to drop everything and to go to a place I never heard of until today." Eartha looked at Bumi, eyes pleading. "I think I need some more time here."

Bumi took in a deep, cleansing breath. "This is unprecedented. This species has a tremendous hold on you." She sighed. "However, it would be detrimental to force you to leave. I can only use the most persuasive language. I can reiterate that you are running out of time. You need to prepare for the trials."

Dana saw an opportunity to help both sides and jumped in. "What will you require of Eartha to prepare for these trials? What do they entail?"

"She needs to learn our history, train like our warriors, learn our etiquette, prepare to rule," Bumi listed off, eyeing

Dana slyly. "And I know what you're thinking, Captain, but it isn't possible from this ship."

"Why not?" Eric asked. "We can help her learn whatever she needs to know. We have people trained to fight on this ship."

Bumi shook her head. "Not in our way. Besides, how will she learn our history and about her people from here? It is not knowledge I can pass on to any of you directly. Your brains could not contain it."

Dana let the insult slide as her eye caught sight of Ari. "Do you have the information in electronic form?" she asked. "Study materials or something similar?"

"Most of the historical information needed is aboard my ship, but how does that help you?" Bumi asked.

Dana gestured his way. "Ari Three, our android. He is quite advanced, and could hold the information required to teach Eartha of your history and ways."

Bumi glanced at the android, debating. Then she looked to the quiet woman on her left, the guard who hadn't spoken a word since her arrival. The two seemed to communicate silently before they both nodded, coming to an agreement.

"Fine. If transferring information to your android is successful, I will leave the information with him. However, her training must be vigilant," she stressed. "If she returns to our home world unprepared, it will be to her detriment and you will all pay the price for that failure. I will leave behind one of my warriors to train Eartha." She raised a hand to encompass her guard. "Zehra is an excellent fighter, and has the patience of her ancestors, the Majiwa, in her veins. She will require her own space and a small pool in which to relax when she is not helping to train Eartha. Can you provide the necessary accommodations?"

Dana looked to Zehra, who still hadn't spoken, and nodded. "Of course. We'll do whatever it takes."

Bumi turned and called Eartha to her, taking her by the hands. The young girl was unafraid as she placed her hands in them and leaned her forehead toward the woman, as she'd done with her before. Something passed between them, and before Dana's eyes, she saw Eartha's hair grow an inch, the shade of purple at her roots lightening another shade.

"I've done all I can for you, my little one," Bumi whispered. "I hope you use this time well. It cannot be infinite." She pulled back. "Your people need you, but you will have one of your known years to prepare on your own. It is all I can give you."

"One year?" Esme echoed, clutching her belly with both hands.

"One year," Bumi said, her voice raised enough to startle them all. "You have no idea what you are asking of us, and what it could mean for you as a species. I suggest you take this gift and use it wisely."

Something tickled the back of Dana's mind at the warning. There was something more behind her words, as if she knew something about their people that they didn't. How was that possible?

Bumi stood from the table, her guard stepping to her side. "Come Zehra, we must prepare. I will bring the android with me now, as it will take time to transfer the information."

"I will send Dr. Noah Walker with you," Dana said. "He is the engineer who helped create Ari. He'll be able to answer any questions about him should the need arise."

Bumi nodded, and Ari followed her out.

Dana made the call as soon as the woman left the room. Eartha went to her family and clutched them as if they were already saying goodbye. Dana wondered what Bumi's warning meant, and decided she would investigate their planet's history for herself. There might be something there they needed to know to protect themselves.

She still held the drive with the new map information on it as well. There had to be a new home for them somewhere out there.

The day was catching up to her, and when Dana checked the ship's time, she realized it had been almost another full day and she hadn't slept. No wonder she was drained. She made her way back to her cabin, and on her way, ran into Rido. He had a pensive look on his face, but he reached out and engulfed her in a brief hug. Dana knew she smelled like dead Buk To, but he still held her close. He was so good to her. He'd used his alternative healing to help her when she was at her worst. She'd always be grateful to him, but it wasn't enough.

"I was so worried when I heard what was going on at the station." He pulled back to look at her. "Are you alright?"

"Just exhausted." Dana looked down, not ready to look him in the eye. The last time they'd talked, she'd said she needed some space. She and Wade had been talking about getting back together. Rido was fun, but they didn't have enough in common to keep them together.

He nodded, holding her for a moment longer before letting go. "Well, I won't keep you. Let me know if you'd like me to come by this week for a healing."

"Rido, I..." Dana couldn't think of how to finish her sentence.

Rido reached out and cupped her face with one hand. "You're still working things out with the Commander. I get it. I'll miss our times together, but there's no need to be uncomfortable around me. We're still friends. I think that's something we'll always be."

Dana remembered her first conversation with him about staying friends with exes, realizing now what he'd meant. It was true. In her heart, she still had room for Rido as a friend, even if she didn't want to pursue a romantic relationship with him. Dana knew it would be far more difficult for her to remain friends with Wade, though if he wanted to pursue a real life with Maggie, she wouldn't stand in his way.

They parted ways. It was nice to have the automatic lights come on when she walked into her cabin. The engines and systems were all quickly coming back to fully operational thanks to the engineering and repair teams working round the clock. She'd been thinking of giving everyone a mandatory day off in celebration of their survival through the Arch and on the Nexus.

Now that they had credits to spend, they weren't in any hurry to leave. She needed to let Chancellor Evans and President Muñoz know they would be staying for at least a week while they prepared for the next leg of their journey. They just needed to read the maps and figure out their path and approach.

She startled badly when she heard a *thump* coming from her bedroom. Her service weapon was in the drawer by her bed. If Peter Barnes was back on her ship, she was going to lose it.

Dana grabbed the heavy, decorative vase she kept by the entryway door and crept along the wall, waiting for whoever was in the bedroom to venture out. She loved the vase, but she'd break it to put Peter back in the brig if he was hanging out in her bedroom.

A second later, a ball of fur came bounding out of her bedroom, bouncing at her feet. The little hairy creature from the cafe had found her once again.

Dana put down the vase and looked around the room to check for anyone else. "How in the *sou* did you get in here?" she asked, lifting him up in her arms.

His little tongue poked out, trying to lick her face, but she kept him at arm's length.

"I better find your family, or you might get the wrong idea here." She looked the little guy over as he wiggled in her arms, sighing. "Though, you need a bath as badly as I do. Let's get you cleaned up."

CHAPTER 29

WADE

Their first night back onboard the ship was the hardest. Wade kept waking up and reaching for Maggie. When she wasn't there, he'd pace his cabin until he calmed down, remembering it was all just a simulation.

But their reactions to the so-called adventure had been real. The feelings they'd had for each other had also been real. Wade didn't want to think about how relieved he'd felt when they'd woken up in that simulation room with Magnus grinning down at them.

At first, it was just that they were both alive, both young again. Then it was the relief of guilt he'd been feeling for moving on without Dana. It had been the hardest choice of his life, and one he no longer had to make. The experience had only clarified his feelings for Dana, but he wondered if she would understand that and forgive him for what it had taken to get there.

There was only one way to find out. Since the ship was docked, the bridge duty rotation had been running drills. Dana would be in her office. There had to be hundreds of reports to go through since their return. While he'd been watching the space station explode, they'd been running from steel-cutting space beetles. If he hadn't seen the carcasses for himself, he'd have never believed it.

Maggie walked around looking as stunned as he felt. The space station hadn't been destroyed. People were going about their business. The ship remained docked. Dana had given him an odd look when she'd dismissed him. He'd realized then he'd still been clutching Maggie's hand in his own. They'd become a couple during their experience, and it was tough to remember that it hadn't been real.

"What do we do now?" Maggie had asked the night before after Wade had walked her back to her cabin.

"Go get some rest. We don't have to make any big decisions right now."

Her door opened, and it was obvious she'd already started packing before her interviews. She'd been so sure she was going to get a new job. He'd glanced at the sealed boxes and half opened bags wondering what she would do now. He didn't have any expectations for her. What they'd had was based on a very large lie. The experience with her confused him at first. Wade knew he would have been with Dana, but when left with no other choice, Maggie had become the love of his life.

Sleep had eluded Wade for most of the night. The silence of the ship was deafening. He missed the wind in the trees, the sounds of nocturnal creatures that filled the night on the planet. The smell of the sea and the shorter days had grown on him. He'd stayed up half the night reading departmental reports, then the other half rehearsing what he wanted to say to Dana. She'd seen some of the footage of the simulation. He knew it from the hurt and disappointment she'd been trying to hide.

That's when he had an idea. He left the ship around three in the morning and returned to Fantasy Adventures.

An hour later, he had what he wanted in the palm of his hand—a small storage device specially made for Dana. Wade couldn't contain the joy he felt as he returned to the ship. There wasn't much time left before his shift, but when his head hit the pillow this time, his eyes closed in peace.

FOUR HOURS AFTER LAYING DOWN, HE WAS WIDE AWAKE. Adjusting to the ship's time again was going to take some doing. A message from Maggie beeped on his device, and after he read it, the weight he'd been struggling with lifted and he leaped out of bed. He picked up the small digital storage device and made his way to Dana's office.

He found her with her head down, pouring over something on a tablet, her monitor scrolling through a spreadsheet filled with numbers. As he entered, she gave him a kind smile that made his heart sing. There was still worry behind her eyes, and he planned to dissuade her of it.

"Computer, continue search on mute," she ordered.

The system beeped twice, and she gestured to the chair in front of her.

"You look better. Did you get any rest last night?"

Her hand reached out instinctively across the desk, and he grabbed for it.

"Not much. I did a lot of thinking."

"I'm not surprised. You've been through a lot."

Dana pulled her hand back, out of reach. Wade sighed. He wanted to gather her up in his arms, but she'd never go for it.

"Not as real as what you went through," he said, pulling his hands back as well. "I've been reading the reports. It sounds like the ship barely made it off the dock and back."

"Thank the Majestic they made it. If not, they might have needed a rescue of their own." Dana turned to the monitor as it continued to scroll through the numbers. "So, what brings you here? You're not scheduled for duty until tomorrow."

"I know. My sleep schedule is off, and there's something I wanted to show you." Wade held out the storage device.

"What is it?" she asked, glancing down at it.

"A montage of clips from my time in the Adventure with Maggie."

Dana's eyebrows drew together, staring down at the device as if it would sting her fingers.

"I think it will explain why nothing between you and me has changed," he explained. "I still want to be with you, Dana. I can imagine to you it looks like I betrayed what we had again, but I think after you see this, you'll know the truth."

"What truth?" Dana bit her lip as she waited for his answer.

"That I never got over you, and despite the life I led with Maggie, I know unequivocally now that she's not the one for me. You are."

"From what I saw, you were happy," Dana challenged.

"To be honest, sometimes I was. But there was always something missing for me, and I think once you watch this, you'll see that I'm right." He set the data stick on her desk. "I haven't given up on having something real with you. If you feel the same, I think we should talk about what it will mean for our future."

"What about Maggie?" Dana asked, careful to keep her eyes on the data storage, avoiding Wade's intense gaze.

Wade reached for her, seeming to need to make a connection as he spoke. "Maggie let me know just this morning. She came to the same conclusion, and wanted to leave as planned. Despite what we had, it was enough to know that we can still be friends, but neither of us wanted to make that life a reality. Strangely enough, it's the kids we miss the most."

Something unreadable passed over Dana's face. "Kids can't be a part of the equation for me. You need to understand that."

"I know," he said. "You can't have a family while in search of a new home. For now, I'm happy just to date you again, if that's all right."

Dana's lips thinned into a straight line. The doubt in her eyes told him he still had more work to do to convince her.

"After my time with Maggie, I learned something," he continued. "You and I can't pick up where we left off. We need time to get to know each other again as we are, and it's my sincerest desire to do that every day from now on."

He stood up and moved to stand beside her. He lifted her to her feet and rested his head against hers.

"Watch the vid, and give me your answer when you're sure."

Wade turned away and walked out the door without looking back. She needed to figure things out, and he'd give her the time to do that.

There was only one thing left to do.

Maggie was standing on the docks directing a couple of locals who were loading her bags and small crates onto a hovering maglev lift. They were the same species as Magnus, and were no doubt his people, as they wore the same flashy clothing and bore the gray skin and pink spiked tentacles of their boss.

"Heading out?" Wade called out.

Maggie turned toward him and gave him a wide smile. She was radiant, and it took his breath away just a little. But things were over between them. He'd known it when he'd seen her message.

"I hope you don't mind. I couldn't sleep. My mind was racing with the possibilities and there's just so much to do."

"So, you've settled on one offer?" Wade noticed that there was a small crowd gathering around them. Their faces were on almost every moving advertisement on the station. The two of them physically together on the space station naturally drew attention.

Wade's jaw tightened. It was the thing he liked least about the entire experience. They had watched him, even in his most intimate moments. Magnus had assured them they showed no mating rituals of any species to the public after some incident in their past, after a secretive and explicit practice that nearly started an intergalactic war, but he had his doubts.

"It took me a minute, if I'm being completely honest," she said. "I mean, after what we went through with Magnus, I don't have warm and fuzzy feelings toward him. But if it weren't for him, I wouldn't have gotten all the offers that came pouring in." She lifted a shoulder in a half-shrug. "Plus, Magnus pays the best, so I'll be working as a liaison for Fantasy Adventures and a news correspondent for the biggest network on the Nexus."

Maggie glowed with joy. He hadn't seen her look that self-satisfied in years, not since their last child was born in the game. She'd been a fantastic mother and wife, and he wanted to tell her so, but the words stuck in his throat. He knew that as much as he'd missed Dana, she'd missed her career. There was nothing in the game that showed off her journalism skills except for the very beginning, when they knew they were in virtual reality. Yet she'd made a life for herself. He didn't want to take anything away from that joy.

"You've talked to Dana," Maggie said, catching his silent struggle.

Wade nodded. "It's been a while since I've had to date anyone new." He laughed, but it was hollow. How did you say goodbye to someone with whom you shared a lifetime of memories?

Maggie took his hand. The small crowd gathering on the docks suddenly stopped moving, and he felt as if everyone who could see them was watching them. They probably were, but he held Maggie's gaze as she looked up at him.

"What we had was amazing, surreal, and an adventure I've always wondered about. But it was my deepest fears realized, too. I'm happy with my choice to move on and do other things. If you're worried about me, don't be."

"I'm not worried about you."

She laughed. "Okay, not so fast. You can be a little worried about me. I mean, we were engaged once."

He noted the way she spoke about their time in the game as real, and yet not real. It was the same for him, and despite his feelings, he was going to miss her.

"Take care of yourself, Mags."

"You too, Commander."

Maggie turned away, noting her things were already being transported without her. She looked back at Wade with a movie star toss of her hair.

"A word of advice. In real life, with other options around, no woman is going to wait forever." Maggie smirked and spoke up loud enough for the crowd to hear. "Don't let her get away this time."

In a flurry of commotion, she was gone, enveloped by the crowd. She was the real star, the crowd buzzing around her as they left. His heart ached a little as she moved on, but he knew she'd be all right. He'd known her long enough to know that for sure. Maggie Brooker was a pro, and this was her new playground.

CHAPTER 30

*The male Forlo's reddish hue darkens when trying to attract a
female. Where the female Forlo's coloring lightens to a pale pink.*
                                                 -A Forlo mating ritual

DANA

Dana watched Wade and Maggie from the window.
It was obvious they were saying goodbye. Maggie
had a huge smile on her face. She wondered if it
was real, or if it was masking her true feelings.

What are they saying down there?

Then Wade turned back and looked up.

It was as if he could see her looking down at them. It
wasn't possible, with the design of the windows, but he
smiled as if he'd caught her snooping. Dana moved away
from the window with a huff. She didn't know what was on
the storage device, but putting it off wouldn't help her decide.

Wade was right, she'd been feeling torn about what to do. Especially after seeing him having children with Maggie. Dana didn't want to see the disappointment on his face once he knew the truth about her inability to do the same.

With a heavy heart, she sat down and inserted the vid into the reader. It projected an image of Wade in front of her in full color. His uniform was torn, and he had set his leg with two small pieces of wood. Everything about the scene was primitive except for Wade himself. Dana couldn't help being impressed by the image quality as she watched him limping away. He made his way through a meadow of trees. The birds and skittering of small creatures didn't get his attention. It seemed he was on his way somewhere. When Wade reached a cliff, the crashing of the waves below drowned out the sounds of the woods around him. Dana wondered what he was thinking, standing so close to the edge.

Then he called her name.

"Dana!"

Dana's heart thudded in her chest at the anguish on his face. He screamed her name a second time.

"Where are you? It's been months. I'm not angry, just frustrated. I miss you. I want to hold you. No matter what we saw leaving that station, I won't believe you're dead. We belong together."

The scene ended, and Dana leaned closer to the image, staring at his face as another began. He was in the same location. She recognized the water and the trees around him, though this time he'd changed. It must have been cold, because he wore some kind of animal fur around his shoulders, and he didn't have the splint on his left leg anymore.

"Dana, you'd have been proud to see me take on this

beast," he said to the sky. "The first thing I had to do was tell you. It's getting cold out here. I'm not sure when I'll be back again. We've got to hunker down to avoid the elements. So here's my chance to say I love you and I miss you, like always. I can't wait to tell you about my survival adventure." Wade laughed at himself and shrugged. "I know you can't hear me, but for some reason, I feel like I can talk to you here. Maybe my words will travel on the sea and reach you on the other side. Crazy, I know, but it's just the way my brain thinks. I started painting the other day. I found some plants and fruits and just started drawing. When I finished, it was your face looking back at me. Don't give up, okay? I'm still waiting for you."

Another cut in the video footage and she was watching him make his way to the cliff again. This time, his head and shoulders were down, and he'd removed the fur from his shoulders. The weather was nice again, maybe even summer, as a fine sheen of sweat was on his brow. How far did he have to walk to get to this cliff?

"Dana," the word was almost a whisper, and she had to strain to hear him. "I need to tell you something. Maggie and I, well..." He looked down, and she could see him kicking at the rocks with the toe of his boot. "We're sort of back together. I don't know what it means, just that we're lonely. It's been years now, and I can't stay mad at her forever. Especially now that I know what it's like to love you and still have feelings for her because she's here and you're not."

Wade shook his head, and she watched his eyes fill with tears as his mouth worked. "I shouldn't feel like I'm cheating on you, but I do. Maybe that's why I keep coming out here. There's an ache inside me that can't be filled for the wanting of you, but Maggie helps me to forget sometimes, and right now that's what I need. Please forgive me."

Dana's own eyes filled as Wade struggled with his feelings. He'd fought against being with Maggie for years. It was a valiant effort, but she saw he was losing, and she understood why. They'd loved each other enough to pledge their lives to one another. It wasn't so much of a surprise for them to wind up together again, especially without anyone else to lean on.

In the next scene, Wade walked in slowly, whispering to the bundle in his arms. Dana let the tears fall even before she could see what he held. Wade walked to the cliff and opened the small bundle. He was openly teary, and his voice shook as he spoke.

"When our first child was born, I couldn't come out here. It was too much. Maggie and I struggled until we worked through our feelings for each other and my remaining feelings for you. I think she finally understands. No matter what happens, I'm going to keep loving you, even if we can never be together. That's why I thought it was time we talked again. Besides that, I wanted you to meet my daughter. We named her Elizabeth for my mother. Her middle name is Dana, for you." Wade's voice cracked hard. He took a deep breath, then cleared his throat. "Elizabeth Dana, someday you're going to meet your namesake, and you'll know why I taught you to be brave and kind."

The video ended, and Dana let out a shuddering breath. Wade had kept her in his life all that time, for what to him had been years. Dana's heart broke for him, and yet she realized his feelings ran deeper than she'd even known.

No matter what came, she knew she wanted to make it

work with Wade. After everything, he might not even be upset with her when she told him about her inability to have children. She just had to find the perfect time to tell him.

The door to her office chimed, and she raced to open it, expecting to see Wade on the other side. Her disappointment must have been obvious as her contact, Rohath Karzenali, stood staring down at her. He seemed taller when they were both standing.

"Expecting someone even more handsome than me?"

"Yes, uh, no," she stammered. "I was expecting someone else, but I'm just surprised that you were able to board without clearance."

"I have that effect on security," he said, giving her a sly smirk.

Dana wondered how a creature like him could get out of anywhere with those distinct black markings on his red face. He glanced down and noticed the little hairy beast prancing at her feet.

"What's that thing doing here?" he snapped.

The look of horror on his face was comical, but Dana kept a straight face. "Can I help you with something?"

He glared down at the little beast for a moment longer before his eyes found hers again. "I believe we were in the middle of a transaction before..." he waved a hand around, "all of this."

Dana nodded and took several steps back, allowing him to enter the room, giving the little creature a wide berth.

"Actually, I have what I came for," she told him. "Your services are no longer required."

He laughed as if she'd told a joke. "I doubt that," he said in challenge. "What, you received a couple of maps and you think you're all set to chart a course through the region on your own?"

"Yes, in fact. It seems our species has already entered this part of space. It shouldn't be too hard for us to find what we're looking for."

"If you want to find your species, I know where they are."

She shook her head. "Most of the humans in this region are not mine. We're not interested in settling with them."

"I've heard you're looking for a new home. A place where you won't be looked down on by your distant cousins. That's not going to come easy or cheap. You're going to need more than maps. You're going to need someone who can negotiate and navigate your path through these worlds."

Dana raised a brow at him. "Are you claiming to be such a guide?"

He inclined his head. "I am."

"We don't need any more help. We have the Fashin Teku."

Rohath laughed again, but this time from the gut. He couldn't seem to get it under control even after she walked away and sat down behind her desk.

Dana looked up at him with her most serious expression. "Well, since you've had your laugh, why don't you find your way off my ship." She looked down in dismissal, but he didn't leave.

"I apologize," he said tightly, clearing his throat before he went on. "It's just the Fashin Teku have a certain reputation that far exceeds the ills of mine. No one will speak to those overgrown cats. They barely speak any of the regional dialects, and the translator module implants only pick up what is intelligible. They're no good to you on this side of the Arch."

Frustrated, she stared up at him, waiting for his never-ending pitch to end.

"I'll get to the point. I'm a skilled navigator and negotiator."

"As you mentioned before, you also have trouble with the IC. We don't."

"No, but there are a lot of other species who don't get along with the IC, and not to be too harsh, you look like them. Half won't speak to the IC, the other half will have nothing to do with the Fashin Teku." He held up his hands. "That leaves me, your Forlo guide. Besides, around the Nexus I'm known as the one who can get things, which could be of some value to you and your ship."

Dana rubbed at the ache growing in her head. She wanted a home, a place her people could settle and end their roaming of the universe. It was too tempting an offer to turn down outright.

"What do you want in return?" she asked.

"Free passage through this part of space. And a private room that can accommodate me and my luggage."

Dana sat back in her chair and frowned up at him. It wasn't an unfair offer if he could deliver on his promises, but she wasn't born yesterday, and wasn't entirely convinced he could do as he said.

"How about I give you a trial run?" she offered. "If things go well, you stay."

He tilted his head, eyes narrowing. "If they don't?"

"You'll be dropped off at the nearest inhabitable planet with air your species can tolerate."

Rohath let out a flat laugh before he sobered. He lifted a hand to his chest. "Deal. As my first official duty, let me inform you there is a group known as the Syndicate of Three. They're three competing mercenary groups with control over the ring of planets in the seventh sector and its trade route, known as the Zeon Cluster. They know everything that's going on here."

"I've heard of them. I'm not sure they're the kind of group we want to get mixed up in. One of their groups may have tried to take over the Nexus," Dana said, thinking of what Kob had told her. She still had intensely warm feelings when she thought of him.

"I wouldn't be surprised if that were the case," Rohath agreed. "The Syndicate are a wildly unpredictable bunch. However, they're always recruiting more help from runners." He waved a hand through the air. "That's not why I mentioned them, though. There's a planet near to one of the Three that is as yet uninhabited. He's taking offers."

"We have credits, but not enough to buy a planet."

He shook his head. "Not that kind of offer. He's looking for an alliance. I believe it's worth further investigation, and it's near here."

Dana took in the information. She made a mental note to investigate the trade route itself and what the ramifications would be of aligning themselves with one group over the others.

"I'll consider it."

Rohath glanced down at the creature near her feet as he turned to leave. "By the way, I'd get rid of that thing if I were you."

"Never mind that. Be sure to check in with security before you board my ship again."

"Of course, Captain," Rohath said with a bow before

seeing himself out. She could hear his low whistle as he
strolled down the corridor. He was a strange-looking creature, but if he was even half as helpful as he claimed, they'd
find a new home in no time.

Dana glanced down at the little creature. "Well, do we
trust him?"

The beast let out a high-pitched growl followed by a bark,
and she nodded.

"Yeah, that's what I was thinking, too."

NOT LONG AFTER ROHATH'S DEPARTURE, THE DOOR DINGED
again, and the small animal growled.

"More from the red-faced devil. We'll see if we can get rid
of him," Dana said to the beast as she moved to open the
door.

It wasn't Rohath this time, but Adrian, her chief of security. The lines on his face deepened with concern.

"Captain, there's a problem. The President and the Chancellor have called for the arrest of Commander Wade Chance
on the grounds that he admitted to being a member of the
CAH and sabotaging the ship."

"They what?" Dana took a step back, the sudden buzzing
in her ears nearly blocking out his next sentence.

"They've secured the Commander in the brig to await
trial."

"How? Why do they suspect him?"

Adrian had apparently prepared for that question, and
handed her the portable tablet she hadn't noticed in his
hand.

It was more of the Fantasy Adventure he'd shared with Maggie. Dana played the footage twice, unable to believe what she was seeing.

He'd admitted to sabotaging the cryopods. To being a former member of the CAH.

A throbbing at the back of her skull warned her of the massive headache that was imminently inbound.

"When is the trial scheduled?" she demanded.

"They're rounding up the Justice Committee now. I believe they'll want to make a decision before we leave port."

"Of course," she scoffed. "If they decide against him, they can leave him here rather than support him in the brig."

Adrian looked at her, frowning. "What are you going to do?"

Dana shook her head. "I don't know. He's admitted to the crime. The question is whether or not they'll believe he's done with them or not." Just when she thought she knew the man... He'd been a member of the CAH until the destruction of their world.

"Do you think he's done with them?" Adrian asked.

Dana remained silent. She wanted to believe Wade's involvement with the Coalition had died with the destruction of their planet, but he hadn't been honest about his association with them. He'd kept it a secret while others had gone to trial for actions he'd done. He'd stood by while they hunted Barnes down. It was obvious he'd had no loyalty to them once the truth of their predicament was out, but would that be enough?

And why hadn't he told her the truth before now? It was clear from the footage he'd had no trouble telling Maggie.

Dana shook off the resentment and handed the tablet back to Adrian.

"It doesn't matter what I believe. I'm not on the Justice Committee, and I haven't been since they tried to put me on trial for being captain of this ship." Dana wasn't sure the Justice Committee, led by the President and the Chancellor, could even be trusted. "He will have to answer for his crimes against this ship and crew. See that the Chancellor and the President come and see me tomorrow in my office at oh nine hundred Nexus time."

"Yes, Captain."

"We also have a couple of new passengers joining us," she added. "Be sure to give them appropriate accommodations, but they are to have no access to crew-only areas."

Adrian nodded and turned to go. The door closed behind him, leaving Dana with her thoughts. The small creature must have sensed her disquiet and moved to her side, nudging her leg. Dana reached down and scratched the light patch of fur under its chin.

"What the *sou* has Wade gotten himself into?"

CHAPTER 31

I t's hard to believe it's only been three days since we've arrived at the space station known as the Nexus. Though we had a rough start, we've left our mark here. I don't think they'll be underestimating our people again in the near future.

We've learned some valuable information about the other humans who were chased off during the Great Purge. They've settled on this side of the wormhole, and there are millions of them. Though they consider us their backward distant cousins, it's a place to start. Somewhere among them may be the other survivors of the Zelenia disaster. If so, we may be reunited with them soon.

The crew and the passengers will avail themselves of the space station's amenities for a little while longer, and then we'll begin our sojourn to find a new home in this part of the galaxy.

We've picked up another Fashin Teku as well. The son of Ashwin Zeppel, who was being held for ransom, has been reunited with his father. The four Fashin Teku will remain onboard, and will carry out their duties until we are in closer proximity to their home world.

Rohath Karzenali, an alien contact from the Nexus, has offered his services as navigator and guide. I sincerely wish to gain even more new allies in this part of the galaxy. Anything to find a new world where our people can settle.

Our stowaway, Eartha MacLaren Singh, has found her original people. She is of the Trellis. Bumi, one of five Trellis queens, has agreed to allow Eartha to stay with her adoptive family for another year. She is to prepare for the trials with the help of a deaf security aid named Zehra from a distant planet called Bolaji. Her abilities are yet unknown, but the Trellis queen trusts her with Eartha's life, which means something, as she was not happy to leave her with us.

CAPTAIN'S PERSONAL LOG SUPPLEMENTAL:

After reviewing the footage from Fantasy Adventures that I received from Wade, I'm confident that he's found his closure with Maggie. He's been arrested on conspiracy charges and despite wanting to help him, I'm biased. There's nothing I can do for him right now. I had to relinquish his fate into the hands of the newly selected Justice Committee.

Wade doesn't know the truth about me yet. Pursuing a relationship with him now would be complicated.

I tried to get rid of the little creature from the cafe that seems to have followed me onboard, but no one has yet claimed it, and it refuses to leave my side. For now, I'm caving to the pressure and naming him after my least favorite food, Pickles.

CHAPTER 32

EARTHA

Bumi returned from her ship and requested to see Eartha. As if they were afraid the queen would abduct her, the Rogans joined her, but it wasn't a big deal. Bumi would never do something like that. She might be one of the queens, but she'd become a friend, and Eartha suspected there was even more to their relationship that she had yet to say.

Bumi approached Eartha in her adult form. Zehra, with a bag slung over her arm, was on one side of her, and Ari, followed by Dr. Walker, was on the other. She saw something different behind his eyes, but was too distracted by Bumi.

Arms wide, she bent down so she could press her forehead to Eartha's and hug her. She spoke in a language that the translators couldn't pick up, like she had before, leaving the Rogans in the dark about what she was saying. Eartha could see the confusion on their faces.

"Why won't you speak so they can understand you?" Eartha asked in her own language.

"What I have to say is not for them, it is for you," Bumi said. Her mouth was tight, resolute. "I've given you everything you need to know about our people within your android friend."

Eartha glanced at Ari. She wanted to ask what she'd done, but Dr. Walker spoke up before she got the chance.

"To be honest," he said, scratching his head, "I was there, but I still don't know what she did to get all that information into Ari. It changed him. He's different in a way I can't even explain. I think it has something to do with the interface."

"What did you do to Ari?" Eartha asked, worried by the doctor's exclamation.

"Your android is unharmed," Bumi said, continuing to speak in her own language. "But he's a primitive machine, and our technologies are not perfectly aligned. I had to give him a way to store all the information that you need, so it required a significant upgrade. However, like Zehra, he will also guard you above all others. That is my compromise."

Eartha nodded, unsure what else to say about what was to come, though her mind swirled with a million questions. Bumi must have read her expression, because she spread one hand out in Ari's direction.

"Ask the Ari anything you want to know about our people's history. Zehra can help you understand the heart of our people, as she has a special connection with the feelings of others. She will also train you in the art of physical defense."

Again, Eartha wasn't sure what she was supposed to say. "If I ask Ari who my parents are, will he tell me?"

Bumi's lips pursed. For some reason, she didn't like that question. "Why are you so concerned about who your parents are? I've told you how you came to be. Is that not sufficient?"

Eartha could hear the frustration behind her words, but she persisted. "You're not happy that I'm choosing to stay with the Rogans. I get that. But you don't understand. They're not the first parents I've ever had. There was another set before them, Michael Singh and Susan MacLaren. They gave up their lives so I could live. You say I need to honor my past and history, and I'm telling you they're my past." Her gaze hardened. "I won't abandon their memory or way of life for faceless people who left me to be raised by others in order to expand their ruling territory."

Eartha's sharp tone startled Bumi into taking a step back. It was the most she'd said to her since she'd learned who Bumi really was. In part, it was out of fear of what she might do, but also out of respect for her position, but Eartha knew it might be her last chance to get the answer to the question that mattered the most.

"Your genetic make-up is from one of our queens and her mate," Bumi said softly. "You will meet them when you come to Trellis. Until then, it will have to remain a mystery as you focus on what's important."

Eartha's chin dropped to her chest, the fire fading out of her almost as fast as it had appeared. "I understand."

Bumi shook her head slowly. "I don't think you do. You have one year before you must undergo the trials to become queen. It is imperative that you succeed. Our worlds are depending on you." She held Eartha's gaze. "Do you understand?"

Eartha's brows drew together. She wasn't sure she did, but she knew she wanted to prepare among the people she had come to know, so she agreed.

Bumi spoke aloud in the language of Eartha's family. "I will miss you, little one. Be diligent in your studies and stay safe." She pressed her forehead to Eartha's again, then embraced her.

Eartha felt something like a warm glow travel through her again, like before when she'd been able to put all the space beetles to sleep. Then Bumi turned and something passed between her and Zehra, who nodded before turning to Eartha and the others. Bumi continued on alone, and soon she passed into the crowd and disappeared.

Eartha felt the loss of her suddenly, tears welling up in her eyes. What if something prevented her from getting to the trials? What if she wasn't strong enough or smart enough to pass the tests? The doubt she'd been suppressing welled up inside of her all at once.

Zehra took a step forward and placed a hand on her shoulder. A feeling of calm swept over her again—different from Bumi's, but still strong. She took a deep breath and led Zehra on board the ship along with the Rogans.

Dr. Noah Walker resumed talking about all the modifications to Ari. "It was the most amazing thing I've ever seen. There's no way I could replicate it, but I think after his enhancements, he might assist me in building more ARIs."

Eartha looked over at the android. Ari seemed *different*. He turned to her and smiled, but she wasn't sure what to make of him. He tilted his head at her, then lifted the sleeve of his left hand, showing her the marking she'd made when she'd first met him. A-R-I was scribbled on his arm.

She reached for his hand, smiling up at him. Whatever the queen had done to his memory, she hadn't erased what he knew of her, and that's what mattered the most.

"We have assigned you a room on our level so you'll have access to Eartha and we'll have access to you," Eric was saying to Zehra.

Eartha watched Zehra's confused expression before she raised her hands and used the signals that Zehra used to communicate as if it were second nature. Zehra's eyebrows raised, but she nodded her understanding.

Esme sucked in a breath. "I guess we're all going to have to get used to the fact that you can do things we can't." Esme winced and reached for her back. She was probably tired from all the standing around. At home, she was constantly complaining about her ankles.

"Why don't you guys head back," Eartha offered. "I'll take Zehra to her room."

Eric exchanged a glance with Esme.

"I'll take Ari with me. I'll be fine."

They both looked at him before agreeing.

Eartha led Zehra through the ship's security and to her cabin, on the same level as her own. She pointed to her cabin so Zehra would know where she lived with the Rogans, then she headed down the corridor and to the left, where Zehra's room was located off the main junction. Eartha showed Zehra where she needed to put her hand, and she swiped her hand in front of the reader, opening the door.

Zehra glanced around the cabin, putting her bag down on one of the empty chairs. She seemed to need to touch everything, even as her eyes scanned the room. When she reached her private bath, she made a sound in her throat that Eartha had never heard before, then there was a splash. A large tub in her bath accommodated her form, and she dipped herself in, not caring about her clothing getting wet.

Eartha laughed, asking, "So, you think you'll be comfortable here?"

Zehra smiled. "I like it," she signed back. "You can go. We'll begin your training tomorrow, early, before your academic studies."

Eartha turned to go, glad that while she was busy training, Zehra would be happy onboard.

Ari had remained by the door, following them in silence. Eartha took his hand and led him out into the corridor, heading back toward her own cabin.

"What did she do to you?" Eartha asked him. "You seem different."

"I am," he replied. "Let's see Captain Pinet. She has requested that I update her as well, and since the information pertains to you, I believe your presence will not be unwelcome."

The Captain was busy in her office when they arrived, a few other officers already with her. She dismissed them as Ari and Eartha entered.

"Perfect timing," she greeted. "I was wondering when I was going to see Bumi's handiwork. How did it go?"

"Well, in my estimation," Ari replied. "Though I'm not entirely sure what she did, as my internal monitoring systems were offline at the time."

Dana frowned. "Was she able to access any of our security protocols, or the information stored in your locked memory?"

Ari made a face that Eartha couldn't interpret. "I think we should assume I've been compromised. I admit, it did not occur to me to be concerned with that part when I went over there."

The Captain rubbed a hand over the back of her neck. "It's something I should have accounted for, but I doubt there's anything we can hide from the Trellis, even if we wanted to. From what I've seen, they are far more powerful than we are. We should be happy they are an ally for now." She sighed. Eartha thought she looked very tired. "I've spoken with Dr. Noah Walker. He mentioned you had a substantial number of modifications."

"The queen amplified my communications systems, upgraded my storage capacity, and improved my deductive reasoning skills."

"She said that you're going to protect me, too, like Zehra," Eartha said.

"Yes." Ari smiled down at her. "Although that directive was already written by me. She only enhanced the parameters."

Eartha thought she understood most of that, mostly excited to be learning about her home world, about the people that were ruled by the five queens.

"So, how does all this work?" she asked. "I just ask you questions, and you give me the history or whatever?"

"You will learn to use the cascade system," Ari explained. "You will learn basic knowledge, passing the knowledge checks to prove that you understand what you've learned, after which another level will be unlocked."

Eartha frowned. "How many levels are there?"

"I am unsure. I only have access to the level that you're currently on."

Captain Pinet rubbed her face with one hand. "No doubt it's a security precaution. Giving us access to information that you understand before it can be told to anyone wanting something more."

"Sorry, Captain," Ari said.

She waved a hand in the air. "It's fine. Have any of your primary directives been altered?"

"My Zelenian directives haven't changed. From what I can tell, the queen added a layer of security for Eartha."

"Good. For now, begin Eartha's studies as planned. I'd like a direct report from you on whatever subjects are discussed in case I have questions."

"Of course," Ari said, but there was something odd in his responses. The tilting of his head had a more lifelike quality than before. Eartha hadn't noticed it before, but the way his eyes met hers had changed, showing more emotion than before, if that was even possible.

The Captain watched him like she was looking for something wrong. Had she noticed the difference, too? "How do you feel, Ari?"

"I feel fine," Ari replied.

She squinted at him. "So you *do* have feelings?"

Ari stopped short. He seemed to be thinking for a long moment before he looked back at her. "I don't believe they are human feelings, but I do have more preferences than I think I had before."

"Really?" the Captain asked. "In what way?"

"I prefer Eartha's company among all others onboard. I

prefer to spend time with the Rogans rather than the other families I've met."

She made a sound in the back of her throat, as if she were thinking about something. "If Eartha was to leave and return to her people, would you go with her?"

"I—" Ari stopped again, considering the question with his eyes on the captain. "I prefer not to say at this time."

Eartha took a step back, as did the Captain.

"Ari, what's that mean?" Eartha asked.

"Well, that's surprising," said the Captain. "Report any other anomalies you've discovered since being with the Trellis queen to Dr. Walker. I'll let him know I want a full diagnostic report."

Ari hesitated, waiting for Eartha.

"She and I have something further to discuss," the Captain told him. "You're dismissed."

Captain Pinet waited for Ari to clear the room before she turned to Eartha.

"Well, we've got a little quandary now, don't we?"

"I don't understand why he would say that," Eartha said, wringing her hands.

"Bumi rewrote some of his higher and lower functions. I know he won't hurt you, but I need you to be careful from now on. Do you understand?"

Eartha shook her head. She had no clue what that meant. Ari was her friend.

Captain Pinet sighed. "It just means that he'll obey your commands over mine, which means I need you to be very careful about which of my commands you choose to disobey."

"I wouldn't—"

"You were a stowaway aboard this ship for fourteen days before we found you. You hid with the Rogans after that, and you protected Peter Barnes's hideout rather than give him up to me. Let's not pretend like you don't have your own mind." She reached out and put her hands on Eartha's shoulders. "I love that about you. I'm only asking you to be cautious. You will have the power to overrule me with both Zehra and Ari. Guard that privilege, and be careful when you choose to use it."

Eartha agreed, but she couldn't imagine disagreeing with the Captain on anything major. Yes, she hadn't told her where Barnes was, but that was because she owed him. He wasn't even onboard now, so he wouldn't be a problem anymore. Everything else she'd done so far had been in self-preservation, nothing that would hurt anyone else onboard.

"Head on home," the Captain told her. "I'll see you for ice cream in our usual spot later."

"Yes, Captain," she said. Eartha was thinking of how adult it felt to hang out with the Captain of their ship when she reached the door, turning back. "Things are going to change, aren't they?"

Captain Pinet nodded. "They always do."

"What if I'm not ready?"

"Then you'll learn from the mistakes you make. We all do. The trick is to not make the same mistake twice. Understand?"

Eartha smiled. "I think I do."

She'd just reached the door when she felt a pain in her gut. There was something wrong with what she'd just said. Was she about to make a mistake she'd made before?

Eartha shook off the foreboding and headed out the door. Ari was standing in the hallway, waiting against the wall.

"What are you still doing here?" Eartha asked him.

"I'm following my directive to ensure your safety."

"Ari, stop following me and go report to Dr. Walker, like the Captain said."

"Yes, my queen," he said, bowing in retreat.

Eartha's mouth fell open. Before she could call out and ask him why he'd said that, he was gone. The Captain's words rang in her mind. Yes, she'd have to be very cautious with her power or someone might get hurt.

EPILOGUE

DANA

When Chief Eric Rogan called Dana to meet him at the scrap yard, she didn't know what to expect. The *Hope* needed extensive upgrades to accommodate the new fuel and adjustments in velocity that their refits had provided. If the reports from engineering were to be believed, the entire ship would exceed their maiden voyage specs.

Dana tried to imagine what the other Zelenian ships had experienced on their voyages, the alien encounters they'd had before arriving at the Nexus space station. The wonder of it all would have sidelined some, but for Dana it was everything she'd dreamed of as a child, looking up into the sky and thinking of her father.

It was because Dana was thinking of her father that for a

second, she thought the man walking along the Ring in the crowd ahead of her might be him. She strained to get a look at the man's face, but beyond the broad shoulders and the long brown coat he wore, there was no indication he was from Zelenia. He might be one of the other Terrans from their original Earth, displaced by the Great Purge, though there was something too familiar about his bearing, the way he shifted from side to side as he slipped in and out of the crowd.

"Captain!"

Dana turned at the sound of Eric's call. He was waving her over, standing in front of the hangar doors leading to the office of what the Nexus called their 'scrapyard'. The man whom she'd been tracking dipped behind a taller group of aliens, and Dana lost sight of him. She shook off the feeling of déjà vu and followed Eric inside.

"You won't believe what we've discovered," Eric said. He'd gone ahead of her with Ensign Dix from engineering to see if they could find anything that could help them on their journey. Esme, still experiencing bouts of morning sickness, had stayed behind.

The two men looked eager to show Dana whatever it was they'd found.

Eric beamed at her. "We spoke to the scrapyard dealer briefly about some parts we need, and you'll never believe what he said."

"There's a ship in this sector with our exact markings and issues," the other man leaped in to finish. "He said the ship comes through regularly to swap out parts."

"Hey, Dix, let me tell it, will you?"

"Of course. Sorry, Chief." Dix clamped his lips closed,

though the bouncing excitement that made him wiggle in place remained.

"I'm aware that there was another ship here already," Dana said.

"Not already here, regular visitors." Eric rubbed his hands together. "He said the guy who does business with the scrapyard comes by every few weeks and he's due today."

"What?" Dana gasped.

"It might even be another engineer from Zelenia," Eric barreled on. "I wonder if it's anyone I've worked with before. There were plenty of renowned engineers in the community. I often wondered if their gifts were lost with the rest of the world. If any managed to get off–world somehow."

"We could meet our people today," Dix blurted out.

Dana gulped down her own anticipation. If that were true, they might add another ship to their journey, which would mean more resources. They needed that in this unknown part of the galaxy. The species here were unfamiliar, and their new path might have something even worse than plant eating ecologies, the mischievous Fashin Teku, or even the xenophobic Begarans waiting for them.

The owner of the scrapyard, a large species of alien with bulging muscles on his two arms and four legs, came toward her, moving like a dog despite his enormous trunks for legs. The form carried a head too large for its small face, made up of the usual two eyes, nose, and a mouth she was used to.

He looked Dana up and down as if she couldn't possibly be the person for whom they were forced to wait. "You the captain looking for more folks from your world?"

Dana inclined her head. "I am. I thank you for any information you can give me about my people."

"About that." He reached up and scratched the side of his colossal head. "Looks like he's not coming to talk with you today."

Dread bubbled in Dana's stomach. "What happened?"

"He came in here, took one look around, and bolted."

"When?" Eric asked, looking around the large warehouse space filled with scrap.

"Just now. He's walking out the door." The man pointed, and they all followed his extended finger.

Dana saw a man wearing a brown coat dashing out the door with a familiar gait. Without waiting, she ran after him. The shouts of her engineers faded behind her as she bolted through the crowd, but the man reached a lift and had entered it before she could clear it. Dana wedged herself between two aliens and pulled herself through in time to see the man's face before the doors closed.

His brown eyes met hers. He frowned at her with the same disapproving look she'd seen a thousand times.

He wore the face of her father.

The world stopped. Dana wanted to collapse to her knees.

How could it be? Her father had been dead for years, and yet this man could be his younger twin.

A million questions raced through her mind as the engineers caught up to her, both panting.

"Captain," Eric gasped, "who was that?"

Dana stared at the closed doors of the lift. "I don't know. But I'm going to find out."

To Be Continued...

DID YOU LOVE IT?

If you liked this book in whole or in part I hope you'll let other people know by leaving a review. The fastest way to get another book from any author, including me, is to review and share the last one. Thank you!

ALSO BY T.S. VALMOND

Starship Hope Series:

Ensign (Prequel)

Exodus

Marauders

Viral

Nexus

Arrival

Verity Chronicles Series

Exile

Divided

On the Run

To be notified about the latest releases, promotions, and giveaways, make sure you're a VIP Reader. Learn more at https://TSValmond.com

ACKNOWLEDGMENTS

Four books into this action-packed *Starship Hope* series, and I couldn't be happier to get *Nexus* to you readers and off of my laptop. If you're excited to see where this series goes, you're not alone. For those of you who've been with me for a while may recognize some secondary characters from other books. That's on purpose and should give you a clue to what's coming up after this series wraps up in book five.

Before we go any further, let me thank the people that made this book happen. I'm ever grateful for my patient editor Jack Llartin, who always finds ways to make my books even better. I want to include my wonderful cover designer, who has the amazing ability to read my mind. He has delivered yet another gorgeous cover for this series, and I couldn't be more grateful for his hard work.

Let me profusely thank my family for their continued kind words and support through the creation and publication of this series. They've been with me through the ups and downs of this year and helped support me during the entire process.

I want to thank my husband, Matthew, who continues to be a shining light during the bright and dark days. Though she'll never read this, I want to thank my dog Cookie, who is always there when the writing gets hard to give me a break.

ABOUT THE AUTHOR

Hi, I'm **T.S. Valmond** the science fiction and fantasy author currently residing in Canada with my husband and dog in an undisclosed location. One can never be too careful when exposing the secrets of powerful governments, worlds, and illegal aliens.

(Yes, they're watching.)

I was into science fiction and fantasy long before Browncoats, Trekkies, and Jedi were cool. Like my readers, I long for the days when Reality TV didn't mean anything and entertainment was entertaining.

When I'm not writing I'm–

Nope. I'm always writing.

TSValmond.com/links